The Marvelous Marvels

KALEIDOSCOPE KYTE'S

J. E. MILLER

www.jemillerbooks.com
@jemillerbooks

ISBN: 978-1-7374735-1-0

CONTENTS

Chapter 1

Take Off

The afternoon we left Merdwick held so many mixed feelings. Walking out of The Old Seawitch, and into the warm humid hallways of Seafarer's Cove for the last time, was bittersweet.

It was a celebration that I had completed a sort of initiation. I made it through auditions, traveled with the Marvelous Marvels to a location I had never been to, and survived my first performance unscathed. Well, not entirely unscathed, seeing as I nearly fell to my potential demise, jeopardizing my way of currently supporting myself and ever making it to Fimaldi Hunu one day.

I had overcome that, some credit to Caroline Mandeville no doubt, and had injected myself into the family of this circus. I had established what I hoped to be lifelong friendships with Shay, Ava, and Zeke and I felt that together we could face the accident that happened and the pitfalls that were sure to come. And last, but not least, I still had Alex.

Sure, we were busy. Constantly rehearsing, traveling, and no longer staying in the same room as we did before we got in with the Mandevilles' troupe. But he was there. We were still together. And I didn't want to admit it but, now more than ever, I knew I needed him. He had more or less saved me from Ceto's wrath, took care of me, and made sure I was safe. Not to mention how he was constantly encouraging me, coaching me, and telling me I was good enough to be part of the show.

Maybe that's why I was starting to feel jealous watching him with Ava. Maybe I felt like she could knock out one of my support beams and I'd fall. Maybe I was just being overprotective of my friend.

I thought about Shay interrogating me as I watched Alex perform at the first show. "Mind readers must think they have it all figured out," I thought to myself in grumbling tones, but I knew deep down I was hiding from the reality of her perceptiveness. I just couldn't mentally afford to have non-platonic feelings for him right now.

In our room, I finished packing my bags and sat on the bed to look around the walls and comforters that had lodged us for my very first circuses. To take in the experience of it, say goodbye to it. It seemed fitting to spend the last bit of time where I first snuck away for solitude; the wooden bench bolted to the ground just inside the great cove's sea entrance on the channel.

I walked down the hall, glancing at the octopus tentacle sconces on the wall, aflame to light the path. Since it was now midday, the cove was well lit and boats were gliding steadily to and from their docking. The sun was reflecting off the water and bouncing up across moss and algae covered stones that stacked and constructed the enormous dome shaped cove.

I plopped on the bench, closed my eyes, and took a big inhale. The scent of salty sea was familiar and warm, nostalgic and calming. And though perhaps I should have been, I wasn't concerned with what I knew was below the waters and beyond the entry.

We were all devastated by the loss of Henry. As I sat there, I tried to sort it out in my mind. It had been an eye for an eye, an attack on Henry for an attack on Ceto. The merpeople had just gotten the better of us. This was no consolation, and it wouldn't help any of us carry the loss, but it helped me to try understanding it from both sides.

For some reason, I didn't feel fearful about the merpeople now. Perhaps Whisper was restoring my sense of strength. Or maybe when Ceto zapped me, it changed my body chemistry entirely. Maybe the vision was actually a gift. Seeing my worst-case scenario of a life played out in my mind might help me be more grateful. Inspire me to do all I can to prevent that from happening. Everything seems to happen for a reason.

"Whisper," I spoke in my head, "I don't know what to make of the vision I saw when Ceto nearly escaped."

"Do you need to make something of it?"

"I don't know. Do I?" I asked.

"What did it show you?"

I thought for a minute. "Well, it showed me bad things. Losing all the things I've worked so hard to get, losing things I loved."

"What did you love?"

"My friends," I answered.

"Your friends…" Whisper knew I was skirting around.

"Yeah, my friends. I was kicked off the troupe and separated from them. Alex got swept away, and then he was with Ava. Shay didn't want to see me anymore."

"What struck you as most painful?"

"It was all painful."

"But what was most painful?"

I hesitated to answer them or answer the question to myself, "I guess losing Alex." It was difficult waiting for a response. "Losing Alex," I tried again. Still no response. "Whisper, what does that matter? What does that even mean?"

Whisper was… is an omnipresent being in my life. Whether I hear them or not, they're present. But sometimes they don't answer right away. And while it can be annoying and inconvenient at times, it's wildly beautiful in a way.

Whisper is unpredictable, but only in a way that's in my best interest. Leading me to clarity with a gentle guiding hand, and wise beyond what I can imagine. However, because they are beyond space and time, I must occasionally wait for them; as patiently as I can manage.

Given the inner dialogue going on in my head, I was just starting to get really aggravated with Whisper when I heard feet shuffling on the damp, water-sloshed surface of the cove entry floor.

"As suspected," Alex said, as he rounded the corner of the bench. "I thought I may find you here."

"Yeah, ya know… just saying goodbye to the blob."

"No longer scared of the blob?"

"Nah, I think it's over now."

"Yeah, me too," Alex huffed as he sat down beside me, a heaviness in his voice. "It's not really the creatures. Reg, Hagan, I blame them. Men of power who stop at nothing. And they're not even doing anything about all of this. They don't even care," he said, as he emphasized his disdain for the situation with his hands.

"I know, I know." I tried to be reassuring.

"A man is down. His life has ended. And it's just—off to the next gig."

"I get it. Our friends get it." I rested a hand on Alex's knee before I realized what I was doing. Once I snapped back to reality, I gave it a firm pat instead. "Henry was a good dude."

"You didn't see it, Janie. When I went back to help, Reg jumped over to Ava and the roustabouts once or twice, tops. He took one look at Henry and knew he was done for. But he was more worried about his precious wagon than anything."

I said nothing. I watched Alex's face as he went back in time and relived the whole fiasco.

"Ava was crying so hard. And Henry just laid there lifeless in her arms. His face was losing all its color and turning white."

I turned my body sideways on the bench to face him. "Listen, we can only do one thing for Henry now. And that's watch out for each other and for our own safety. Reginald Mandeville is out for the Mandevilles only. We know that now more than ever. And this Mr. Kyte character doesn't sound good from what Shay has told me. We've been in two shows so far and I nearly fell and we're down a man. I've been thinking about how the rigging slipped during our act. I'm pretty certain Henry checked it. And Reg was quick to come and berate me after it happened, very quick."

"You think someone tampered with it?"

"I don't know about that, but I do know this. I don't have an extra special talent. You, Zeke, Ava. You all have a unique act. And Shay has many talents. I'm like an add on, maybe even a two for one to get you on the troupe. And I'm starting to wonder if Reg was trying to trim some of the fat."

Alex was reeling at the idea I had just proposed. "People make mistakes all the time. Henry may have really missed something," he shrugged.

"Alex. The look on Henry's face when he ran to us afterwards was more confusion than apology. Shay and Ava say he was an exemplary roustabout. I just think there's more to the story. What if it's not a coincidence that he's the one that led the wagon in the water first? What if Reg ordered him to help?"

"Reg did order him to help. The other men on the scene talked about it."

We stared at each other, blank faced, trying to process what each other was saying. Alex propped his elbows on his knees and ran his fingers through his hair as he dropped his head to think.

"All I know is we have to be careful. We have to be so careful. Honestly, I'm freaking out right now." My heart was speeding up and my palms were starting to sweat.

"No no no, don't freak out."

"What if he tried to kill me, Alex!" My thoughts were racing. "What if he was mad that Henry got in the way, and leading the wagon into the water was his consequence." Now would have been a good time for Whisper to speak up, but they didn't.

"I promise I'm not going to let anything happen to you. We just need to be mindful and aware," Alex said. "We need to stick together, all of us. Watch each other's backs. We'll be fine. Maybe there is another explanation for this."

"Oy!" a voice called from down the walkway, "You kids don't want to be left, do you?" Mr. Habbershack was hobbling in our direction, lamp light swaying and one eye squinted. "Your lot is about to head off, you know."

"Oh yeah, thank you, sir. We were just about to leave," Alex shouted back to him. Mr. Habbershack jerked his wrist in a dismissive wave and turned back in the other direction.

"A send off as pleasant as the welcome," I said.

"No kidding. Poor guy. I'd be pissed if I had to stay in this damp tunnel every day too."

After the two of us had gathered all our belongings, we exited the cove on the street side entrance, and waited with the other performers on the grassy area near the shoreline. The sun was still blazing and everyone was looking off to the east. Alex and I followed suit.

Way in the distance, I could see two brown and silvery dots moving slowly. In ten minutes time, they had grown in view from dots to massive globular mechanical creations. Dangling ropes and flags waving in their wake. As they got closer, you could see that the brown coloring was rust, which was slightly unsettling; yet no one around me seemed concerned. They were zeppelins.

The geometrical lines that radiated from the tip of the zeppelin to the back tail wheel were more visible as it approached. These things were massive. Beyond what I could have imagined having never been very close to one before. Perhaps these particular ones were extra huge in order to carry our giant party as well as horses, big cats, and a full-grown elephant.

"How can Reg afford this kind of travel? I thought he needed money?" I asked quietly amongst our group.

"These are Mr. Kyte's air ships. We're indebted to him already," Shay answered.

"Nice," I said sarcastically. There was our first cue to take caution in using this crazy contraption. Not that I knew what to do in the case of a zeppelin emergency anyway. But we needed to keep in mind that, in his eyes, we already owe this guy something.

Alex and I watched in wonder as these great blimps slowly floated down to a landing. Like a giant bubble you blew from a wand on a summer's day, steadily sinking to a halt and pop. I so hoped there would be no pop while we were on board.

Reginald marched out toward the zeppelins first, chest high with a determined look on his face and Caroline trailing behind him. He gruffly shook the hand of the pilot, who had just opened the boarding doors. There was some back and forth between them that couldn't be heard from our distance. Then the Mandevilles strode inside without a glance back at the troupe at all.

The performers watched for a minute, looked at each other, shrugged, and threw their bags over their shoulders. Slowly, they fell in line to board. As usual, our group were the ones to bring up the rear. That gave us plenty of time to watch the roustabouts lead our reluctant circus animals into their own adjacent floating transportation. Eloise was particularly apprehensive and Daniel wandered over to help her calm down and walk in. It made sense that an elephant would not be too keen on flying or floating, or doing anything without at least one foot on the earth. Eloise had defied all kinds of gravity, but this would be next level.

Our group was approaching the boarding area when the pilot's assistant noticed Tombo and promptly notified Zeke, "No animals on this airship. Take him to the next one." Zeke looked at Anthony worriedly.

"We've been cleared by Mr. Mandeville. I'm sure if you could run it by him he could clarify," Zeke said.

The assistant looked at him with an aggravated expression and wandered inside. When he re-emerged he said, "Mr. Mandeville says no animals of any kind, no exceptions."

Anthony appraised Zeke's horrified face and wrapped an arm around him before quietly saying, "Come on. We'll get him set up. He'll be fine. Don't worry." Though Zeke's countenance exuded the definition of worry.

"Scumbag," Alex said under his breath. "He's just going to throw his weight around now, huh."

We tried to show our most encouraging expressions to Zeke as they turned to walk to the other zeppelin.

"What's the point of that?" I said angrily.

"He's doing it because he can," Ava replied and rolled her eyes, "and because he's in a foul mood."

Once we had all stepped inside the boarding zone doors, the assistant beckoned us towards the promenade, where the rest of the performers were huddling. He closed the boarding doors and fastened some sort of lock. Then he disappeared and must have given the pilot an all-clear signal because I felt slight movement beneath us.

We were slowly and gradually floating up. We looked at each other with wide eyes, since they gave us no forewarning. But overall, the movement was so slight you could barely notice.

"Pick your own cabin down that hallway." The assistant had reappeared and instructed us as he gestured.

"There's two bunks per room. You'll only be aboard for one night, so don't make a fuss about who goes where."

We all looked at each other, aware of the challenge for even pairings, and wondering how to decide who lodges with who.

"I'll bunk with Shay," said Ava quickly.

"I'll go with Daniel," said Zeke. "For discretion," he added, as he winked at Anthony.

"We could bunk together. Like old times." Alex turned to me, "You do have seniority over Anthony." Alex nodded at Anthony apologetically, though Anthony obviously couldn't care less.

"Sure," I said.

It was one night. I would be fine. The only reason it slightly embarrassed me was because Shay knew my feelings; better than I knew them myself to be honest. But thankfully, she remained stone-faced. She wasn't the type to make googly eyes, like girlfriends do in high school when your crush walks by. That would've been Ava, but when I glanced at her, she was stone-faced too.

Chapter 2

Floating

As the other performers shuffled toward the cabins, we got a glimpse of the windows. I walked closer to look out the forty-five degree angled panes. Huge, puffy, cumulus clouds, white as cotton, were all around us, and I could see the grassy area we'd just left beneath. The cove growing smaller, The Old Seawitch being occluded from view by the longleaf pines encasing it.

Though Merdwick grew smaller in view, the trauma of it still loomed large in our minds and hearts. Floating above and away from it brought a little serenity, but not enough. We were headed to uncharted territory.

I had spent my time freely traveling where ever I so pleased with Alex until we were employed by the Mandevilles. I thought it would be fun to move around more frequently and with someone else worrying about lodging and transportation. But now we were sort of slave to the Mandevilles' decisions of where we go next, and in the short time with them so far, we had discovered they may take us to places of uncertainty. Places unsafe, unfamiliar, and you didn't get a say about the when, where, or who. So, though it felt nice to float away from Merdwick, apprehension and caution were almost tangible around me.

"Pretty wild, huh?" Alex said, as he approached the glass next to me. "Guess we can mark blimp travel off the list."

"Yep. It should feel more exciting than this, though. The experience is tainted with anxiety about the destination," I replied.

"Ahh." Alex waved a hand dismissively, like there was nothing to worry about. "You know these things can explode mid-travel, but we'll be fine." It was true, and it surprised me he was so cavalier about the risk, but I guess he knew there wasn't much he could do now. "Let's go dump our stuff and explore," he said.

I followed him through a very tight hallway to a door with rounded corners that was still open. Stepping through the threshold, I scanned the tiny room. There was not much to see. Two slender and hard looking bunk beds with old metal stairs to the top one.

"Preference?" Alex asked.

"Bottom. Definitely bottom," I replied.

He slung his bags up on the top bunk and moved about a foot further in to make way for me. We pretty much had to turn on the spot, shuffling in baby steps, to come in and out because it was so snug.

"Well, it could be worse I guess. But I'm glad it's only one night of living in a shoe box," I said.

There was no bathroom, obviously. Community toilets were downstairs. And the only thing in the room, other than the bunk beds, was a tiny fold away table. It was currently secured to the wall with a closed folding stool leaned against it. Tight quarters.

I dumped my bag on the bunk bed and exited our tiny room, Alex following. Continuing down the hallway, to the other side of the zeppelin, we found the dining room. A long slender table with chairs all around it; family style if you were an incredibly large family. The dining room had angled viewing windows lining the side of the airship, like the ones in the promenade.

We walked downstairs to find a smoking room, a bar, and a piano lounge. All of which were dated and dusty like they had not seen a patron in years; though now they were flowing with members of our troupe.

A door in the bar room opened and led to a patio area where you could look at the inside of this great metal cylinder. From our lodging area, it would continue a length of about two hundred yards of metal matrix, looking like a geometrical work of art composed of truss and duralumin walls. I looked at it in awe of the creativity and imagination required to dream up and construct such a massive thing. Furthermore, it gave me an odd feeling to view it and know it confined us to such a small section of such an enormous space. I found that surprisingly metaphorical. But after a minute, it started to give me the creeps, so I walked back to the piano lounge.

"I wonder if the animals get such lavish digs as a piano lounge?" Alex said. He sat on the bench and began tinkering with the keys.

"It would have to be customized for animal stalls, wouldn't it?" I tried to imagine the interior of the airship that housed a five ton elephant. "I wonder how Eloise is handling it."

"That is one smart elephant. Daniel has told me story after story of all the incredible things she has done. I bet she's figured out she's floating. Hopefully she's chill about it."

"You think Zeke is okay? You know, being apart from Tombo," I asked, knowing that Zeke would be wrecked with worry. I mainly wanted to see if Alex had any inkling of insight about Tombo's secret abilities.

"The man loves his monkey. But he'll be fine."

I nodded in reply.

"Speaking of Zeke. This recent development with Anthony. I think that could be good for us. Anthony will know things about the Mandevilles that the other performers don't. I mean, I'm happy for Zeke and Anthony in general. But you know, added bonus having somewhat of an insider to the Mandevilles' agenda," Alex said, after pausing the little melody he had been stringing together on the ivories.

"I bet he still keeps it close to the vest," I countered.

"Yes, but if there was real imminent danger, which sounds probable, maybe he would inform us," Alex said. The risk analyst part of him was taking over.

"Yeah, I'm sure he would. So maybe it won't be so bad after all. Zeke would relay important information to us. And maybe White Cap Peaks will be a nice change." I tried to be optimistic.

"But if not, we've got each other. The group. We'll be fine." Alex tried to follow suit.

It would be tough to have enough self-control to stop constantly worrying about our future. But worry leads to the death of imagination and adventure. Wasn't that what this whole decision to become part of the troupe was about?

"We just need to take it one day at a time," I said. "Let's try to enjoy this new mode of travel."

I propped my elbows up on the edge of the piano and focused on my breathing for a few minutes as Alex kept pinging keys.

"What do you think, guys?" Ava came bouncing through the door first, Shay following.

"It's a first," I said.

"We're just trying to enjoy drifting through the air in this giant metal tube, hoping the super flammable hydrogen that's lifting us doesn't set us all ablaze mid air," Alex said.

Ava clicked her tongue a few disapproving times. "You need chill music." She played the intro to Beethoven's fifth symphony with heavy pressure on the keys until Shay swatted her. It was momentary comedic relief.

"Fine," Ava said, sarcastically frowning at Shay, and began to play a beautiful melody that was not what a beginner pianist could achieve. Alex and I were surprised.

"I didn't know you played," Alex said to Ava as he scooted over on the bench to make room for her fluidly moving hands.

She raised her eyebrows at him as if to say, "surprise," and continued. I watched the two of them with great scrutiny of every movement or expression.

Shay leaned over the opposite side of the piano from me, propping her elbows as well, and watched them. "Good," I thought to myself, "She's getting all the information out of their heads."

Shay then looked at me with a raised eyebrow as she heard my thought. I had forgotten her rules. She didn't want to be the go between. She would not divulge other people's thoughts unless it was to protect someone from harm. I rolled my eyes at her and thought, "okay, okay," in defeat.

Ava's melody came to an end, and we all applauded her. When all of us finished clapping, the sound of thick callused hands continued to smack somewhere behind our huddle.

"Oh, what a group. There certainly is a lot of talent in this room, isn't there?" Reg stood in the doorway to the piano lounge with a cigar hanging out of his mouth. He must have heard us from the smoking room.

"Miss Ava, I too did not know you had other gifts besides hooping and balancing. But look at you, quite the pianist. And Alex, our rockstar," Reg beamed at Alex like a proud father. "Perhaps a fellow musician would be a good companion for you, but I'm no matchmaker," he chuckled.

Alex attempted to laugh for the sake of politeness.

"Shay, our exquisite swan. Full of mystery and grace, not to mention knowledge and insight." Reg tapped his thick finger on his temple. Shay's eyes grew slightly more alert, but she maintained a poised smile.

"And Janie..." Reg continued, "You've shown progress, girl. You've got a little moxie, I'll give you that. I may keep you."

I was shocked initially, but snakes can turn direction on a dime. This was a drastic change from the last interaction with Reginald Mandeville. He was being strategic, methodical.

"I certainly appreciate that, Mr. Mandeville. And I do promise to maintain the moxie." I spoke before I realized the words were coming out of my mouth; more snide than I meant to. I don't know what came over me. Here I was, thinking that this man may have tried to hurt me, or worse, just a few hours earlier. My response must've come from divine intervention. And the others must have been surprised at me too, because after I spoke, they all turned and stared at me.

Reginald chuckled and growled, "Atta, girl." He swiped his hand through the air casually. "You kids enjoy your down time. It'll be back to work tomorrow." The end of his cigar glowed red as his cheeks sucked in a drag. He turned in the doorway and walked back out towards the bar.

"What the hell was that?" Alex whispered in the circle as he cut his eyes at me.

"Yeah, why is he being nice?" I used my fingers to air quote the word nice.

"Not him, you!" Ava whispered.

"Oh. I dunno."

"I've never seen you assertive," Ava replied.

"I liked it," Shay piped, "but you better use it sparingly with Reg."

"You're right. I will," I replied.

"Geez. The balls on you, man," Alex said to me.

I tried not to smile, but if I was being honest, I was a little proud of myself. Ordinarily I would have reamed him for the vulgarity, but I was feeling somewhat euphoric.

I reined it in the rest of the night and tried to keep pretty quiet. Over analyzing and picking apart all the variables in our current situation was useless at the time, anyway. They served a humbling dinner to all the performers who sat around the long skinny table in the dining room. Zeke looked particularly somber. No doubt worrying about Tombo floating in the sky behind him. Daniel, on the other hand, never missed an opportunity to enjoy food and must've felt confident that Eloise was okay because he was the most joyful member of the troupe at the table. I giggled as he lightly elbowed Alex and asked, "Are you gonna e-eat that?" To which Alex responded reluctantly, but gave up his bread roll.

As the table dispersed, I made my way to the window. The night was crystal clear and gorgeous. Black, tinged with a heavy blue, and dotted with luminescent sparkles. Hundreds of tiny glowing stars just across my view from up high in the air. Like I could reach out and swirl a wispy cloud around my hand, or poke a bright little star.

"You are always with me, aren't you?" I said to Whisper in my mind. "Look at your artwork." I felt at ease in the awe of the night's beauty. A shooting star whizzed across the window.

I had tuned out the sounds of ending table conversations, but was brought out of my gaze at the bidding goodnight from Shay and Ava.

"I guess I'm about to call it a day," said Alex.

"Yep. Me too." I took one more glimpse at the sky before following the rest of them to the cabins.

Alex kicked his sneakers off under my bottom bunk and climbed up to the top bunk. There wasn't any room to sit around, so that was our only option. He laid back immediately, folding his arms behind his head. There was hardly a spare foot between his face and the ceiling. I sat on the bottom bunk with my head about five or six inches from hitting the bed frame above me.

"Interesting day. Airship travel. You back talking Reg," Alex spouted off above me.

I ignored the statement and seized an opportunity to further my subtle interrogation. "My back talking Reg was way less impressive than how Ava played that piano. Wasn't it amazing?"

"Yeah, she's really good."

"Now that Reginald is aware of the hidden talent, he may have you two forming some sort of crazy circus rock band. Ava could do electronic keyboard attached over your head or something."

"I don't know about that."

"Anything that's lucrative, Reginald is up for it. Besides, he seems to think you two would make a great pair." I tried my hardest to sound indifferent to the topic, but I couldn't help but mock Reginald's tone when quoting him.

"Reg just talks to hear himself talk," he countered.

"Don't you think Ava's pretty?"

"Sure."

"Well, you two have hung out a bit," I pressed.

"Yeah, so."

"So. You haven't really dated anyone since I've known you. What about Ava?" I held my breath.

"I haven't really thought about it. She's a nice girl. Talented. Kind. But I don't know," Alex said, his voice already exhausted by my nagging. "You haven't dated anyone either. Maybe I'll start giving you the third degree. Try to set you up with one of the fire breathers."

"Relax," I said. I didn't like this thing being turned around on me.

"Hey, you started this," he defended. "So what's your type?"

"Type..." I rolled my eyes as I answered him. "I don't think I have a type."

"Oh, come on, Janie."

"Alright then. My type is kind, loyal. Gotta be adventurous. Must be funny."

"No standard aesthetics?"

"I'm not telling you that. Besides, looks are only skin deep," I replied. In reality, my mind filled with images of Alex's sweaty determined brow and glistening arm muscles after playing a set.

He quieted and I knew I should let it go, but what if the topic never came up again. "Why haven't you dated anyone?" I asked. It was like ripping off a bandaid.

"Because I'm busy, alright. You usually have to be settled to date someone. I'm moving."

"That doesn't count out Ava," I quickly countered.

"Janie, enough. I'm not talking about this anymore," he said, agonizingly annoyed.

I hated when his voice got like that. It made me feel like he was playing dad and I was just a dumb little kid. For some reason, it always stabbed my pride.

"Fine. Geez," I laid back on my stiff bottom bunk bed and seethed indignantly. Why did he have to avoid me so hard? It was just a question.

"Goodnight, big mouth," he said in a tone that implied somewhat of a truce.

"Big mouth?"

"Yeah. You smart off to Reg. You won't shut up around me," he trailed off like he could name more reasons.

"G'night."

I rolled over and shut my eyes. He liked Ava. I knew it. That's why he was so closed off. I rolled over to the opposite side restlessly. I was defeated and I felt like this was the beginning of the end of our friendship. All those years together and this one little thing was going to drive the wedge to end it.

I steamed about the frustrating nature of friendships. You invest all this time into a person. Caring about their likes and dislikes, their input on decisions. Seeking their advice or approval. And then something happens. Maybe you get displaced from each other. Maybe your values and preferences change. Or maybe they move on to someone else. Someone more interesting or fun. And there you are, back to square one. Looking for another companion to invest all that energy in while taking the risk that they do the same thing. It's maddening when you think about it.

Wouldn't it be easier to go rogue? Be a lone wolf. But if you did that, who would you share life with? Who would be your partner in crime or help you out of a tight spot? People need people, that's how we are created. Unfortunately, it was a challenge whichever direction you chose.

Chapter 3

White Cap Peaks

The next morning, I woke up to Alex shuffling in and out of our tiny cabin.

"You better get up and hit the showers if you want any lukewarm water. You can forget hot," he said grumpily.

When I finally sat up at the edge of the bed, I immediately noticed a major change in temperature. It was super cold, and all that knobby metal we kept bumping into as we scooted around was like ice.

After the uncomfortable experience of showering in a cold zeppelin, everyone congregated in the dining room and promenade. They held their arms tightly to their chest as they munched on apples, bananas, or toast with butter. I went straight for the windows first.

There was a mountainous range of forest covered in fresh powder beneath us. Everything was white and crisp. A river peeked through, winding between the trees toward a large frosty lake. From up high, the sky was crystal clear periwinkle blue. All was calm and magnificent. As the snow continued to fall, I wondered how it would affect our metal balloon, other than obviously turning us into human ice cubes in a floating freezer. What if we froze, grew heavy, and fell right out of the sky?

Caroline came sweeping through in an impressive black mink overcoat. She peered over the angled window next to me, but her expression was as if I didn't exist. She turned around to the horde of performers.

"Alright, troupe. We are another hour away. You've no doubt noticed it's very cold. Better bundle up because it's going to get much worse before it gets better. Fortunately, Mr. Kyte has been very generous and agreed to house us in one of his three star mountain lodgings near the park. When we land, we will check in to unload there first. Animals will be unloaded at the park's menagerie. Lunch will be provided at the lodge and then we will visit the park's performance facilities." Never one to stick around, she nodded politely to the lot of us and left.

I already packed everything in our tiny cabin. There was nowhere to scatter it all out in the first place. So Alex and I sat at the promenade and played blackjack as we waited. Shay and Ava reappeared after the first two hands and commentated as we played. Daniel and Zeke showed up about fifteen minutes later. Zeke was chomping at the bit to land and get Tombo back, but the wrinkles of worry on his face were softening. Being their assistant, Anthony had to maintain proximity to the Mandevilles. I could easily imagine Reg ordering him around in my head. Making Anthony pack all of his things while he sat back and puffed on a cigar or that pipe of his.

When we were about fifteen minutes away, you could see a clearing in the mountains through the promenade windows. The trees dispersed and created an opening at the foothills. Smoke was rising from several chimneys, factories, and warehouses. Though caked in snow, you could make out little houses and buildings from the glow of the lights within them.

As we drew nearer, Shay pointed out Mr. Kyte's amusement park, a quickly departing look of apprehension skirting across her face. She would, of course, remain strong. But strength can wisely coexist with caution and suspicion. Even the most mighty still need to be smart in order to stay on top.

The sky was clear and the morning rays of the sun were showering everything around us with a welcome and pleasant glow. Beams of light caused the snow to sparkle. At this time of day, the mountains cast little shadow, and the town was alight. From the distance, I could make out a giant Ferris wheel, a single blue coaster track, and a tall tower of a building. We steadily floated closer in the rusty metal balloon. Several tent tops, large and small and in a rainbow of colors, came into view and shined in the morning sun. The park stood out like a child's dreamland amongst the normally constructed and currently snowy buildings of White Cap Peaks.

We descended towards a snow dusted airstrip and landed next to a unique-looking helicopter made of shiny silver and brass colored metals, with a very round cabin and asymmetrical porthole windows.

It was surprising how softly we stopped moving, and when we had all stepped out the door of the zeppelin, we got our first taste of how cold it really was. They reported the temperature at twenty-five degrees Fahrenheit, but it felt much worse, and we weren't exactly prepared for the arctic tundra.

The Mandevilles, of course, were dressed in weather proof winter wear that was actually quite fashionable. I squeezed my torso to hold as much warmth in as possible. Huffing and grumbling that they didn't give us any more notice. But that figured.

Leaving Caroline and Anthony to manage the lot of us, Reginald strutted out in front of the troupe towards the nearest building, which was humble in size but ornate in appearance. As he neared the door, a tall, slender man stepped out to greet him.

The man was just a few inches taller than Reginald and about half the width of him, Reg being so burly and he being skinny. The man was dapper. He dressed in an unconventional style, yet it suited him. A black felt top hat with bronze Victorian driver's goggles resting on the brim. A white pinstriped button-up and collared shirt peeked from under a gentleman's vest, which was woven with swirling filigree in shades of amber and gold. There was a pocket watch strung through the buttonholes. Black pants, leather gloves, and a crimson swallowtail coat, the tails of it blowing in the snowy breeze. Still intriguing, and maybe most of all, was the elaborate workmanship of his beard, which was as white as the falling snow. It was trimmed like a musketeer, with a curling mustache and boxed around the goatee.

The two men exchanged hearty handshakes and smacks on the shoulder. Both smiles capped under a bushy mustache. They seemed sort of cut from the same cloth. Reg swung his arm back at us and the man nodded still smiling. If I didn't know better, I would have relaxed by watching their interaction. Laughing amongst themselves, they made their way over to our assemblage.

"Troupe, for those of you who have not yet been to White Cap Peaks, let me introduce you to Mr. Kyte," Reginald said.

"Welcome, welcome to you all. I am so pleased to see that you've made it and am looking forward to each of your performances. We take entertainment very seriously around here. You will undoubtedly see sights you've never witnessed before." Mr. Kyte spoke with a smile on his face, but in a direct tone.

"Yes kids, Mr. Kyte has taken his shows to what were once unreachable heights," Reginald added. And at this point, the two men looked at each other and burst out laughing. We all looked at one another confused.

"Mandeville, I've gotta watch you." Mr. Kyte was working on catching his breath from laughter. They were unfazed by the fact that they were the only two people laughing while we stared blankly like a confused herd of sheep. "Anyway," Mr. Kyte continued, "we will house you guys at Frigid Ridge lodge while you work for us."

"And we so appreciate you accommodating us, sir," Reg interjected.

"Oh, it's nothing. I saved the four and five stars for tourists." Mr. Kyte's chin rose a little higher. "I understand you've encountered a major climate change. I'm afraid we didn't name it Frigid Ridge for nothing," he chuckled.

"We'll acclimate. No worries," Reg said.

"You had better. Parts of the acts will be outside, variably."

"Not a problem, sir."

"Good. Well, let's get you guys unloaded. You can follow me to the transport track."

The transport turned out to be an old trolley car, and the track was like a little railroad through White Cap Peaks. The outside of the trolley was like the zeppelin, rusted metal. We all loaded into the trolley as they took the animals to the park by an old freight liner that had large metal pens attached to the back of it.

I took inventory as I watched through the smudgy windows. We entered the city's main street to find the usual shops like a grocery, butcher, bakery, and hardware store. But there were also some unusual businesses there as well. A blacksmith, a mechanical repair shop, a cobbler, and a clock shop, amongst a few other oddities. The mountain air was clear and crisp above us, and over the tops of the buildings you could see the snow-capped mountain ridge that this place was named after, but the store fronts and city streets were dingy with dirt, soot, and grime.

The people traversing the sidewalks were in a similar style of dress as Mr. Kyte. The women in Victorian era garb, some in bodices and dresses. Others in something similar to the men's wear.

It was a shaky and bumpy progression along the track. Within five minutes we were approaching the outskirts of the main street, where the houses were of asymmetrical architecture with curling decorative trim and beaded railing on the porches. They were a variety of colors, though my favorite was the maroon one. It had black and gold framing that turned this way and that, all around the windows and awnings and along the rooftops.

There weren't many houses and soon we began passing through more open and snowy areas around the mountains that encased the trolley track. It winded back and forth through white dusted rock. From my window, I watched twiggy gray tree limbs that were topped with white powder glide past my line of sight.

A little further, we came to halt at a drop off point in front of a long skinny lodge made of brick. Over the main entryway door was an emerald green fabric awning with Frigid Ridge scrolled across in a calligraphy style font.

The herd of us shuffled through the entry after the Mandevilles had gone inside. There was a lobby with an open sitting area in one corner near a grand piano, and a few cafe style tables and chairs in the other. The front desk was long as a bar and had curved arched doorway sections, with more beaded spindle atop it. The floor was black and white checked tile, and three chandeliers were emitting a warm and welcome glow from the ceilings throughout the extended room.

The Mandevilles had us grouped by the same rooms as our Merdwick stop. So Shay, Ava, and I would again be a dynamic trio. Alex, Zeke, and Daniel in a room. Poor Anthony on his own since they made him constantly available as the Mandevilles' assistant. I was excited and relieved to be with the girls again. The receptionist behind the desk directed us to room nine, and we carried our bags down the narrow hallway in a single file line.

We entered our room to find three beds with not only a wooden headboard but a footboard as well. They had tall dark stain bedposts at each of their four corners. Cornflower toile bedspreads lay atop each mattress. Another chandelier hung in the middle of the room, and the curtains were tied back with rope and tassels. Never in a million years would I have decorated a room this way, but it gave off a surprisingly tasteful aesthetic when contrasted with the cold snowflake covered view out the window.

"What a charming little room," said Shay.

"It certainly beats last night's quarters in that rusty old balloon," Ava replied. "Speaking of which," her smirk emerging, "how was your night, Janie?"

"Fine," I said, rolling my eyes.

"Co-ed is always fun though," she probed. Shay merely listened and shook her head as she placed some of her garments on hangers.

"Why are you always pestering me about this?"

"I guess because you have nothing else interesting to pry about," Ava replied.

"I asked him about you, you know," I shot back at Ava. Shay's eye grew big and confused as she looked at me from behind Ava's line of sight.

"What?"

"Yep," I said smugly.

"What is there to ask?"

"I thought you said you were interested? And you guys have spent some time together. And you're always asking me about him. I thought I'd see if he was interested in you two dating," I said.

Ava looked a little embarrassed, and I slightly regretted my statement. "Well, what did he say?"

This put me in a weird predicament that I hadn't thought through. I didn't want to make this overly easy for Ava and Alex if I was right in my verdict that he was interested in her. I didn't want to lose Alex's friendship. And on top of that, through painful self admission, I had surrendered to the fact that I might have feelings for him. But with all that in mind, I still didn't want to tell her he hadn't thought about the two of them dating. Afraid it may somehow hurt her feelings.

"He wouldn't say. Told me it wasn't my business," I said. Not a total lie, but not a total truth. And at this Ava looked further confused.

"Okay, new topic," Shay took the wheel of the conversation. "More important topic. We are about to go to the park, and look at this." She threw a newspaper down on the bed between us. The front-page headline was bold and large.

Body found in frozen river behind Kaleidoscope Kyte's not yet identified.

"Great. How relaxing," I said sarcastically. "We're about to head straight to a crime scene."

"Keep reading," said Shay.

The article continued to describe how the mayor had responded to this incident by stating that the body was most likely a drifter. That there were no missing persons reported in White Cap Peaks and that therefore it was not a local.

"This is what I was talking about. Kyte has the mayor. So being fastidiously careful begins now," said Shay.

"This is terrible. We just got here and my nerves are already shot," said Ava. "What are we gonna do?"

"We're going to look after our own, that's what. We're going to do our acts and stay out of the way otherwise." Shay, our fearless leader, ever poise and even toned. "We need to show this to the boys, too. So they're aware."

"It's almost time to load up. I got it. I'll be discreet with it," I said. Snatching the paper off the bed, I shoved it inside my jacket under my arm. "I'll get it to the boys and then dump it on the trolley floor."

We all wandered back down the hall to board the trolley once more. I found the boys sitting near the grand piano as they waited and plopped down next to Zeke and across from Alex.

"Ready for the grand adventure?" Zeke asked sarcastically. Tombo must've already been taken to the park. Which would be wearing his nerves already.

"Not really," I lowered my voice, "I need to show you guys something when we board the trolley. Try to sit as far away from the trolley man as possible."

"Alright," Alex answered worriedly.

I went back to rejoin the girls. We waited another couple of minutes before the trolley rolled into view outside. In the usual sea of acrobats, jugglers, and sideshow acts, we bumbled up to get on.

Chapter 4

Kaleidoscope Kyte's

We went as far to the back as we could and, thankfully, the boys followed suit. Daniel and Anthony were with them too, which was good. That way, everyone would be informed. I walked towards the back and pretended to ask Alex for a pen for my fake crossword; I didn't have a crossword on me.

I felt guilty about not getting the information out to the performers seated all around us. Maybe eventually we could, but for now, we needed to be careful. It was a local newspaper that anyone might find strolling through White Cap Peaks' main street. But the Mandevilles couldn't be trusted right now, and it was best that they didn't know how aware or unaware we were about the goings-on around Mr. Kyte's enterprises.

I discreetly pulled the newspaper from my jacket and shoved it inside the right breast of Alex's, and then went a few rows up to sit with the girls again. After all that stealthiness, it turned out the Mandevilles never even boarded the trolley. They went ahead of us in some fancy car with a driver provided by Mr. Kyte.

We wound back around the track between the mountains as the snowflakes continued to build heaps outside. When we reached the east side of the main street, the trolley engineer switched tracks to turn north. Evidently, this area was the poor side of town. Dilapidated homes, dirty streets lined with garbage. My hearted grew heavy as I wondered if any of the children that lived here ever got to go inside Mr. Kyte's place.

Further north, we saw peaks of the roller coaster and Ferris wheel of the park. The parking area was quite large and there were all sorts of odd forms of transportation resting in the lots. Old model T looking vehicles with exposed engines and more mufflers than could possibly be needed, cars with wooden panelling along the back and metal in the front that made them look like a boat on wheels, what appeared to be an actual tank, and another mode of transportation that looked like a rocket laid horizontally with wheels placed under it. They were fantastic creations. I looked back at the boys who, despite their look of apprehension from reading the paper, were wide-eyed as children gazing through a storefront window at Christmas time.

The next thing to catch our eyes was an expansive and ornate sign across the entry of the park that said Kaleidoscope Kyte's. Each letter was constructed of gears, springs, tools, pulleys, and a variety of other metal pieces that I had no idea what you would call, and backlit by red and blue bulbs.

We came to a stop in front of the magnificent sign. I walked back to the boys, to feign giving Alex his pen back, and took the newspaper from him. I sat down next to the girls and stealthily moved it from my jacket to the trolley floor underneath our bench. But what happened next sent a jolt of panic through my insides.

Reginald and Mr. Kyte came up the steps inside the trolley. They walked up the middle aisle until they were about six feet in front of us. Caroline followed in and wedged herself next to a dancer who had room on her bench. I glanced down at the paper on the floor surreptitiously. The headline would be in view if they looked at the ground. I froze, not wanting to bring any more attention to it by moving.

"Well kids, you've made it to the grandest amusement park known to man. No matter how cold it is, it's unmatched in architecture, creativity, and entertainment." Mr. Kyte was beaming. "You're going to see things you've never thought possible." His face grew more serious as he continued, "And here's the thing, when you perform here, you need to become a part of it. I must make the demand that you all step beyond your comfort zone."

"We can do that, can't we troupe?" Reginald asked, coercively. He looked determined and his snarl, the one he thought was a fake smile but was actually quite horrifying, was more overbearing than usual. Like one peep of cautionary questioning would get us shot.

As they stared over our heads, very slowly, I moved to place my foot over the headline of the newspaper on the floor. My palms broke out into sweat when I noticed Caroline's eye trail down my moving knee to my foot. I held my breath. Her eyes moved back up to my face. She held eye contact and then flicked her gaze to Shay, Ava, and then to the other side of the room as if she had seen nothing. I just knew she was going to poke Reg and the jig would be up. But she didn't move a perfectly postured muscle.

They exited the trolley and beckoned us to hurry up and follow. I looked at Shay and Ava with wide speaking eyes who returned something similar. Why didn't Caroline say anything? Without saying a word, we rose and walked the single file line down and out of the trolley. Despite the slight hiccup with the newspaper, we had to remain flat.

Upon the first view of Mr. Kyte's extensive grounds, even from outside the gates, you could tell immediately that it was a masterpiece. From there, it evoked the childlike sense of whimsical wonder one experiences the first time they lay eyes on a striped rag top circus tent. We were all filled with excitement to know what was inside, just as any kid would be. But as adults, however mature an adult we may vary, we were all in an alerted state considering all we knew about this place. It called for some complicated feelings. Kind of like when gambling. Maybe you know you should stay away from the casino, but it keeps drawing you in. There's allure in unpredictability.

"Alright kids, let's head this way." Mr. Kyte's voice was assertive and demanding, but coated in a facade of hospitality, not too unlike the way Reginald spoke to us. He gestured at the entrance. "I will introduce you all to my assistant, who will give you a small tour of the park and loop back around to the theater."

It was a midweek day, and therefore the park was in full operation. People were swarming around everywhere. Kids running wild-eyed and parents screaming at them to, "Get back here, right this instant!" The smell of buttery popcorn, cotton candy, and soft pretzels was warm and inviting at the front gate concessions. There was music in the background, but it was nothing I'd ever listened to. It sounded like some sort of techno classical with piano and string instruments sped up and thumping to a electronic beat.

The troupe followed Mr. Kyte and the Mandevilles inside the gates and stopped in front of a giant eagle sculpture made entirely of random pieces of scrap metal. It was probably twelve feet in height and had an open wingspan of more than double that. At the eagle's feet stood a tall and slender Native American man, his skin dark and his hair long and black, though age had given him a few gray streaks. He wore a bearskin coat, which was an extraordinary sight to behold. His face was solemn and his affect flat, a protection of all the knowledge and vision behind his gaze.

"This is Gray Cloud. He'll be the one giving you the tour. He has known this park the longest and these mountains behind it even longer," said Mr. Kyte. He turned to face Gray Cloud and lowered his voice to him. Gray

Cloud nodded once, and Mr. Kyte turned his attention to the Mandevilles. "Let's go find a drink, shall we?" And with that, they left us staring at the mysterious and ceremonious figure who was to be our guide.

Gray Cloud slowly and gracefully extended his arm toward the east before turning to lead us. As he walked through the crowd, I could see that his pace never changed. He flowed like a river as people of all ages ran and skirted past him. Any glimpses of his face that I caught were of unwavering calm and without expression. I couldn't decide if he was to be feared for his consistent coldness or pitied for his apparent repression.

The first attraction we came to was the roller coaster, but it was nothing unusual other than the fact that its aesthetic, like everything else there, comprised metal and iron, steam and rust. Regardless, there was a long line of people waiting to ride it with exhilarated looking expressions. The second exhibit on our path, however, was something to behold.

We all stopped, including Gray Cloud, and marveled at a landscaped sitting or viewing area. Short, about two foot tall shrubs, created intricate maze-like patterns of curved half moons followed by cross hatch or intersecting lines. It spread all around tables and chairs so that patrons could rest and contemplate the intricacy of creating such a thing. Though it would have been green, it was currently caked in snow by about two or three inches, which gave it a lace like appearance. But that wasn't all to this area.

Over head were floating rock formations as if blown from a bubble wand and then stopped in place across the air. They hung in the sky freely. Iced in snowfall like a chocolate donut with cream spread on top. Patrons sat beneath them sipping hot chocolate or cider or coffee while taking in the view. I had never seen anything like it and didn't believe it was physically possible. Though we all stared and mumbled bewilderedly, the park guests seemed perfectly content believing such a thing existed so easily here.

"Sky gardens," Gray Cloud stated.

We were still perplexed at the sight of the gardens when everyone in the troupe jolted at the sound of a squeeze bulb air horn. Our eyes found the source of it. A dapper-looking man with a very thin mustache pedaling by on a high wheeler bicycle. Its front wheel rising about four feet, about fifty inches in diameter, and its back wheel maybe a foot. The whole troupe laughed and waved as the rider tipped his hat to us. And I could've sworn I saw Ava wink at him.

Gray Cloud's face was unchanged, and he continued to lead us onward. I had seen what I thought was a Ferris wheel from far away during our trolley ride to Frigid Ridge, but seeing it before me was totally different than I had expected. After all, a typical Ferris wheel has only one wheel.

Mr. Kyte's Ferris wheel seemed to be composed of four wheels and in front of the entry gate was another giant scrap metal sculpture; a compass. Each wheel was positioned in a different plane. Think of a compass face and imagine you can somehow place it on top of the Ferris wheel. If you were looking down at it from an aerial view, a wheel would rotate in the north to south plane, the west to east plane, the northwest to southeast plane, and the southwest to northeast plane. This made Mr. Kyte's Ferris wheel look more like the rotating skeleton of a globe than a mill wheel.

There was no paint or lights on the Ferris wheel. Only metal and iron, grease and rust. It moved as slowly as a typical Ferris wheel, but somehow I thought it would make a person dizzier to watch all the adjacent movements. Nevertheless, the guests riding it were gleeful. They shouted down to their waiting family members when they reached the top of the arch. Children waved to kids riding in the other planes as they rotated over their head or beside them.

"Do we get to ride this stuff?" Alex asked with a hopeful look on his face.

I shrugged, and we continued the tour. What we saw next was undoubtedly one of the reasons Mr. Kyte could state that there were attributes that were seemingly impossible in his amusement park. Straight ahead was another sign that said Sky Wire made of shaped woven fencing wire in cursive. At first glance, you would wonder what you were supposed to be looking at. Next, you would find a few bubbles floating down here and there. And then you'd look up to investigate the source of these bubbles.

Everyone's eyes slowly rose and travelled upwards, squinting against the rays of the sun and falling flurries. Way up high in the air was a man in a white suit who appeared to be stepping across an invisible path. He held a long, white balancing pole and had something odd strapped to his head. It was a bubble machine. It was amazing to think one of those bubbles could sink so far down to us before popping. The wire walker almost blended in with the white mountainous landscape behind him, like a snowy owl. We watched in awe as he slowly stepped across the Sky Wire and eventually realized what the wire was attached to.

On either side of the wire was a hot air balloon, stabilized in place by ropes reaching down to the ground we were standing on, so that it wouldn't float away. The man in the white suit was walking across a wire that was attached to each of them. Both balloons comprising a rainbow of dyes in a prismatic design. A big pop of color amongst a sea of iron and rust below, and white mountains beyond.

I looked through the crowd for our own high wire performer. When I found his face, I saw it was a countenance riddled with anxiety.

"We've never had a wire that high," Shay said quietly.

Gray Cloud wordlessly continued walking. We weaved through an area that had several scrap metal sculptures, like the eagle where we first met our quiet guide. A standing grizzly bear, a pegasus about to take flight, and a commanding elephant with its trunk raised high. A buffalo in mid gallop, a male lion complete with springs for his mane, and a crouching dragon with a twenty-something foot wingspan you had to walk under. Each of them made of hub caps, metal pans, gears, springs, rods, bolts, tin, fencing and baling wire, graters, old utensils, and an assortment of other hardware.

To salvage left over metal that others would deem garbage, and patiently piece them together, welding and bending until you have formed the silhouette of an actual creature scaled to size or larger. We were in awe. It was spectacular. I would have never dreamed up the idea, but someone around here was a master at it.

We continued moving and passed a very antiquated carousel. It was not metal, just the usual sort of mediums that made carousels. The horse were very worn by adoring riders over many, many years. But to me, their look of wear gave them more appeal and evoked the wonder of how they had survived all this time. Each horse was once hand painted with smooth curving shadows along the horse's muscles, highlights in their flowing manes, and intricate designs on their saddles. They were now chipped and nicked, scratched and scuffed, but still beautiful in their aged state. Palomino, Appaloosa, Buckskin, Clydesdale, Dapple gray, Chestnut, and Bay, all winding in their singular circular path.

The anticipation grew as we were led to the front of the theater. It was a colossal building near the center of Mr. Kyte's park, and it grew in aesthetic enormity as we were walking closer and closer to it. The exterior walls were painted a robust magenta and there was gold filigree trim, winding and scalloped and lining every edge and corner, giving it a kingly and royal look. Gothic architecture surrounded the windows. Gold painted columns connected to each other by archways and book ended the main entryway, through which a crowd would enter. To enter you passed through red wooden doors with ornamental wrought iron curling and waving across its bright paint in pleasant and electrifying contrast. Above that was a giant retro marquee sign that spelled out Kastle Theater in giant Edison bulbs; and of course, the change from C to K was for Kyte.

It took a minute for the troupe, who were all still taking in the building's luxuriousness before them, to realize that Gray Cloud had stopped and now had his arm extended towards the theater doorway.

His face never changed. It appeared worn and hardened from years of dissatisfaction and toil. A quiet display of perseverance. There was no cue on it that told you to engage with it, elicit conversation with it. But as I looked at it, I felt drawn to the story behind the man's eyes. There was something captivating there, probably all kinds of untapped treasures and wisdom.

We all poured into the theater to find a huge open space right through the center that would be the performance floor. Red vinyl chairs for seating went on in rows and rows, jumping up to higher tiers and continuing up the walls on the right and left sides of the room.

At the back end of the stage floor sat an enormous display that spanned across the back wall. In the center was a shiny brass colored scrap metal sculpture of a pretty woman's face. She had gears of different sizes and designs all around her, and silvery piping that hung in bunches around her ears and missing shoulders. She looked like a metal princess with gears for a crown and piping for hair. Around her were painted clouds. To her left was a giant moon, to her right a sun, both of which looked like there were made by patchwork in complementing colors and patterns. On either side of those were faux hot air balloons, a blue one by the moon and a red one by the sun. The entire display was lined with gold filigree like a Victorian picture frame.

Underneath the princess was an archway with a lit sign that said Kastle Theater in bright golden yellow. And the archway was covered by a thick red velvet curtain. A source of entry for the king of the Kastle himself.

Currently, Mr. Kyte and the Mandevilles were standing in front of the display in deep discussion of the logistics. When we all poured in, Mr. Kyte made a welcoming gesture to usher us forward. Gray Cloud steadily walked toward them.

"Well, what did you think?" Mr. Kyte asked as he swept his arms through the air. Everyone in the crowd mumbled a number of adjectives in response: great, amazing, beautiful. The Mandevilles smiled warmly at him.

"It'll be your home for the next two weeks," Mr. Kyte continued. "You may as well enjoy it. I'll make sure you all get ride passes."

Everyone cheered at this. And if I was being honest, I felt a jolt of excitement too.

"Now, in exchange, I'll make some minor adjustments to your routines. Give them a bit more shock and awe, a bit more flair. Zhush it up some. And you need not worry. Reginald here says you'll have no trouble at all with it," Mr. Kyte said. To which some looks of excitement and cheerfulness faded, but quickly adjusted to maintain the facade of calm.

"They'll be great," Reginald piped. "I haven't invested in them for nothing." He smiled that scary fake grin of his, the one that threatened us through his teeth.

"Oh yes, that makes sense knowing what you're after." Mr. Kyte chuckled as he looked from Reginald to Caroline and back to Reginald. "Those things are expensive, you know?"

"Yes," Caroline breathed through a strained laugh. She looked like she wanted to change subjects.

I looked at Shay with suspicious eyes. What in the world did that mean?

"I'll give you guys a day to get..." Mr. Kyte paused and looked slyly at the ceiling, "acclimated."

We had been freezing all day. I could imagine what it would feel like to be in the park wearing only a leotard or body suit.

"Oh, how silly of me. I forgot to show off one of my most grand performers," Mr. Kyte said as he placed a hand on Gray Cloud's shoulder. "He's been right under your nose all day."

Gray Cloud's placid expression did not change, and he slowly turned to face Mr. Kyte.

"Give these kids a small taste. We've got to teach them something. How about a bolt?" Mr. Kyte asked this of Gray Cloud in a self-assured manner, more like a sugar-coated command than a request.

Gray Cloud slowly lifted his hands until they were straight out in front of him. Electricity popped and glowed between his hands. The theater lights flickered in reaction. Gray Cloud held lightning in his palms like a plasma ball lamp. He thrusted his wrists upward, and it shot above us in the air of the domed theater and a clap of thunder resounded as it disappeared. Its echo rang out afterwards.

We all stared at Gray Cloud with mouths agape. An illusion of this nature was unprecedented. Even the Mandevilles looked shocked. But Gray Cloud remained unfazed, a sense of stoic on his face.

"Lesson number one, kids. Never piss off a man who can control the weather," Mr. Kyte laughed openly.

I didn't know Gray Cloud from Adam, but my heart ached for him. Thoughts solidified in my mind as I watched this interaction. His face was confirmation. It told me to be wary of Mr. Kyte.

Chapter 5

Taking A Ride

Our gaggle of people started to spread. A lady had entered the theater bringing ride passes to hand out to all the members of our troupe. After each of us got one, we scattered throughout the park like ants. Our small group of friends wandered around together.

The park had a few stores within it. A coffee shop, a souvenir shop, a small restaurant and, thankfully, a quirky little vintage clothing shop. I stopped in and bought the biggest jacket I could find with the tiny amount of pay we got from our Merdwick stop. It was an olive green asymmetrical button front coat lined with sherpa. My legs would freeze, but maybe my torso would be warm.

The rest of the group bought unique pieces of winter wear too, but Alex and I were the most under prepared. Alex skimped a little and bought a well-worn black bomber jacket for cheap, and though it was not the thickest option, it was attractive on him. I raised an eyebrow when he took it to the counter.

"What?"

"That's not near warm enough for the arctic tundra outside," I said.

"I don't like my arm movements restricted. Plus, I'm saving."

"For what?"

"For whatever we may need as we stay aboard this crazy train," he mumbled under his breath for discretion.

"Leave him alone, Janie. He's hot blooded anyway. Always complaining about our room temperature. And you do see how perfect that looks on him, right?" said Zeke.

"Don't encourage him," Alex said, his brows playfully lifting in disbelief as he looked at Zeke.

After we had all paid, we walked out and immediately put on our new clothing items, stuffing the bags in the nearby trash cans. The purchases helped some. It was dreadfully cold outside, but at least the sun was beaming. And the excitement of getting to ride the rides was growing. As a group, we decided to start at the Ferris wheel.

Each car had room for two, so we paired off. Alex and Daniel, Ava and Shay, me and Zeke. After being locked in, we rotated up the creaking black spider of a frame.

"So, where's Tombo now?" I asked.

"Anthony is supposed to be taking him back to Frigid Ridge today, when he gets done being the Mandevilles' puppet. God bless him," Zeke said, with a sense of worry on the edge of his tone.

"That's good. How on earth is he working this out, though?"

"Anthony pleads the case that we have to practice so much more than others to get the timing right for the ventriloquy. Reg gives him a pass," he brightened. "And it helps that Reg thinks we are a big money drawing act."

"Does Reg ever talk to you about it?"

"Sometimes. He checks in and seems genuinely concerned that we are being supplied with all we need for our act." Zeke paused and sighed with frustration. "I don't know what to make of him. I know you've had a rough go with him, but he can be supportive at times. Then he blows up and throws Tombo in with the other animals. But Anthony says he's not so bad if you know how to work him."

"How are things with Anthony?"

"Good. He still struggles with what happened in Merdwick. Like post traumatic stress. He has bouts of guilt. But he's slowly getting better."

We paused our conversation to wave and yell at Alex and Daniel, who were passing over our heads in the opposite plane.

"Well, that's good, but I meant things with you and Anthony," I said.

"Oh." Zeke couldn't help but blush a little. "It's great. I'm damn near head over heels. I've never been in a relationship that felt so comfortable. Having a real partner, being in this thing together. I spent so much time hiding who I was, shoving away that part of me. Because my parents were so... unable to understand. And then it was so hard to know where to even start once you decide to be who you are born to be. How do you know who is safe to talk to?" He stared in thought momentarily. "It's just nice to have someone that's easy to be around, feel safe around. To travel with, explore with, share with. On that note, you should be able to relate a little."

"Yeah, well, maybe a little. But it sounds like you've got a better deal than me right now," I said.

"You know, communication is everything. And life is short," Zeke began, but I stopped him.

"I know, I know. It's just hard and weird." Paranoia struck me. "Please tell me you're not having conversations like this with him," I said. The him, of course, being Alex.

"No, no. I wouldn't do that. That's your business."

"Good." I breathed out in relief.

"I'm glad you were on that train, Janie. I'm glad we met. You're alright," Zeke said.

"Same here. And so are you. Otherwise, I wouldn't be hanging out with you," I smiled teasingly.

We had descended toward the platform, and the wheel was slowly coming to a halt to unload our section. Zeke and I waited for the others to exit their cars. We all headed to the carousel. I picked a gray horse with black hair that reminded me of the hobby horse I used to bounce on as a little girl. Back when times were simpler and I had no worries. I wondered what my parents were doing now. It had been so long since I had seen them.

The tethered hot air balloon rides were next up on the path through Kaleidoscope Kyte's. There was a bit of a line, but we talked and joked as we waited. Shay wanted to ride with me this time. When the riders before us drifted down and landed, a little pang of fear hit my stomach as I watched the fire bursting up inside the balloon. I had seen pictures of baskets on fire from hundreds of feet up. Nevertheless, I followed Shay and boarded.

As we lifted, when the tether was barely off the ground, I thought, "This isn't so bad, pretty smooth." But as we continued to climb higher, I got squirmy. The operator informed us we were only ascending one hundred feet, but twenty or thirty was quite enough for me.

I watched as the rest of our group grew smaller and smaller, like little dots on the black and snow blotted pavement. Shay had her elbows propped on the side of the basket, completely unfazed, actually rather giddy.

"Ahh, it's great being up here. A relief not having to tune out all the voices. I wish I could stay up here all the time," she whispered.

"Uh huh," I gulped.

"When I was a young, and figuring everything out..." She winked at me so I would understand, but the operator would remain clueless. "I used to wish so hard I could fly. So I could get away from everything at a moment's notice. Make things quiet, turn the noise down."

"I haven't thought of this until now, but what about the animals?"

"I can't hear them," said Shay.

"Tombo?"

"Nope, there's something different about animals." Shay went back to her daydream. "Anyway, one time I asked my grandmother if she could work some of her magic to make me fly. She told me I didn't need any magic, but that focus would lend me wings. She was trying to encourage me to become more disciplined with controlling my gift. But of course, her answer disappointed me," Shay laughed lightly as she thought. "And then The Carnival of Wonders stopped just outside of Blue Smoke Bog. One evening, I took my piggy bank money and went all by myself to see it.

The noise was something awful because there were so many people all around me. I wasn't as adept at tuning it in and out as I am now. I had a hard time even paying attention to the show. But then the aerialists came out. From way up high in the air, they perched on hoops or tied their feet up in silk. Such grace and fluidity of movement. It was so alluring that when the show was over and most every one had left, I searched the ground looking for one of them. Finally, I found a girl named Daphne and begged her to teach me how to do it."

"She was your mentor?"

"No. She told me she'd be outta there in two more days and that I should pick something other than the circus to aspire to do," Shay laughed. "Prophetic maybe, don't you think?"

"You could say that."

"I was just a kid then. But I trained and tried to get my strength up in the coming years. I made my own hoop out of an old clothing rack and tied it to a thick tree limb. Practiced on it as much as I could."

"You were determined," I smiled.

"I was. By the time I was sixteen, I was working at a diner in that little town outside the bog. At nineteen, that same circus came back around and Mr. Carlyle, the owner, came in the diner one morning. Everyone eating there was in a tizzy over him and his circus, and I just happened to be his waitress. He was a little much, calling me sweetheart and honey when he asked for more coffee or butter. But I told him I wanted to be an aerialist and asked him if I could audition for his circus."

"You got in?"

Shay lowered her voice. "Yep. My gift served me well in keeping away from a nasty old man, but I learned a lot from the other aerialists in the troupe. Then, about six months into gigging, the circus started losing steam, wasn't making enough to keep traveling. They found Carlyle dead and Reginald Mandeville came swooping in. Of course, he picked through the acts, dumping the ones he deemed lackluster. But I made the cut."

"And here we are," I said.

"And here we are. Way up high." Shay smiled, "What about you? How'd you wind up an aerialist?"

"The story is not as cool as yours. I just saved up and took classes. There was a studio in the town where Alex and I first met. I practice there for a few years before we started traveling."

Shay nodded and operator let us know we were about to descend. It was a pleasantly graceful landing, like a butterfly lighting on a flower. Shay stepped out of the basket with ease and our friends clapped and giggled as I bumbled out like a newborn baby calf. I executed a mocking curtesy once my feet were on the ground.

I looked at the faces of my friends. We were happy, at the moment, not worrying about our past or the dangerous future. Each of us carried so much of our own personal history, that created our perspective and who we were as a person. Talking to Zeke and Shay had reminded me of that.

Everyone is a product of their experience. Their perceptions, values, and traits come from the past. Their childhood most importantly, and the experiences they grow into adulthood with. We all had baggage, and we all wanted relief. That goes for all humans, really.

Their faces didn't show it at that moment. Even though it was freezing, and snow was collecting on top of our heads, we were as happy as the little kids running through the park surrounding us. That's the wonder of the circus. Of a fair, or a park. It momentarily transports you.

"Us next!" Ava exclaimed and dragged Alex by the arm to board the balloon. I looked at my feet and tried to adjust my new jacket to keep from showing my flabbergasted and wounded expression.

"You knew this was coming," I thought to myself, "Suck it up."

I must've put on a good face because Shay, Zeke, and Daniel began conversation like there was nothing the matter, which was good.

It seemed like they were up there for ages. What would they be talking about? My heart lurched as I imagined her slapping his shoulder flirtatiously. I felt like my body and soul were shrinking.

They finally landed, exited the basket, and walked back over to us as Zeke and Daniel went up in the balloon. Ava began talking nonstop, which was not unusual, but Alex didn't say much. I smiled and nodded intermittently during Shay and Ava's chit chat.

When Zeke and Daniel returned, Shay reported the time and we all made our way back to the trolley station. Everyone sat on the bench except me and Alex. We stood to face them. I half listened as I looked at the park from the distant station. It was a sight. Since it was growing dusky, the lights were turned on and the park was now illuminating. The Ferris wheel still turning, the coaster still zooming up and down its track.

Toward the right side of the park's exterior, some unusual movement caught my eye. It wasn't a person walking, or a car driving. I squinted to focus. It was a horse, an actual horse, and a rider. I knocked Alex's arm and pointed, and everyone on the bench slowly turned around.

"I think it's Gray Cloud," I said. I watched as he looked over his right shoulder, bouncing along on his horse. He rode around the corner of the park's edge and up toward the mountain.

"Where's he going?" said Ava.

"Maybe an errand for Kyte. Checking on the decaying bodies behind the park," said Alex.

Zeke looked at his watch. "Maybe home," he said.

Chapter 6

Come To Collect

When we got back to Frigid Ridge, we found Anthony seated at the piano in the lobby. Beside him was Tombo, tinkering on the keys as he played. Zeke was thrilled at the sight of them.

"My two favorite guys!" Zeke exclaimed as he hugged Tombo's hairy body.

"This favorite guy has a special request," Anthony said as he nodded to Tombo.

"Oh yeah. What's that?" Zeke asked.

"Maybe we need to convene in you boys' room. Girls, I'll explain later. No need to worry," Anthony said. Zeke raised his eyebrows at Alex and Daniel and pointed his arm toward their room. Us girls shooed them along compliantly.

I sat down at the piano when they had left. Ava sat down beside me.

"Want me to show you a little nocturne?" she asked, warm and friendly.

There was a struggle inside me to allow her anywhere near my vulnerable inner feelings. But she had done nothing wrong. She had done nothing against me. We had discussed Alex so many times now. She had every right to do as she please since I acted so uninterested in the tiniest of subjects related to him.

"Sure," I said.

Her fingers moved slowly, lightly landing and pressing atop a few keys, and then pausing to allow me to imitate her strokes. She played the high end while I played the low. Together we took turns playing the melody of Chopin's nocturne number two.

Ava was a patient teacher. When I jumbled a progression or missed a key, she would say, "it's okay, just keep going." We completed the abridged version and repeated it again so that I could try to memorize its flow.

Though occasionally staccato at times, it should flow or pause and fall in with the timing. At last, my fingers had stuttered through the little melody. Shay clapped lightly behind the piano bench in approval.

Ava wrapped an arm around my shoulders. "See! It's not so tough. You got it," she said.

"Yeah," I slowly breathed, as if I was just starting to believe her statement myself. I felt a little crumby for not envisioning that Ava possessed the kindness to share something with me. To lend her hand at teaching me something beautiful instead of lording her talents over me. My ego was trying to pit me against her, but I knew it was wrong. "Thanks for showing it to me."

"Keep it up. I'll show you some more along the way," she said as she stood up from the bench.

I kept tinkering through the nocturne as Ava and Shay headed to the room. I wondered if I was annoying the receptionist at the front desk, but whenever I glanced at her, she seemed to smile encouragingly. As if to say, "Go on, it's okay." An elderly woman with kind eyes, maybe she played too.

Steadily, Chopin filled the air more fluidly as I went through the progression again and again. The flow of the activity was good for my soul. To focus on memorizing and executing something new, to hear the soothing notes of a seasoned piano, to feel the warmth of the lobby that sheltered us from the freezing climate outside. It sort of transported me away from the negative headspace we were all forced to now live in.

The music, paired with the glow of the chandeliers overhead, evoked a wondering of how long this place had housed such a grand piano. How many pianists sat at her bench? How many years of her singing rang through this hotel? In this strange place of industrial metal and steam. Something so beautiful and calming in juxtaposition with the rumored dangers surrounding Mr. Kyte, his park, and maybe his properties, too.

I was concentrating so hard on the black and white rectangles spread out in a line before me. It took me an extra few seconds to process that someone had sat down in the chair just beside the piano bench; the chair for the listener. My eyes flickered up once, back down, and then quickly back up again in a double take.

Sat with her shoulders back and relaxed, her head turned slightly to the side as if listening intently, and her right leg crossed over her left. Donned in a burgundy evening dress, her blonde hair half back in long, flowing waves.

I immediately thought, "This is it. She's come to call me out on the newspaper." I stopped plinking the keys, but Caroline swished her hand as if to say I should continue. But when I tried, Chopin was really out of sync and in complete disarray. In surrender, I put my hands down in my lap and swiveled on the bench to face her expectantly.

"New to the instrument?" she asked.

"Yes. I can't really play. Ava just showed me this bit."

Caroline relaxed further into her chair and stared off at an invisible daydream. "I always thought it would be nice if my mother had taught me an instrument. Any instrument. Because it would be something you could take with you where ever you go." She paused thoughtfully, "Your mother ever teach you anything like that, something you could take along?"

"Uh, well she taught me how to cook. A couple of card games." As my words came out they seemed ignorant. I hadn't really thought much about what kind of folklore was imparted to me by my parents.

"My mother didn't really stick around to teach me much of anything," Caroline breathed. I dropped my head in a nonchalant nod, but instantly felt like garbage.

"That's out of my control," Caroline continued. "But when I have a child of my own, I'll be to them the mother I always wanted."

I remembered how Shay had first told me that the Mandevilles were trying to have children, but currently to no avail. And I didn't know where to go from there. Caroline had just more or less confided something huge to me, made herself vulnerable in a way. Instead of playing it cool and waiting for her to continue, I awkwardly fumbled to a new and more dangerous topic.

"Listen, Caroline, I'm sorry about the newspaper. We had just heard some rumors..." I sputtered.

"I'm not here about the newspaper."

"You're not?"

"No. I don't want this troupe in a chaotic mess over that article, but that's not why I'm here. I needed to talk to you about something else," Caroline said quietly.

"Oh... okay."

"You remember the slip up in Merdwick? When Reg got so angry with you about the aerial cube routine."

"Yes."

"And I calmed him down. Got you a second chance." Her voice was slow and flat and even, unemotional to a point that conveyed control. Firstly, control of her own emotions and secondly, control over me.

"Yes."

"I said you would owe me a favor..." Her eyes were like that of a lioness watching the prey it intends to feed its cubs. "I'm here to redeem it."

"I understand," I said slowly. My mind reeling in search of what I could offer Caroline. What did I have to give? What could she ask of me? This time I waited for her to go on.

"The chance to be a mother has evaded me for several years now. It's drove Reginald into a madman. We've tried, painstakingly. Paid endlessly for tonics, treatments, and therapies." She was frustrated and her face looked agonized as she spoke. "We got word of something, while we were in Merdwick. A friend reached out and told us a rumor they'd heard about an incredible doctor, one with special abilities. Unconventional compared to your typical fertility specialist, but efficient and legendary in his success. We heard he lived here somewhere, in White Cap Peaks. So Reginald went straight to contacting Mr. Kyte, to ask him for work. To get us here to the location... and to get away from Mr. Hagan."

As she revealed this, it enthralled me to know how Reginald and Caroline were truly operating. Shay was on to something. She was right in her assessment that the Mandevilles had other motives than just making money and owning a circus. They were methodical, working to get what they wanted. It was alluring and terrifying all at once, because I still believed Reg may have set up that accident in Merdwick. That maybe he was trying to make me fall and get rid of me. But the good news now—was that he might be preoccupied with this fertility situation.

Caroline continued, "We sought information from Mr. Kyte once we got here, after we got him loosening up on drinks. Kyte says that the rumor seems to be true, that he heard around town of a special doctor for women. But apparently the doctor is quite secret, elusive really. He's not doing this for money so he's not advertising or broadcasting where to find him." She breathed out a sigh of exhaustion. "Now Reginald is already on the search. But he's going at it like a heat seeking missile destroying everything in its path. He takes the strong arm approach to getting information. But… Have you ever heard the expression, 'You catch more flies with honey than vinegar'?"

 "Uh… yes."

Caroline looked me in the eye and said, "This is where you come in."

My mind was a whirl. This doctor didn't even sound real. How could I do anything to aid her cause?

"I need to know who he is, where he is, and what I have to do for him to help me," Caroline said.

"Caroline," I proceeded cautiously, "I would love to help you, but how can I?"

"I've watched you since we brought you on. You're a driven person, and loyal to your friends, your group. You guys trust each other. All good things, all more honey than vinegar."

"I guess so."

"You and Shay have been with each other from the start. Grown close, roomed together," Caroline continued.

"Yes."

"Then you know Shay can find the doctor," said Caroline.

The pieces of the puzzle fell into place, and I understood.

"I want you and Shay to do reconnaissance throughout town. To help me find this doctor."

"Why didn't you ask Shay?"

"Because Shay doesn't owe me a favor, you do. You can convince Shay to help you."

"How will we get away from the park? To have time to do this?"

"I'll take care of that," said Caroline.

I starred at my knees and shook my head, "I don't know." I felt overwhelmed.

"Please," Caroline said as she put a hand, with perfectly manicured nails, on my knee, "I need you to do this for me. All I've ever wanted was a chance to be a mother. And you can help me."

Her eyes were misty, and her tone was genuine. I truly wanted to help her because it was my nature to help people, anyway. And to help a woman achieve motherhood, that was new, but I was already dreaming up how good it would feel to help her succeed.

"Janie, you have to." Caroline's eyes had turned stern. "If you don't, I will not vouch for you again. And I know you want to stay with us, with all of your friends."

She maintained eye contact as she slowly rose to stand. Then she left me on the piano bench and went to her room.

I sat there, unmoving and processing, for a minute or two. Somehow, though it seemed to me unwarranted, Caroline had decided we would be allies. With sinking eyebrows, I glancing from right to left across the checked tile floor, trying to think. My face propped up by my left fist, I decided I really didn't have a choice in the matter. I had to stay in the circus. I couldn't watch them move on without me. I could just imagine seeing Alex trailing off in the distance. Not only that, but Caroline was right. Shay was now one of my greatest friends; and what about Zeke and Ava, Daniel and even Anthony? And Tombo! I was happy with my little circus family.

"Whisper, what am I gonna do?" I thought in my head. "Even with Shay's help, how are we going to find some secret fertility doctor without Reginald going berserk if he notices us missing at practice? I'm overwhelmed."

"You're right, you know. You don't have much of a choice," they seemed to reply.

"This is going to take so much time, a lot of time. And we don't have time."

"It will take the time it will take. You can only do your part."

"Why me, though?" I thought, exasperated.

"Janie. You were made to show light. You were made to help others. You're very well suited to help this young lady find her happiness," Whisper said inaudibly.

It didn't make me feel much better; it didn't make the task ahead any easier.

"You won't be alone. Shay will be an extraordinary help," they continued pressing. "Plus, I'm here too. On your side."

"Yes, and I'm grateful." I relaxed my face and neck. I dropped my hands to my lap with my palms up and exhaled. Still sat on the piano bench and facing east of it. I closed my eyes for a minute and let my head tilt back. "Breathe in, breathe out, this is not your first rodeo," my inner dialogue talked to myself.

"Dear… are you alright?"

I popped open my eyes to see the lobby desk receptionist looking at me funny.

"Oh yes. I'm fine. I'm just heading to my room now," I said as I stood up. I bet it must've looked strange, a girl in her own little world perched on the piano bench no longer playing but sitting there like a meditating monk. I walked into the hallway where my room was as quietly and normally as possible.

Chapter 7

The Ante Upped

The following morning, our gang sat together at a pair of tables in the dining area of the Frigid Ridge. Though we were stuck in the coldest climate yet, I was thankful to be lodged there; it was warm, cozy, and homey. But what really sold me was the food we were being served at the lodge. It was the best breakfast spread that I had the pleasure of partaking from in years. The entire room smelled like maple syrup and hot butter.

Alex did not spare the chance of gorging to a maximum, given free breakfast on the Mandevilles. As usual, he ate several plates piled high with pancakes and sausage, biscuits and gravy, a mountain of fried bacon, an apple, a banana, and lastly a small cup of yogurt, which he force fed himself for health reasons. Where all that food went, we'll never know. He was still slender as a cheetah.

"Well ladies, the cat is out of the bag. Or monkey, I should say," said Zeke. Shay and I smiled and nodded as we continued nibbling bagels with cream cheese and spooning down brown sugar oatmeal.

"What?" Ava said, looking confused.

"Oh! That's right. There's one more we missed." Zeke lowered his voice to a whisper. "Sit by me on the trolley and I'll fill you in."

Apparently, Tombo was fed up with the secrecy. He told Anthony that if he was going to stay in the hotel with the rest of our group; he wanted to share his own two cents as troubles or dangers arose. Considering what had happened at Merdwick, and the discovered rumors of White Cap Peaks. Tombo felt he could be a spy for us, unsuspecting eyes and ears within the park and whenever the Mandevilles were near.

Zeke was not exactly thrilled with the proposal. But half of us already knew about Tombo's secret abilities anyway. He trusted Alex and Daniel and would be relieved if he didn't have to hide his most precious secret from his own roommates, especially with Tombo being in the same room with them. And Tombo wouldn't have to spend all that time without speaking. So when Zeke filled Ava in, all of us knew.

The group of us swore to honor the secret and protect Tombo to the full extent of our capabilities. Alex was thrilled and spent nights asking Tombo loads of questions as Daniel listened and watched wide-eyed. Ava adored the fuzzy little chimp all the more.

As dangerous as it was to let anyone else know about this secret, it would be beneficial to have Tombo around. To be another watchful and cautionary investigator of this unique little town at the bottom of the snowy mountain.

"Is there anyone else who has a cool and useful talent that they'd like to share with the group?" Alex said in hushed tones lined with sarcasm and a goofy grin. He thought he was being cute.

The trolley ride was uneventful, thankfully, and we arrived at Kaleidoscope Kyte's by nine o'clock in the morning. With our gaggle of circus folk, we walked straight to the theater to find the Mandevilles and Mr. Kyte talking animatedly in the center of the room. Near the back, Gray Cloud was pushing a large broom across the floor with the same stoic countenance.

"Ah, they're here." Mr. Kyte's smile spread across his face under his white curling mustache. "I hope you all had a great time enjoying the park yesterday, but alas, it's time to get down to business. We will now inform you of your assignments," he said, glancing at Reginald and Caroline. "Remember, as I mentioned to you upon arrival, we want to take it to the extreme, and we want to capitalize on the climate."

"Let's start with side shows," said Mr. Kyte. "Now Reginald has already acquired such a delightfully shocking group of acts, but we're going to amp it up by having you all on exhibit just after the path of metal sculptures and before the theater. Additionally, you will be wearing scrap metal covers. Think of a bathing suit."

I scanned the group to see the performer's responses. Their faces were stony, but they couldn't stop their eyes from widening.

"This goes for Big Bertha, Strong Man Kai, the snake charmer, and the secondary sword swallowers," Mr. Kyte read off a list.

The look on Bertha's face was as stoic as Gray Cloud's. Her enormity was already on display, but now she would face wearing some type of metal bikini in the freezing cold to amplify it.

Mr. Kyte handed the list to Reginald. "Alright. Animal acts including domestics, equestrian, big cats, Eloise, and Tombo. You will perform inside Kastle theater during the second part of the show. Mine and Caroline's act, contortion, and the aerial drumming act will also be in the theater." Reginald looked over the top of the list with glaring eyes, knowing there would be bickering over whose acts were inside versus outside. The look said not to dare thinking about objecting to him. He handed the paper to Caroline without taking his eyes off of our crowd of performers.

"Great. Where does that leave us you think?" I mumbled to Shay. I didn't think there was any way she could have heard me, but Caroline seemed to zero in with her icy gaze on me. It felt like a lengthy pause before her perfectly painted red lips moved.

"Tight rope walkers. You will be performing outside on the tethered hot air balloon line, the height of which will be increased to fifty feet," Caroline said calmly.

"That's thirty feet higher and between balloons," whispered Ava.

Caroline continued, "Trapezes will be attached under these two balloons, where flyers will perform in succession. Fire breathers will perform underneath these acts on the ground as usual."

I looked down at my boots and tried to focus on my breathing. If the tight rope walkers and flyers were going to be heightened, there was no way our aerial act would not be.

"Aerialists," Caroline said flatly, "You will perform a silks routine rather than the aerial cube. You will follow the trapeze flyers from the same balloons."

I looked at Shay who was still facing forward. She cut her eyes toward me, only for a moment. I thought about the tight ropers. If they were at fifty feet, the top of the silk would reach forty-five. And I hadn't done silks in a while. I would be rusty. My grip would be weak. The panic was rising as I fought to shove it down and maintain a facade of apathy.

"Ava's hoop and balancing act, as well as the jugglers, will take place prior to intermission and outside the theater entrance," Caroline said with finality as she folded the paper list.

Mr. Kyte spoke up with gusto and enthusiasm, "Oh, this is going to be grand! Aren't you guys excited? A new challenge set before each of you. You're upping your game here!" Though his face was bright, it seemed more like acting than a genuine call to inspiration.

All this time, Gray Cloud was slowly pushing the broom across the theater floor. Now Mr. Kyte shouted,

"Gray Cloud, would you come here?" He propped the broom against a wall and slowly walked over.

"I want you to be in charge of monitoring their practice and report back to me. I give you full liberty to enforce compliance with the new format of each act," Mr. Kyte energetically spouted.

Gray Cloud gave a small nod and walked away. I watched him go through the front entrance and outside. I assumed he was going to inform the folks running the Sky Wire.

"Practice begins now. Chop Chop." Mr. Kyte smiled as if he had just said that everyone got free ice cream cones, rather than implying that everyone would now submit to potential hypothermia or death by fall.

His facade made him look blissfully ignorant to how horrified we would all be, but we knew better. His white curly mustache wiggled while his eyes were aglow in anticipation. His chin jutted and raised so high I thought his top hat might fall off backwards. I kind've wished it would, though I don't think it would have really fazed him. He nodded enthusiastically toward the Mandevilles and sauntered out of Kastle theater.

The troupes' eyes were darting around, trying to get a feel for what would happen next. Those that were still performing on the ground, in the usual fashion in which they always had, only had to worry about the temperature outside. The animals would be fine. Zeke and Alex's acts would be pretty much the usual. It was the aerialists and tight roper walkers who were the most uneasy. These were dangerous heights to be performing at. Were we being singled out?

"Alright, troupe," Reginald stepped forward and spoke loudly, "You're aware of your part in this show. Now I know we had a time with the fiasco in Merdwick. And yes, you were skimped on pay. But you will follow through on this gig, and at the end of it, you'll receive full pay plus what we owed you from the Merdwick shows. Alright?" He paused and scanned our nervous congregation. "This is no big deal for you. You're a part of the Marvelous Marvels. A few feet higher or degrees colder can't deter you."

Never in a million years did I expect some sort of motivational speech from the likes of Reginald Mandeville. And I was starting to be leery of his mood swings. One day he was agreeable, the next he was a holy terror.

"Everyone, begin splitting up to do your stretching protocols and warm up..." he paused. "Warm up," he chuckled to himself, "while you can because we begin choreography and prep outside in an hour."

No one laughed, but Reg didn't mind. Shay and I picked out a corner of the theater to loosen up. I watched Caroline shoot me a glance as we sat on the floor and began straddle stretching. I felt her sense of urgency almost telepathically. I scooted in straddle stretch until I could prop up on my elbows close to Shay's face.

"I need to talk to you," I said as I scanned the immediate area around us. Ava and the jugglers were about ten feet away but preoccupied with each other. Zeke and Tombo similarly spaced in the opposite adjacent direction.

Shay bent further down to mirror me so that we looked like two very flexible girls gossiping at a slumber party. "What is it?"

"Last night, after you guys left me at the piano, Caroline spoke to me."

"Oh?"

"Yes, you know when I almost fell off the rigging at the Merdwick show, and she stuck up for me when Reg was so mad?"

"Yeah," Shay said, growing suspicious.

"Well, she came to me later in Merdwick and said I would owe her a favor."

Shay didn't respond. She only cut her eyes and turned her head apprehensively.

I looked around again, taking inventory of whether or not anyone was in earshot. "She's come to collect."

"Okay... and?"

"And I'll need your help," I said flatly.

"Janie," she drew out the last syllable of my name as if she were exhausted already.

"Listen. Apparently, there is some kind of special fertility doctor around here. And she wants to see him. See if he can help her, you know, conceive finally."

"Well, why does she need us to be involved in that?" Shay looked confused at first, but I watched her expression change as she sifted through my mind. Her face softened as she realized why. Before I had even said another word.

I had finished my spill anyway. "No one knows who this doctor is, what's his name, where to find him. She knew you could work around that. She came to me because I owe her the favor. But she knew you would help me."

"And she will cover for us while we're away trying to solve her dilemma."

"Yes," I whispered.

"When?"

"I don't know. I guess in between practices," I answered.

Shay was in thought, working out the logistics of the task like a scientist, "We can sneak off after the choreography. Sounds like the trapeze flyers will need to use the same hot air balloons that we're rigged under. We'll have to take turns anyway. While they're practicing, I guess we could take the trolley into town. But what about Gray Cloud?" Shay said.

"Shoot." I hadn't thought about Gray Cloud's task of monitoring us and reporting back to Mr. Kyte. "Think we can make friends with him?"

"He doesn't look all that friendly," Shay said with a dubious expression.

"I'm sure he has a plethora of reasons why. I'm going to try anyway," I said.

"Alright," Shay said incredulously through closed teeth.

People began crowding us as those who would be performing inside the theater began practicing their routines. We finished stretching as we watched Daniel lead Eloise into the center and start signaling her through tricks. His smile uninhibited, as if nothing could ever go wrong in our current scenario. Roustabouts began setting up Alex's coaster track, so the noise of lifts and heavy machinery made it hard to hear or have a conversation.

Caroline entered the main doors and whistled through her fingers so loud it halted the commotion. "I want all aerialists outside. Silks are up first."

Shay and I walked toward her. "Wouldn't it be a nice day to explore the shops in town?" I said to Shay as we neared Caroline. Shay and I both appeared in usual nonchalant conversation, but we both made eye contact with Caroline as we slowly walked past. Caroline nodded only once.

We stepped outside to be greeted with a thirty-six degree smack to the face. At least the sky was clear and the sun was out. Though it wasn't much help in the area of heat, it did at least improve the aesthetic. I began rubbing my hands together to produce some warmth from friction.

"I've got a routine we can do. It's a simple one that looks more impressive than it actually is. I'll walk you through it," said Shay.

"Good. I can't handle complicated from forty-five feet in the air," I replied with chattering teeth.

Gray Cloud stood at the base of the tethered hot air balloons. He signaled the controllers within them by slowly raising one hand. When he did so, two bright fire engine red silks tumbled down from the base of the balloons. They swung and jostled momentarily in the light breeze until they straightened and stopped due to their weight and gravity.

I had to admit it. The presentation of this act would be spectacular. The colossal peaking mountains, topped with crisp white snow, were in the background. The magnificent and brilliant colored hot air balloons were in perfect symmetry and now had bright red tails that reached all the way to the earth. An eagle soared across the mountain tops as I was taking it all in.

I began to understand why our acts would go first. They needed sunlight to display this work of art. They showed how distinctively remarkable this show was and would be. If I didn't suspect Mr. Kyte to be a killer, I might think he was a genius.

Removing our coats and pants until we were in the usual leotard and leggings was rough. I jumped up and down in place, trying to get my blood flowing. When using and performing with silks, it works best when tying foot holds to have bare feet. As we took our shoes and socks off, even Shay, in her multitude of strength, could not help but shiver.

"Let's do a few climbs first," Shay said. Climbs were taxing and doing several reps up and down, up and down, would fatigue the body quickly, but also warm it up. "You may as well climb all the way to the top to get used to it," said Shay.

I yanked the silks as hard as I could a few times to see that the rigging was secure. I began the first ascent with a basic climb, which would get my blood pumping. Twenty feet up, I looked down below me. It was the usual view. Thirty feet up, looking down began to be a little uncomfortable.

"No more looking down," Shay shouted. Parallel to me about fifteen yards away, she was keeping my pace so that we were increasing in height together.

I nodded. Forty feet up, I was starting to get slightly warmer, but the lump was growing in my throat.

Forty-five feet up, max peak, I looked up to see the woven basket just above my head. Through a hole in the bottom, I saw the controller propped in a corner and the fire from the propane burner under the center of the balloon.

"Hello there, Miss," the controller said politely.

"Hi," was all I could muster. About that time, a bird flew past me about five yards ahead, which drew my attention and caused me to realize the full magnitude of how high I was. This viewpoint of the mountain looked quite different.

"Alright, descend," Shay shouted.

I slowly loosened grip and foothold and sank back to the earth. The friction of the silk against the top of my foot was actually very welcome due to its warmth. At twenty feet up, which was significantly more comfortable, I switched legs to warm the other. When the ball of each foot pressed into the cold cement ground, I finally took a breath. I dropped my hands and bent forward to place them on my knees and focused on breathing. After a minute, while still in that position, I turned and squinted at Shay.

"Terrifying," I said to her.

"Gotta get back on the horse," she said as she got in position to climb again.

We did seven climbs total. By the time we were finished, I felt like I could at least move through some choreography.

Shay began walking me through fairly simple and familiar poses and transitions at the center mark. That was about twenty-five feet from the ground and passably comfortable. We slowly worked through splits while in double foot knots, fanning our free arm in a slow, wide circle like a ballerina. Candy cane pose was next, which required that you rotated through the silks, wrapping your back leg until the force of the silk pulled it into as much of a split as your groin muscles could handle. It hurt, but at the end of it you looked like some sort of maiden head on the bow of a pirate ship. Following candy cane would be a cross-back straddle. From this pose, we hung upside down in a very limber sort of seated teddy bear looking pose. Once we held the edges of the silk that spilled over each foot, we could flap the tails and transform into a radiant butterfly. I knew this trick would be a pretty one, as snowflakes fluttered down in front of the shimmering red silks. The mountain behind would beckon nature and we would look somehow more a part of it.

Next, we worked through some more daring tricks, poses, and drops, but remained close to the center point of the silks for our own safety. A creature pose which looked sort of like an upside down and sideways back bend in mid air. A belay that transitioned to a neck hang. Neck hang sounds so scary, and really it was very dangerous, but it more cradled the base of your skull than your neck. And last but not least, we ended with a beautiful angel drop.

For this we climbed a little higher than usual for dramatic effect. The drop required a lot of silk wrapping around the pelvis and legs to set up. Just before the drop, you would perch at the highest peak, which we adjusted to be at about thirty-five feet above ground, and hold a sassy little mermaid looking pose. You held the silk poles above your head and arched your back through the middle of them while your legs were straight behind you, parallel to the ground and wrapped like a lollipop stripe. Then, after a deep breath, you would shut your eyes and release your grasp. Your face hurtled straight forward until you were heels over head, and after making a three hundred and sixty degree flip, you would be back upright again; legs still beautifully wrapped in scarlet candied apple silk.

I felt a sense of pride. There we were, with the elements against us, yet still very poised, very graceful. Fluidly moving and twirling through the crisp atmosphere. I had forgotten most of the bitter cold by now. I felt a sense of honor or reverence towards the aesthetic. The mountain remained solemn and commanding of respect as we danced in front of it, but it shared its grandiose beauty with our routine.

We went through the routine once more. And I noticed Gray Cloud monitoring from a distance. He propped himself against the scrap metal sculpture of the standing grizzly, which I thought was optically appropriate. If I hadn't been comfortable in candy cane pose, I might not have been scanning the park to see him.

We finished the angel drop and descended to the ground for a break. It didn't take long for our unmoving bodies to grow cold again, so we threw on our coats and pants.

"You two! You're definitely not done with practice, and that most certainly won't be all to your routine." Reginald was shouting at us as he stomped briskly towards the balloons from the direction of the theater. It was embarrassing.

"I beg your pardon, sir," said Shay in even tones.

"You heard me," he spat, "that is not going to cut it. You didn't even do any drops."

"We did an angel drop, sir," I chimed in, trying to mirror Shay's attitude of poise.

Reginald's head snapped in my direction, "I wasn't talking to you. If choreography was up to you, we definitely wouldn't have a silks routine worth a damn."

"Okay," I said sharply, but quietly under my breath. To which he responded with an unmerciful glare.

"You'll do at least two more. I want a star, and I want a bullet. And the bullet should be a long one." He turned his chin as he eyed Shay for a response. "Ten feet minimum."

"But we've never dropped that far. I'm not sure it's safe." Shay could barely get out the last few syllables.

"I'm not concerned with safe right now! You heard Kyte. This is supposed to be extreme. And your pay check depends on it." Mr. Hyde was out to play this time. Only a few hours ago we had seen Dr. Jekyll. Quickly he had swung from encouraging his troupe to admonishment for our caution.

"Yes, sir," said Shay. Reginald turned to scorch my face with his glower until I responded as well.

"Yes, sir," I mimicked.

He looked at me like I was the lowest of low and walked back towards the theater. I think I held my breath for another twenty seconds after he was out of sight.

I let out a heavy exhalation and slung my heavy head towards Shay, "What's a bullet?"

She started taking off her coat and pants again, "I'll show you a normal, safe one." I watched her bounce, alternating her feet to get her blood flowing again. She climbed the silk about thirty feet, inverted, hooked one knee in a catcher's hang, and wrapped the other but created a lot of slack in the silk. She looked like a beautiful upside down gazelle. Then she let her top hand go and rapidly slide straight down as far as the slack allowed.

"Great. So you're the bullet, and your head is the tip of the bullet, and he wants you to shoot ten feet towards the ground." I was talking fast and losing oxygen at the thought of it.

"Pretty much. The star drop is not so bad, you can't really fall out of it. But the bullet causes the occasional friction burn and we're going to have to be very mindful of the slack."

Shay instructed me on how to perform the new drops and spotted me from the ground as best she could. True, the star drop seemed fairly secure no matter what height, but it left me dizzy at its end.

We started slow and small, steadily increasing the slack as we continued trials of the bullet. And I gradually realized how horrifying a ten foot drop of this nature would be. Plus, I had yet to see Shay actually execute it at that length. The longer the slack, the more friction I felt on my thigh and the more I jolted at the end of the drop.

We diligently worked at the additions to our routine until Caroline arrived with the trapeze flyers. She told us we'd have to share practices and to use our ground time wisely, which meant we should start focusing our efforts on her favor. We gratefully donned our coats and moved to a bench nearby to work out logistics.

"I think we need to do one more thing before we head to the trolley station," I said, and I beckoned Shay to follow me. We went inside one of the little cafes in the park and Shay looked at me suspiciously when I ordered three hot apple ciders. I handed one to her, slung my bag over my shoulder, and held a cup in each hand. Her eyes continued to inspect me warily as I briskly headed across the park.

I was relieved to find that he was still there when I reached the scrap metal sculptures. And Shay understood. I headed toward the grizzly bear.

"Gray Cloud, isn't it? I'm Janie. This is Shay." I tried to be as warm as possible. Gray Cloud didn't really move, he barely nodded his head in acknowledgement that I had spoken. "We're with the Marvels. You gave us a tour," I smiled, but still there was minimal response. "Well, I had an extra hot apple cider. The other friend I got it for doesn't like it. Do you like hot apple cider?"

I waited for words, but none came. A small nervous laugh creeped out of me despite using all my might to stop it. This happened to me sometimes when I was really angry or nervous. And though I knew it would most likely be awkward, facing the interaction in reality rather than in my mind elicited the odd response.

Gray Cloud glanced at the cup and opened a hand. In my mind, I thanked Whisper in relief. After I passed the cider to him, he gave the slightest nod once more.

"Alright, see you around," I spluttered, and turned to walk back toward the park exit.

After we had walked a few paces, Shay said, "Smooth…"

Chapter 8

Reconnaissance

Shay and I discreetly meandered through the park and out to the trolley station. Luckily, we only waited about five minutes before the trolley's tedious journey halted in front of Kaleidoscope Kyte's. A swarm of fifteen or so eager amusement seekers flooded out of it and made their way to the park gates. We were the only ones heading out.

"Do you think we should take the first stop on main street? We can check out all the shops, investigate the area," I asked.

"I guess that's a start. You know, this may be harder than you think. I have to be pretty close to people to hear their thoughts. We're going to have to stand or walk right beside them somehow. And you're going to have to engage in conversation with them."

"Me?" I was a little apprehensive since I wasn't exactly skilled in initiating conversation with total strangers.

"Well, we have to draw information out of them. Get them thinking about the topic you're investigating. People don't just walk around thinking about the town doctor," Shay said.

"Ah man, small talk?" I grimaced at the thought.

"Yeah, initially. Leading small talk. Just do what you did with Gray Cloud." Shay laughed at her own sarcasm.

I rolled my eyes at her, "Maybe if we start inside the shops. With the employees, possibly even the owners. That way I can at least talk about whatever it is they're selling."

It was still a bright sunny day, despite being viciously cold. We entered town to find a decent amount of foot traffic on the sectioned sidewalks beside the cobblestone street.

The old trolley screeched as it grinded to a bumpy halt at the first station off main street. Shay and I clambered out of it and stood on the street trying to gather our bearings. The smog was dingy in town, especially when compared to the being near the mountains in open air. The smell of gasoline and ash was pungent, and the hazy fumes seemed to rise from each building. It slowly drew your eye and attention to those diligently working with steam and fire, smoking iron. As we walked down the sidewalk, it didn't take long to notice the watchful eyes of locals appraising newcomers, a pair of oddballs.

What's funny is it didn't seem to me that we were the oddballs. The patrons of the town were the ones who looked strange. In their flamboyant vests and bodices, their gadgets swinging off hats, jackets, and belt loops. But this was a culture. This was their normal. Who was I to decide who was conventional and who wasn't? It's all about life experience and perspective, after all.

∞

When you put two very different groups of people together, it usually yields one of two types of responses. The first being intrigue, curiosity, wonder, and a sense of wanting to understand and discover a new way; a new way of thinking, acting, living. The second response yields no growth or any sense of adventure. The second response is fear, apprehension, to judge immediately that a way different from your own is not right or that maybe it's even bad, wrong, or less than. Simply because you know nothing about it. I could only hope that they were as intrigued by us as we were by them.

Ahead there was a sign hanging over the sidewalk that said Attoman's Groceries, and Shay and I decided it may be a good start since it was larger and likely held more people.

On our way, we walked slowly past the blacksmith. Through the entryway came a great wafting smell of unnameable solvents and oils, burning iron, and the sweat and human odor of five or so men. I could see them forging, bending, and welding a variety of different objects that looked like tools, sculptures, gates, and perhaps furniture. It did not seem inviting to two strange women, yet I was mesmerized by the ability to control molten metals and form them at your will. The careful skill and artistry it required.

A little boy, maybe seven, wearing suspenders and a newsboy cap, walked with his mother. He grinned at Shay as they passed by us. Undoubtedly stricken by her beauty.

I pulled open the door of the grocery and let Shay enter first. "Okay, what now?"

"Let's just take our time, act like we're looking for a particular item," she said.

"I don't need a particular item." I was already feeling caught as shoppers sneaked glances at us.

"I know that!" she hushed me, "Pretend. Listen around."

We weaved in and out of aisles around people preoccupied with their quest to acquire all the items on their lists. Then we loitered around the bakery as two women behind the counter discussed something they saw in the newspaper.

"I can't believe that place is still open for business. What more could it take to warrant a real investigation?" The gossiping little lady in a hairnet, and a very odd pair of glasses, looked frustrated.

"They're in cahoots, I tell ya," replied a tall, skinny lady.

They went on in lowered voices, discussing what the papers had said about the body that was found.

"I heard it was Drusilla Perkins. The body. And that the old Indian assistant of Kyte's is the one who carries out the hits," said the little lady.

"Drusilla Perkins!" Apparently this came as a shock to the tall lady. "I heard she moved to Relonia to pursue a law degree." She thought for a minute and then continued rolling out dough. "Well, I guess that would be quite a change in career path. Acrobat to lawyer. She always wore the most ghastly costumes. It showed everything."

"If she's dead, what does it matter what she wore?" said the little lady, her eyes bugging through extremely magnified lenses. "Shouldn't speak ill of the dead. Anyway, I bet that girl down the street knows all about it. Being Indian and all."

"What girl down the street?"

"The one in the clock shop. I bet she knows exactly how he did it, that assistant of Kyte's."

I looked at Shay blankly, hoping my eyes would speak for me. I had forgotten our whole mission of reconnaissance for Caroline. Now I was reeling at the fact that I had potentially attempted to shoot the breeze with Mr. Kyte's hitman and given him hot apple cider. And if there was any truth to this story, wouldn't it make sense? Gray Cloud knows the mountain. We saw him riding a horse back and around the park where automobiles couldn't go, not far from where the body was found. And Kyte seems to have such a power over him, maybe Gray Cloud would do anything he asked.

Shay pulled me by the arm, around the produce and to the next aisle. "Relax. Women in small towns talk like this. All the time in the bog when I was growing up. Starting rumors. They're speculating."

"You don't think we should check it out?"

"What do you mean check it out?"

"I mean go to the clock shop," I said. I wanted to investigate further, otherwise I'd be losing sleep tonight.

"What about Caroline?" Shay hissed.

"Well, we were going to check out the entire area. The clock shop is in the area. Maybe we'll hear something there," I said.

"Alright."

"Did you hear anything else in their thoughts?"

"No. Just the obvious insecurities. If you attack a person's appearance, it's usually because you feel less than that person," Shay replied matter-of-factly. She thought for a moment, "That and unfounded assumptions about Native Americans."

I started back up the aisle and toward the door to leave. We stood just outside, on the sidewalk, next to the entry of the grocery store. Scanning for the clock shop. Across the street was a butcher's meat market, the cobbler's shoe repair, a hardware store, and a mechanical repair shop of uncertain function. Maybe it was a general fixer upper for all things rusted metal or fuming.

We walked further along the sidewalk past some boutiques filled with odd looking attire and garments hanging in the window. And then what claimed to be a dentist's office, though there were odd vials and test tube sets, along with unusual tonics in dark brown bottles, for sale in the window. We thought about going inside, but a dentist wouldn't know anything about fertility. Plus, the sight of the window sent the hairs on the back of my neck to standing.

"Look," Shay said, pointing to a sign ahead. It swung on its wrought iron arm in the slight breeze and alerted passersby to Felix's Clock Shop.

"Okay. I guess we'll just go in and browse. I don't know anything about clock repairs. I don't even have a watch," I said.

"Remember, you're going to have to draw it out if you want me to hear any helpful information," said Shay.

I took in a deeper breath and blinked, "Right." I pulled open the door and a bell clattered overhead.

As soon as my foot stepped through the door, my eyes started whirring in every direction, not knowing where to land. The door opened to a square room with clocks covering every wall. Grandfather clocks, mantel clocks, cuckoo clocks, kitchen clocks. All sorts of designs and objects composing them. Pendulums, candles, digital, electric. Modern and antique. Iron, porcelain, glass, and wood. Some with elaborate paintings, some with little sculptures. They were intricate and unique, a masterpiece from the hands of a fastidious and patient crafter. They were fascinating, alluring.

In the back of the room was a counter, and behind which sat a dark-skinned man wearing a pair of magnifying binoculars and using some sort of tweezers to operate on a beautiful old clock. He didn't look up when we entered. Yet promptly after the noise of the bells had ceased, came a most interesting looking woman from a curtained doorway behind his counter.

"What can I do for you, ladies?" the woman said, though her voice was muffled behind a brown leather face mask that covered her nose and mouth, the ventilation holes of which were small and few. We could only see her dark brown eyes, which told us she was beautiful despite most of her face being covered. Her hair was black and wavy under a cream-colored cloth, tied around her head like a pirate. She wore lots of bronze colored chains around her neck and bangles on each wrist, and a leather vest that matched her mask. Her long bohemian style skirt swished and skimmed across the floor as she moved.

"We were just browsing." I tried to bluff as nonchalant and unintimidated, though I felt completely otherwise.

"You two are not from around here, huh?" she said.

"How could you tell?" I said.

"For one thing, you stick out like a sore thumb just by your outfits alone. And for another, most people around here don't come in to browse."

"What do they come in for then?" I asked.

"Repairs mostly."

"Right. Well, your shop and the clocks are beautiful," I tried to pivot.

"Thank you, ma'am. Felix expresses his appreciation." She gestured with a hand at the man behind the counter who appeared completely devoted to the clock in his hand, and had not so much as grunted or moved in the slightest to acknowledge her or our presences. The girl huffed a dry laugh, "He's a busy man, as you can see."

"Yes," I replied cautiously.

"What about you, you haven't said a word either," the girl said, eyeing Shay.

"I don't know much about clockwork," said Shay politely.

"Well then, what are you ladies in town for? What do you do?"

"We're performers. From the Mandevilles' Marvelous Marvels. We're here to perform at Kaleidoscope Kyte's for the next two weeks," I answered for us.

"I see. What do you think of White Cap Peaks so far?" the girl asked. She was super focused on our facial expressions, but I hoped Shay was now getting a read on what she was thinking. And I hoped it was information about the park.

"It's interesting. I've never been to a place like this before," I said. We walked further in the room towards the counter, pretending to be keenly interested in all the different clocks.

"Yes, interesting for sure. And what do you think of Mr. Kyte?"

"We've only just arrived yesterday. Been around him very little so far. But I suppose he's a very creative man. Based on what I've seen of his park," I said, with what I thought was perfect etiquette. "I'm sure the community loves having an amusement park nearby. It seems very crowded."

"You would think that, yes," the girl replied, "but there's more than amusement to that park. And something tells me you already know that."

"We did hear some strange things about it. Some folks in the grocery store down the block were talking about something that was in the newspaper," I said.

"Let me guess. In the bakery, perhaps?" Even through the leather face mask I could hear the upturned tone.

"Uh, yep."

"Of course." She slapped a hand on the counter and her bangles clattered on it loudly. "Those old bats do nothing but jabber. Our people have nothing to do with any of the stories you've heard."

I turned to face her, "Your people?"

"Yes, our people, the ones from the mountain."

"People live in the mountains?"

"The Native Americans. The Indians." Her speech was becoming passionate. "My uncle is a good man," the girl said. At this statement, Felix finally moved. He stopped working and sat up straight. That was all he had to do to communicate with the girl to mind her emotions. "I'm sorry, dad."

"We didn't mean to upset you. We were just worried about our own safety. Being outsiders and all. Not knowing what to make of the rumors. Or of Mr. Kyte," I earnestly confided.

Shay was attentive to the girl now also. Her eyes conveying empathy and concern in her genuine and angel like way.

Felix looked at the girl and seemed to talk to her with his eyes. It was like they had their own security system by wordless expression, and he evidently conveyed some sort of permission.

The girl took a deep breath, "It's alright." She came out from behind the counter to approach us. "I'm Felicity," she said, extending a hand to me and then to Shay.

"It's nice to meet you, Felicity. I'm Janie. This is Shay."

"Right."

I proceeded with caution, "So, Gray Cloud is your uncle?"

"He is. My dad's side." She jerked her thumb over her shoulder back towards Felix. "Regardless of whatever it is you heard, he's a good man. Maybe the most kind and selfless of all the people I know."

There was quiet thoughtfulness for a moment. "I know we're total strangers to you, and maybe you don't want to have a conversation about this with outsiders. I would totally understand that. But I am curious…" I tried to read her eyes, which were the only part of her face I could really see, to see if I could push any further. They were as deep and dark as the honey from buckwheat blossoms, wide and expansive. I continued, "Ya know, just so we have an idea of what we could be up against. What do you think about the newspaper article? About what happened to the body?"

The eyes didn't move or even need to blink, and she spoke low and slowly, "I think one should try not to get in Mr. Kyte's bad books. I think he's power hungry, political, and dangerous. And I think there's no coincidence in finding a body behind his precious park."

"I was afraid you'd say something like that," I responded. Shay cracked a half smile and exhaled at my candid response.

"You two are strange birds," said Felicity, "But I guess you're alright. You'd best watch yourselves though, for however long you're in this town." She went back behind the counter and sat another clock next to Felix's right hand, as he finished winding the one he had been working on since we made our entrance.

"We'll keep that in mind," I said, glancing at my feet and then the door. "I guess we'll get out of your hair. I hope we didn't outstay our welcome. Thanks for the, uh, tips."

"Not a problem. Oh and uh, I know my uncle is pretty quiet, kind of aloof and standoffish. But he's not a bad guy to have on your side in the park. He likes hot chocolate, if you need a peace offering."

"Really? Does he like hot apple cider?"

"Oh no. Hates it. Says apples should be bitten, not drank."

"Oh," I shriveled, and Shay rolled her eyes at me. "Alright, thanks."

I nodded and tossed up an open hand awkwardly to communicate my fairly wells. We walked out the door and down the block so we wouldn't be seen through the shop windows.

"Well, Felicity thinks Gray Cloud is being abused, controlled in some way by Mr. Kyte. She's worried for him and feels like there's nothing she or her people can do to help him. But you didn't prompt anything about the doctor," said Shay, somewhat frustrated.

"I know, I know. But what is a clock maker going to know about fertility doctors? We got some useful information anyway. And now we have further insight. The case for avoiding Kyte is growing. We're on our own and we need to better plan for our safety. Especially with this new silks routine."

"Yes, okay. But what are we going to tell Caroline if she asks us about our day in town?" Shay said, checking the time and trying to convey the need for urgency. We had been in two establishments and learned nothing about the mystery doctor.

"Well, let's try one more before we head back to the station. Look, there's a pharmacy up the block. They take consultation all the time. Let's try there," I said.

We headed up the sidewalk past locals in Victorian attire and mechanical trappings, and entered the pharmacy. It was odd and reminded me of the window of the dentist's office we had passed earlier. Tonics and vials and tubes. There was a short line that queued fairly quickly, and then we faced the man behind the counter.

Jittery as a weasel, he looked at us suspiciously, but spoke very politely and professionally. Time was dwindling, so I skipped most of the charades and asked him if there was a fertility doctor in town. Simply on the basis that my non-existent husband and myself we're seeking help. And that my friend here, which was Shay, had suggested we talk to the pharmacist for guidance first.

He told us there was not a working fertility specialist, that he knew of, in the immediate area. I prompted him further on any sort of alternative or unconventional medicine that could aid me. But he looked at me worriedly and said he was sorry that he did not.

We thanked him and pretended to be very interested in a tonic for fast hair growth, then moseyed away stating we didn't need to spend that much. After our exit, we headed to the trolley station at a brisk pace because we needed to be back in time to look like we've been practicing or stretching or whatever the rest of the troupe was doing. To blend our arrival back at the park before taking the evening trolley back to Frigid Ridge.

"Did you hear anything when I asked about a fertility doc?" I asked Shay after we sat on the old lumpy cushions of the trolley bench and waited for it to begin clicking on the track.

"Just that he knew about the rumor. He didn't have any information about it," Shay answered. "You think we're going to have to come back to town tomorrow?"

"I don't know. We'll see how Caroline reacts, I guess."

We sat quietly for a while, so the adrenaline could lower back down. All the thinking fast, and speed walking up and down sidewalks, and entertaining strangers.

"I wonder what's really going on with Gray Cloud," I said.

"Maybe we can find out. If only you had gotten him hot cocoa instead," Shay smiled.

I rolled my eyes at her little jab. "I like his family. Felicity was the only one we met today that didn't look down her nose at us," I said.

"Yeah, she's tough but loyal. Maybe even a leader," Shay replied.

When the trolley slowed to stop at the station of Kaleidoscope Kyte's, we scanned the area from within its dirty windows. Taking care to walk close to anyone in the parking lot, pretending we were additional family members, we slowly made our way back inside the gates. The bored and weary ticket takers at the gate didn't so much as flinch that we had special passes, they merely shuffled us inside.

Chapter 9

A Spot Under Stars

The air felt heavier and it was growing cold as the sun set behind the gigantic mountain peaks. The sky was glowing in a soft orange and seemed to electrify the white piles of snow on caps of the mountain tops. The snowflakes had let up at the moment and everything was crystal clear.

We walked to the deep purple theater building. Its gold filigree trim seemed to sparkle and glow, even in the night. From a distance, we saw Alex and Daniel walking back in.

Once inside, we scanned the room, which was bustling with our troupe. The ones who had been outside most of the day were standing under some overhead heating vents and rubbing their palms up and down their arms. Ava was laughing hysterically at something one of the jugglers said. Zeke and Tombo were still practicing some choreography, and Anthony was arranging some mobile clothing racks full of sparkles and feathers, spandex and silk, ruffles and tulle. Our costumes for the coming shows, in a wide array of saturated colors and hues.

We dropped our bags in the same area where we had stretched in the morning before practice. Isn't it funny how people seem to call a spot from the first time they use it? I always thought it was a great example of just how much most people don't like, or aren't comfortable with, even the slightest of change. They'd rather stick to the routine. Maybe it's human nature.

"Where have you guys been?" Alex asked. He and Daniel had meandered through the globs of performers to our supposed stretching spot.

"Practicing," I said, without making eye contact. I was a terrible liar.

"In your coats?"

"Oh, we just went to get some cider afterwards. Not everyone in this circus is lucky enough to get to do their act indoors where it's warm." I tried to use the usual banter, but he was already squinting at me with a cocked eyebrow of suspicion.

"Uh huh."

"I like h-h-hot apple c-cider. You don't get us any?" said Daniel. He crossed his arms and shook his head, but couldn't stop the smile for long enough to pretend he was mad.

"I owe you, Daniel," I said.

"T-trolley be here s-soon," said Daniel, then he and Alex went to gather their bags.

By the time we were all seated in the trolley, in route to Frigid Ridge, the sky had become dark shades of indigo. Dotted with hundreds of stark white stars. They streaked across the air occasionally, if you were watching close enough to spot their rapid fleeing. And once away from the lights of the park or city, the night sky was on full display, in all its glory and wonder. The atmosphere was so calm and clear. If it wasn't so cold, the night would feel like an embrace.

When the trolley skidded to a halt in front of our new temporary home, we poured out of it like ants from a hill. Alex followed behind me until we entered the lobby.

"How about some hot tea and cookies?" he asked and said it was on him. Having Kyte's guest concierge benefits, no Marvelous Marvel had to pay for refreshments or complimentary beverages. He was trying to be cute, or intentionally annoying.

A few people lingered by the piano, or the cafe to get a snack, for a short while before retiring to their rooms. Alex and I chatted about the construction of the coaster track and the new silks routine until most everyone had cleared out. It sounded like those who performed in Kastle Theater had it made in the shade. I was, self admittedly, extremely envious. But regardless of routine, and location thereof, no one was really safe. I worried that those practicing inside would become too relaxed. Well, except Alex. The risk analyzer in him was in full effect.

"Alright, it's pretty much empty in here," he whispered. "What have you really been doing? And don't try to tell me extra practice or shopping with Shay. I know you went missing today for an extended amount of time. And you should have told me. I was nerve-racked all throughout practice. You basically screwed up my whole first day in the treacherous tundra."

I laughed and a few drops of tea leaked out of my pursed lips. "I'm sorry," I said in a tone that was not at all sorry sounding.

"For real, where were you?"

"Hmmm, where to begin with you?" I ducked my head in and low toward the cafe table and whispered, "Caroline has demanded a favor from me."

"What? Why?" He looked appalled.

"Because she says I owe her. For speaking up to Reg and vouching for me. Getting a second chance to stay on."

"That was nothing, she's playing you."

"Well, I don't have much of a choice. Do I?"

"I guess not," he answered quickly. "What kind of favor?"

"It's a long story."

He stared at me blankly, "Go on."

"I'm afraid someone could hear us in here."

"Okay," he said, frustrated and impatiently, "where do you wanna go?"

"I don't know where to go. There's people everywhere in here."

"Okay, let's go outside." He pushed his chair back and was champing at the bit.

"It's so cold," I whined.

"Suck it up," he piped as he stood up and headed for the front door. I huffed a sigh, followed him, and was super annoyed when he opened the door, held it for me, and swung a hand at me to lead the way. As if he was herding a pest out of a place it wasn't supposed to be in.

Outside Frigid Ridge, and a couple of yards up, there was a tree line. Alex stomped into the cover of it, through the thick accumulated snow. The sound of it crunching under his boots and the air sharp as a knife. The ground seemed to glow in juxtaposition to the thick, black shadows of the pine trees surrounding us. I would have been kind of creeped out, had it not been for the fact that I could look up and see the beautiful star sprinkled sky, all purple and navy.

He stopped about fifteen feet in and turned to face me. I was walking in his foot trail and looking straight up, so I slammed into him when he stopped abruptly.

"Ow, geez."

"Sorry, sorry."

He straighten his jacket out, "Okay, spill. What's the favor?"

I took a deep breath and let my shoulders fall. "She wants me to find some special fertility doctor that's said to be around this area. The guy's supposed to be the best, and people know about him, or have heard rumors anyway, but no one knows where to find him."

"Why does she need the doctor?"

"Because she and Reginald have been trying to have a baby for years with no luck. All she's ever wanted was to be a mother," I stated, as if exhausted.

"Okay. But how are you going to help them find this doctor?" he looked bewildered.

"By convincing Shay to help me," I drawled.

"Shay?"

"Mind reader, duh. She can hear people's thoughts," I said. "So we're sort of investigating the town's folk. I go strike up a conversation and try to lead their thoughts to the subject. Shay listens to what they're thinking."

"Why didn't Caroline just ask Shay, then?" he asked.

"She didn't think she could convince Shay to help her. But she knew we were friends, she knew Shay would help me."

Alex scratched his head and pushed his hair back from his face. "So, what have you found out?"

"Not much of anything yet. Not about the fertility doctor, anyway. We did find out that a lot of townspeople think Gray Cloud had something to do with the recent murder. That he's sort of Kyte's puppet. But at the clock shop downtown, we met his niece and brother. They own it. And they said their people live in the mountains and have endured prejudice for years. Felicity says Gray Cloud is a good man." I finally stopped to breathe, but by now my teeth were chattering.

"Who's Felicity?"

"The niece, Gray Cloud's niece. Felix is his brother. They work at Felix's Clock Shop." My shoulders were shaking uncontrollably.

"Come here," Alex said.

"What?"

"Come. Here." He opened his jacket and ushered me in. I stutter stepped forward and paused just in front of him. He pulled my shivering body into his chest and wrapped his jacket around me by way of pocketed hands.

Obviously we had spent tons of time together filled with bumping elbows, his arm wrapping around my neck and jerking me around, like a cartoon character yanking someone with a shepherd's hook. We'd sat next to each other on piers with dangling feet, on buses shoulder to shoulder. We'd hugged on occasion, the one-armed side hug in good times, the two arms in bad times. We'd shared the same room, of course in separate beds like a brother and sister.

But in that moment, within the freezing cold forest under the stars, it just felt different. It didn't feel platonic, not just a friend helping a friend. It felt like I needed him to really be whole. And it was terrifying and wonderful all at the same time.

I tried to shake it off and continue. "Felicity said that it's not safe around Kyte. In his park. She said not to get on his bad side. And that it was no coincidence that a body was found around his park."

He said nothing.

"Some lady in the grocery market said it was a female body. A girl that was supposed to move away. She was going to be a lawyer or something. Apparently she was an acrobat that worked for Kyte."

"Then you need to be more careful sneaking away. If Kyte finds out you're not working on his dime," he exhaled worriedly. "You and Shay need to find this damn doctor quick. So that you can stay near the group. We need all eyes out for each other."

"I know," I huffed. I was just starting to get annoyed at his patronizing, then I felt his chin rest on top of my bowed head.

"What's next then? Do you and Shay have a plan?"

"I guess we'll go back in town tomorrow to do some more digging. Also, Reginald is apparently getting out and about, to try to find the doctor too. But Caroline insinuated he's using more of a mobster approach to get answers."

"Well figures. Maybe I can keep tabs on Reg while you guys are in town," he said.

"I don't know. You don't need to get mixed up in this."

"Janie. Come on. You need some help. Why can you never admit it?" he huffed.

"I can admit when I need help," I hissed.

"Since I've known you I've never heard you ask for help." He shook his head above mine. "I'm not getting into that now. It doesn't matter. This needs to be a team effort."

"Alright," I drew out the second syllable irritably.

There was a sound of a tree branch cracking a little further in the forest. I jumped and squeezed Alex's torso reactively.

"What was that?"

"It's okay, chill. Look."

I peeked out of Alex's jacket and saw two deer passing through the trees.

"I think I need some sleep," I said.

"Alright. Hey, has Shay ever told you she's read my mind?"

"No. She's real private about some things. You know—she says she wants to be treated normally and have normal conversations. She doesn't want to share thoughts within the group unless it's absolutely necessary. For safety or whatever. It's so annoying," I said.

"That's good. That's very, er, noble of her," he breathed.

"Relax," I said, "We've got a lot more to worry about than your thoughts." I pulled back and felt the freezing air again. In the shadows, I watched him close his jacket. His face in hues of blue under the dark sky, it was difficult to make out his expression. He looked up at the stars for a moment.

"I kinda like this spot," he said.

"It's pretty. But I'm really missing the pier at sunset lately, when it's pushing eighty degrees and everything is warm and breezy."

"I would gladly take that. Maybe we'll get back there one day."

We trudged back up to the lodge and turned in for the night. When I walked into my room, Shay and Ava were still up, going through their usual bedtime routines. Ava's nightly skin care ritual was elaborate. She was about halfway through it. And Shay was in her bed reading a book.

"Finally, you're both here. I've been waiting all day to tell you girls something," said Ava excitedly. "Guess what I'm doing in the theater sets of the shows?"

"What?"

"A tumbling routine! Apparently Mr. Kyte was short an acrobat," she said.

Shay and I looked at each other, apprehension spreading through the atmosphere like smoke.

"It's gonna be fun. Something new. I've been trying to maintain my gymnastic skills for years with no opportunity to show them off." Ava's smile started fading as she appraised our faces. "What is it? Why are you looking like that?"

"Ava, who asked you to do this?" Shay said softly.

"Gray Cloud! I didn't know he could talk. But he told me Mr. Kyte wanted to know if I did any acrobatics. Said he needed me to pull it off. Something about being the same size as the last girl, or resembling her. Thought I would fit in her costume."

"Ava, you've got to be really careful," I breathed.

She jerked her chin back and gave me a puzzled look. "Okay..." she said slowly, "I'm always careful. It's just a tumbling routine."

"I don't think you should be anywhere near Mr. Kyte alone," said Shay firmly.

"Girls, I haven't even seen him. I just got word from Gray Cloud," she grinned. To lighten the mood, she struck a straight arm, flat face, semi-scowl pose, intending to imitate Gray Cloud and get a laugh.

"It's just that we heard..." I started, but was interrupted by Shay.

She abruptly spoke up to say, "You saw the paper. We can't trust anyone in White Cap Peaks. Just be overly mindful and listen to your gut. And you better tell us if you hear or see or are told to do anything out of the ordinary."

Apparently, Shay wasn't ready to let Ava in on our main street investigations. Which I was fine with, but thought it a little odd since we had been preaching that everyone in the group had to work as a team and watch each others' back. But Shay would only do this to protect Ava somehow.

"Yes, mother," Ava said sarcastically.

Chapter 10

Don't Talk To Strangers

The next day consisted of a similar routine to that of the first day of practice in Kaleidoscope Kyte's. Shay and I took our turn of choreography practice on the silks, which hung beneath the hot air balloons outside Kastle Theater. It wasn't snowing that day, which was a small reprieve, but the temperature still had to be in the thirties.

Shay talked me through the aerial drops that Reginald was demanding of us, though we practiced them on a smaller scale. I knew it would be set up in the same fashion, but allowing enough slack to drop ten feet head first toward the cold, hard cement was still quite daunting. We had been practicing with up to five-foot drops. Today we would shoot for eight feet. Got to get used to it. And the first show would be tomorrow night. That left only one more day of practice in between.

Caroline arrived on the scene and beckoned for us to cease our practice by clapping heartily and saying, "Nice work, girls. But you gotta share. Trapeze is up. Let's have a word before you're dismissed."

We slid down the silks, put on our coats and walked over towards her. In an extravagant fur trimmed Prussian blue overcoat and black leather boots, Caroline looked like a movie star. Her blonde hair was shining in the sun like the beacon of a lighthouse. I noticed the usual cigarette holder was gone. She now wore a gold-colored holder that you place on your finger like a ring. On top of the ring, it had a post that rose about three inches and clasped around the skinny white cylinder that billowed a gray fog. It shouldn't have, but somehow it made her look so cool to me.

"Do you ladies have need for another trip?" she asked. As I examined her expression, it seemed like she might have hoped that we didn't. That would mean we have answers.

"I think so," I said, and her face sank ever so slightly at my words. Raising the ringed hand delicately up to take a drag, she turned to face the mountain and slowly exhaled the silvery plumes with a small nod.

"Well, then. Get going," she said.

After a lingering glance, we turned to prepare for a camouflaged exit of the park to the trolley station. Even though I didn't trust her, I didn't know if I even liked her, I still couldn't help feeling sorry for her disappointment.

We made it to the trolley, and then the short ride to main street, unscathed and undetected. This time, we went to a bakery, the automobile repair shop, and even the blacksmith. All of which were very awkward and yielded no pertinent information.

By noon, we were becoming frustrated and doing all we could to push away the inner monster of doubt that was trying to steal our hope.

"I don't know what to do," I said to Shay, feeling drained. I flopped down on a bench by the sidewalk. Shay floated down to land next to me.

"Why don't we try Felicity again?" she replied.

"And say what?"

"Maybe she knows something about the rumored doctor," said Shay.

"Maybe she does, maybe she doesn't," came an only slightly familiar voice from behind the bench we were resting on.

Shay and I both turned to face each other and then behind the bench. Felicity propped against the brick wall. She balanced on one foot, the other knee bent and stabilizing her balance with the bottom of her boot on the dingy red brick. Her arms crossed as if she was kicked back and slightly amused, or at the least entertained by the fumbling of two out-of-towners.

"You two again. What on earth were you doing at the blacksmith?" Felicity moved around to the front of the bench to face us and leaned against a streetlight pole.

"Hello again, Felicity," I answered, trying to sound hearty. "We just went in for a look at how they craft. Amazing isn't it?"

"I saw you inside, ambling around like you wanted to talk to someone but were mute. Pretty much how you were yesterday at Felix's," she said, her arms crossed again. She still donned the mask that left her face, from the eyes down, a mystery. I was growing very interested in its purpose, but annoyed that it made it hard to determine her facial expressions. But no matter how much of her appearance was hidden, her personality still made her ferocious.

"Oh. You were inside," I said, feeling caught red handed.

Felicity shook an odd looking key on a chain. "Clock key repair. This is a special one. Only key to wind a particular clock. Not that you'd know anything about clocks or their keys, much less how to wind them."

"True," I mumbled.

"So. The one that rarely talks said something about trying me again?" Felicity looked at Shay. The upturn of her voice posed the phrase as a question.

Shay smiled at Felicity serenely despite the subtle antagonizing, and I tried to think quickly of how asking her about the doctor would be the least awkward. Given the nature of the subject, that was quite difficult. So I went out on a limb and half way told her the truth.

"So, we have a very dear friend. She's back in Aspirlington, if you know the area. Big city. Anyway, she and her husband have been trying to conceive for about two years now, no dice. And when this friend heard we were gigging in White Cap Peaks, she freaked. Apparently, she has heard some rumor about a special fertility doctor around here. She begged us to see what we could dig up on him." I stopped speaking to appraise Felicity's immediate response to the anecdote I had just fed her. She hadn't budged, so I continued. "We haven't been able to find any information on the subject and thought maybe you would know something about it."

There was a longer than usual wait for a response. Felicity moved to the side of the light pole, leaning on a forearm braced up the edge of it, and rolling her fingers across the metal.

"I think you're lying," she said, "At least about the chick in Aspirlington."

I tried to speak up, to double down on the story I had just pulled out of thin air, but Felicity stopped me and said, "What makes you think I know anything about a fertility doctor? I work in a clock shop."

"Well, you're just the only person on main street who has given us the time of day."

Shay spoke up, "And you seemed to know about the newspaper rumors. Maybe you know this one too." She was engaged with fastidious observation. Trying to sift through the sand in Felicity's mind.

"Maybe I do know a little about that rumor. But I'm late for work. And my mother always said not to talk to strangers. So." Felicity was pivoting around the pole to walk back to the clock shop.

I jumped up. "What do you want?" I called after her.

"A little respect for my people," she answered without stopping or turning back around to face me.

"What do you mean?" I shouted, but received no answer. I flopped back down on the bench, my hand heavily thudding against my lap.

"Her mind is all over the place. Much of it laced with anger at the town's folks for their view of her family. But I think she knows something. It wasn't clear, but I feel like it was lingering a little deeper," said Shay.

"We're out of time again though," I muttered. "We have to get back on the trolley. What am I going to tell Caroline?"

"Tell her the truth. Tell her you might have a source."

"The show is tomorrow. We can't come back into town."

"You're exactly right. So we have to put this on the back burner for now. Neither you nor I can make answers appear out of thin air just because the Mandevilles ask us to. We need the day to focus on the show tomorrow."

On the trolley again, empty-handed again, sat amongst excited families headed to the park again. Shay was quiet as I was. I looked out of the dirty, grime cornered windows and tried to figure out what the next move should be. Outside the sun was pouring golden light all over the valley, the mountain tall and proud. There was no snow floating to distract the viewer. It seemed too pretty a day to be so doom and gloom.

"Whisper, look at this beautiful vista. How can I be so down?" The inner dialogue began in my head, "Show me what to do next."

"You can only do so much."

"What if the worst should happen? What if I don't find the answer?" I said to them in my mind.

I noticed Shay flinch slightly in the seat next to me. Maybe she was listening to my private inner conversation with Whisper, but I didn't really care. I was too exhausted and worried to care about that. And I wasn't trying to hide Whisper.

"You have all the answers you really need," came the answer. "You remember the fog, don't you?"

"Yes, I remember now. You know I forget sometimes."

They said, "Even if you don't know what to do now, you will when the time comes. For now, let me lead the way through the fog."

"Alright, alright. I'll try. I'm going to try to relax," I answered.

Just as I had many times in the past, I pictured myself in a forest. It's the very early hours of the morning and there's gray mist and fog as thick as the smoke off a burning house enveloping the whole wood. It's all throughout the forest, and I must travel through it. All I can see is the nearest tree, its bark dark and grooved into aging ridges. I put a hand on it to get my bearings. I stare as hard as I can. I squint and furrow my brow intensely but can see no further than the twelve inches ahead of me. All that's there is dim swirling haze. Then a hand appears in front of me, extended, its palm up and open. It beckons me to take it, so I slowly reach forward to do so. When I grasp the hand, it's warm, and it seems a feeling of peace passes through the center of it and into my own hand. It travels up my arm and spreads slowly until it warms my whole body, erasing anxiety and fear of the unknown. Then, it slowly starts to pull me forward until I have to let go of the tree I'm bracing myself on. We keep steadily moving onward, and I am following blindly through the thick, opaque air.

The trolley screeched to a halt, interrupting my meditation. We were back at the park and, thankfully, able to blend in with the crowds to sneak back in. Around the Ferris wheel and through the scrap metal sculptures, we briskly paced to the theater. Again, inside, there was the usual hustle and bustle after a long day of practice. People were ready to get back to Frigid Ridge for the night. To wind down before the big day tomorrow.

"You guys missed it," came a quiet and lowered voice. Alex had pounced on us right as we got inside the door. "Reg has been on a war path all day. I even had to come up with some bogus story about where you guys were."

"What?" I hissed, growing paranoid.

"Yeah, he was outside at the balloons looking for you two around one o'clock. Asking Caroline for updates on your routine. She tried to fend him off."

My heart was pounding, and my hands started to sweat. Gulping, I asked, "Well, what did you say?"

"I acted like I casually overheard them as I was walking by and told him you guys went to the changing rooms for costume alterations. When he stomped off in the opposite direction of the theater I figured we were clear."

Shay and I exhaled, finally.

Alex continued, "That's not the worst of it. He's been on Zeke's case all day for some reason. Really giving him hell."

I scanned the room, looking for Zeke and Tombo. My eyes found him slouched against a wall in the back of the theater, Tombo and Anthony standing beside him. He looked like he'd been through it.

"How? Why?" I asked.

"I dunno. Reg came in to watch their practice, and nothing seemed to be good enough. He criticized their every line, trick, and move just about. There wasn't any rhyme or reason to it. And they were great of course. So It looked to me like Reg was taking his aggression out on them or something."

"Why them, I wonder?" said Shay. "Reginald loves all the boys' acts. I could see him doing that to us, but not Zeke and Tombo."

"Maybe because he couldn't find us," I snorted.

"There's more. But I don't think we need to talk about it in here," Alex said looking around apprehensively.

"Where then?"

"Janie, let's meet in the woods again. I'll go first. You follow ten minutes after," he said.

"Uh, alright," I wondered why we needed to go separate. I wondered what on earth he could know.

Back at the lodge, we waited around the piano's sitting area. Alex nonchalantly stepped outside. The ten minutes that followed seemed like hours, and I squirmed and fidgeted in my seat, waiting for them to pass. At their end, it was all I could do not to leap up and run.

The snow was thick and crunchy again, and I sunk a little with each step. Unfortunately, clouds had masked the night sky's great beauty and it gave the walk past the tree line an uneasy feeling. I was quick to whisper, "Alex? Alex?" I couldn't easily see him waiting for me.

"Here," he replied, and I cautiously stepped toward the sound of his voice.

"Not as aesthetically pleasing out here tonight," I said.

"No, it's creepy, actually. I thought I heard all kinds of things waiting in here for ten minutes. Not that you could do a damn thing, but I'm glad you're here," he half laughed.

"I can admit it's nice to not be in here alone, but I could fend for myself. I could at least climb a tree." I smarted off, "What would you do? Thrash around blind and aimlessly?"

"I guess so," he answered quickly, unwilling to delve any further into a hypothetical argument. "I overheard something else from Reg today."

"Okay, what?"

"Him and Kyte were backstage at the theater. Someone must've left the door cracked that led to the hall of back rooms. I was onstage messing with the drum platform and

I heard—well, not yelling, but raised voices. So I snuck towards the door to try to listen."

"Go on."

"I heard Reg asking Kyte, 'How am I going to get in there?' and 'I've run down half the blowhards in this town. Now I know where to go but can't get in.' And then he asked Kyte about using Gray Cloud."

"For what?"

"To get in this place I guess."

"Did he say anything else?" I asked eagerly.

"Kyte said, 'I can get Gray Cloud to do a lot of things, but I can't get him to do that.'"

My mind was racing. Caroline said Reginald was out looking for the doctor too. He must have meant he knew where to find him, but couldn't get in.

"Why wouldn't he be able to get in? Why would he need Gray Cloud?" I mumbled quietly to myself as Alex stared at me blankly.

I continued mulling things over. "Gray Cloud. Get in. Is it the mountain? Felicity said her people, which would include Gray Cloud, live in the mountains. We saw him ride a horse that way."

"So the doctor is in the mountains?" Alex tried to help me fill in the blanks.

"Maybe. I need to see Felicity again," I breathed.

"The first show is tomorrow night! You can't run off to town. Reg will definitely notice if you're gone, Caroline probably wouldn't let you anyway. And you need to get focused. For your own safety," he preached. "Tomorrow, no investigating."

"You're not my dad," I smarted.

"Janie!" He was getting worked up.

"Okayyy. Yeah, yeah. You're right. Yeah, I can't go tomorrow," I was talking to myself as much as I was him. "It'll have to wait."

"Okay… good," Alex was scanning my face for authentic yield. "You know, we could get attacked by a bear out here and none of this would matter."

Even though he wasn't wrong, I rolled my eyes. He couldn't see in the dark anyway. "Let's go back then. I'm not in the mood for any more drama."

"You go first. I'll follow a little later."

When I pulled open the large brass doorknob of Frigid Ridge and went back inside, there were still several people circulating through the lobby for snacks and teas and whatever else they did as nightly routines. But no one seemed to notice me coming in, which was good. I went to get a complimentary cup of chamomile myself and sat at the cafe table to wait for Alex to come back. Once he had made it back inside, we bid each other a modest goodnight, as if we hadn't seen each other in a while and were apathetic to whether or not the other person actually had a good night. It was kind of fun having the secret between just the two of us. For the night anyway.

Chapter 11

Transformation

It was Friday and the weather was picturesque. Although the light flurries would make performing difficult if they didn't let up, and the sun was beaming across the snow-capped mountains. Hawks with white dotted underbellies were floating and swerving past its rugged terrain, searching for a snack. A turquoise sky, crystal clear and more expansive than ever, in the wake of my anxiousness.

We were at the park and practicing by nine o'clock in the morning. During our silks practice, Caroline covertly asked if we had gotten any more information. I told her we had a lead but nothing solid yet. And as Alex and I had hypothesized, Caroline knew and understood it would have to wait for the next two days due to all the hustle and bustle of the shows.

By ten o'clock, the crowds were filing into queues at the entry gates, eager to come inside and enjoy the thrill rides and fantasy land made of metal. Shay and I went into the theater to avoid them and keep stretching. It didn't take long after passing through the doors to find absolute chaos.

The first horrible sight our eyes landed on was of Tombo standing on a stool and Reginald stabbing a pointed finger towards him as he screamed at Zeke.

"That's not good enough! What do you think this is? This is to be a step up from Merdwick!" He roared each syllable he enunciated. "If you can't up your game here, you're not gonna make it to the next port! And I would've expected better from you!" Reginald shouted just before he stomped off.

All the other performers surrounding had paused what they were doing, hunching their shoulders like scared dogs and averting their eyes as fast as humanly possible whenever Reg's head turned anywhere towards them.

"Ava! What the hell are you doing in here? I told you to get to the menagerie, you're riding Eloise tonight! Are you too stupid to understand the words when I tell you to do something?" Reginald spat. The tirade continued as he strode through, scanning each person and undoubtedly processing their every fault or flaw.

Ava was biting her lip to keep it from quivering and Alex tried to pat her shoulder as she briskly passed. Her face scrunched and ponytail swishing, she made a beeline out the door for the menagerie.

By this point in our observation, Shay and I were frozen solid in space, scared to move any further into the theater.

It looked like Reg was heading to the backstage rooms. He swiped at a bowling pin a juggler was tossing from mid air. It hurtled into the front of the stage with a loud thump, leaving the juggler as frozen as we were, the rest of his pins tumbling to the floor in succession. And Reg did that for nothing, it was just to release some of his frustration.

He was out of the room, but everyone looked much smaller and slower for the following few minutes. It took time to process what was said and then psych yourself back up to get refocused on the task at hand.

"Dang. That was rough. Poor Ava," I said.

"Ava's never rode Eloise. I mean, she'll be fine, but I wonder if Reg just changed that on the fly. She didn't mention it yesterday," Shay pondered aloud. "And why is he singling out Zeke?"

"I don't know."

Apprehensively, we made our way to the stage and sat under the center sculpture, the metal princess' solemn countenance, to stretch. I figured we could follow Alex's lead and inconspicuously listen for any dialogue coming from the backstage rooms. I stared at the sculpted queen of Kastle theater, the gears that composed her cheeks and the piping bent as wavy flowing locks of hair. She shined in yellows, reds, and blues as the roustabouts tested and checked the spotlights.

"So, what did you find out last night?" Shay asked in a whisper.

I leaned closer, under the facade of a straddle stretch, toward the side closest to Shay. "He's in the mountains."

"Who?"

"The doc," I said and curved to the opposite leg.

"Are you sure?"

"Well, no, I'm not positive. But I think so. We need to talk to Felicity again," I whispered.

Shay nodded and dropped the subject. Zeke and Tombo were walking up the steps of the stage. Zeke plopped down to stretch in a straddle just as we were and was surprisingly flexible. Then again, he was a dancer too.

"I need a break," he said as Tombo mouthed, "me too."

Shay and I both look at him pitifully with concerned maternal facial expressions.

"Ladies, stop that. We're fine. After yesterday—I decided I wasn't going to let him affect me," Zeke said matter-of-factly.

"Well, it's affecting me," whispered Tombo, "that snide, despicable…"

"Enough adjectives," Zeke interjected, "they'll get us nowhere."

"He'll get what's coming to him one of these days," mumbled Tombo. I held back giggles as I listened to his perturbed English accent.

"I hate that he's picking on Ava too," said Zeke. "I wish she wouldn't let him get the better of her."

Shay looked at Zeke with confidence. "She'll be over it by noon. And she'll be mad as a hornet too. He embarrassed her."

"So, where have you guys been? I haven't seen you around very much," Zeke asked.

"Can't tell you. I'd have to kill you," I said playfully.

"Oh, look out world! Sass from Janie Morgan at last," he said as he flung the back of his hand to his forehead dramatically.

"Alright. How about, 'Can't tell you yet.'"

"Fine. Fine. I'm no good at waiting but I'll give it a try."

"How's Anthony doing?" Shay asked. We all looked in Anthony's direction to find him glasses donned and scrambling with different fabrics, appearing to be scrutinizing their sheen and colors.

"A dream, if you're asking me personally. But otherwise, he's a little worn. Reg has been on his case too. He's been on everyone's. I'm surprised he hasn't been on you guys yet," he eyed us suspiciously. "Guess you heard about Alex getting berated."

"What? No."

"Oh yeah. Yesterday during his practice. Alex smart mouthed him, just once, you know how he does. And Reg went off. Broke one of the cymbal stands. I heard him tell Alex to mind his own business."

"What does that mean? Why'd he tell him that?" I asked.

"I dunno, I didn't hear the beginning. Everyone was practicing until the cymbal crashed to the ground."

I looked at Shay and wondered if that was all our fault.

"Don't worry. It didn't even faze Alex. He actually looked kind of happy about it."

I sighed, "But that'll just make Reg worse."

"He'll be fine. We'll all be fine. We're all in this thing together," Zeke spoke is if reciting a mantra to encourage us. "You guys ready for a performance in the great outdoors?"

"As we'll ever be," I replied.

"This will be a first, for sure. Even for me," Shay added.

Given the state we had observed Reginald was in, we dodged him as much as we could all day long. And the roustabouts were avoiding Mr. Mandeville as well. They scrambled throughout the theater setting up stage boundary rings, checking the big cat cage for weak links. Their heads were down and they busied themselves continuously. No breaks, it was show day. On top of that, they were told to be extra careful not to damage any of Mr. Kyte's property or else they'd be fined.

The theater was again in a tizzy. People were running around every which way to prepare for the night. The interior was coming along and most of the props, equipment, and cages were in place. Set up was almost finished. I watched the light check overhead, colors spinning and swinging across the room, some slowly, some quickly as lasers. They danced across the center stage scrap metal head and the gold filigree trim around the theater.

Lunch was a small reprieve for the performers, and then came time for costume and makeup. Anthony was holding it together pretty well and the world's fastest makeup artist was in full swing; that's what I called her anyway.

As I waited, performers queued through an assembly line of transformation once again. At the start of the line, they were clothed in stretchy work out clothes with messy hair and plain colored faces. When they came out of the other side of costume and makeup, they emerged looking like they were ready for dystopian battle; but in a very manicured and fashion forward type of way. They looked tough yet captivating, strong and aloof in dress but enticing in face and body. Oh, how I hoped they could turn me into something like that.

Ava reappeared in a cream-colored corset top with tiny gold buttons down the middle and white doile like lace trimming the edges. A mauve colored tulle tutu and neck collar capped the corset in each direction, and she now donned white gloves and stockings. Her platinum blonde hair was curled and pinned so that it looked more like a bob and her face was the most intricate of all. It was now ivory and shimmering at the contours, with exaggerated eyelashes painted in black onyx, and pouty pink lips.

I could tell that Anthony had ensured that Zeke's look would suit him completely. He looked like a futuristic version of himself. It was very charming. Zeke wore a black bowler hat as usual, but with additional gears and a pair of goggles around the band. His shirt was a crisp white button up and over it was a deep forest green vest that really brought out his hazel green eyes, which were accentuated with black liner and a little bit of red rust color in the crease of his lids. His pants had thin vertical stripes and he wore several different sized belts, maybe three or four of them, and some with looping bronze chain.

Tombo followed in a matching green frock coat, tailored especially to him, and a top hat. The coat had gold shoulder pieces with fringe and trailed just above his knobby knees. I couldn't wait to hear his commentary on it because I had a feeling he wasn't enthused. He and Zeke looked like some sort of postmodern pirate duo.

"I guess I'm going to have to go first again?" Shay teased.

I gave her a look of thankful satisfaction as she moved that way. If Shay went first I wouldn't be as nervous because we were usually costumed similarly.

Alex came through the door as I was anxiously awaiting to see how Shay would emerge. I flicked my hand at him and he came over.

"So. What's this about you getting berated by Reg yesterday?" I asked.

"Uh, I don't know if I'd call it a berating."

"Okay, what would you call it?"

"He was just perturbed that I had input to share on how he's been leading the troupe." Alex shrugged his shoulders like they had been weighing him down day.

"So you shot off at the mouth to him? You know we've got enough going against us as it is," I huffed.

"He was yelling at Daniel. Shoved him too."

I gasped, "What? Why?"

"Well, Daniel had came to help me fix a lever on the drum platform. Reginald went off saying he was supposed to be in the menagerie and that he didn't have the brainpower to help me fix anything anyway."

My heart lurched as I listened.

Alex continued, "Daniel told him he was just helping and Reg took it as insubordination, I guess. He shoved him toward the door and told him to get going. He said that if it weren't for Caroline, Daniel would have been replaced a long time ago." Alex was getting steamed again just thinking about it. "Well, you can imagine. That killed Daniel's spirit. And it was so unnecessary. Reg was just being an ass because he felt like it. So I told him to back off, and that I asked him to help me. It successfully diverted his attention from Daniel to me. He told me to mind my own business, and I stepped up to him. I didn't say anything, just moved closer to him. Then he kicked the cymbal stand over and left."

"That jerk," I said through my teeth. The hatred I was harboring for Reg was building as images of all the times he sneered at us flashed through my mind. I refocused on Alex, who looked like he was thinking the same thing. "Why didn't you tell me about it?"

"You've got enough going on."

I was ready to punch something and then I saw Shay was finished. She looked amazing, and it momentarily distracted me from thinking about Reg.

She was wearing a dark body suit that had mesh down the middle, undoubtedly to show off cleavage if you have it; I did not. A burgundy corset around the waist. Knee pads with yellow and black biohazard stripes were held up by a strappy garter contraption that you step into like a pair of shorts. It looked like it was gear used to carry weapons. Her hair was fully teased and in dutch braided rows, four on top with lots of lift, and the temporal sides were slicked down and pinned giving the illusion of a mohawk. The makeup artist had created an intense smoky eye that lined all the way across the bridge of her nose and temples. And finally, the craziest addition to her get up occluded her mouth and nose from view. They were covered by a two filter chemical gas mask. She also wore some combat boots that rose to the knee. There was no way we could wear them during the silks routine, but we were instructed to have them on otherwise, for aesthetic. With the ensemble complete, she looked like a post apocalyptic warrior.

Since I had seen the magic that Anthony and the makeup artist could pull off in Merdwick, I was eager to be next. To have them catalyst a sort of metamorphosis that would turn me into something unique and other worldly.

Shay approached us, "Little hard to breathe in this thing but kinda cool." She took off the gas mask, no sense in wearing it until show time. "You're up," she said to me.

"Gah, I hope I look that cool when I come out," I said before rushing to the queue. When it was my turn, the makeup artist shoved my shoulders down to sit me in the chair without saying a word. Her head cocked to the side as she appraised my bone structure. Behind me, someone had gone warp speed in brushing all the knots out of my hair and separating it into sections. I felt them part it down the middle and begin to braid from the bottom of my neck to the top of my head and secure the hair tightly. Meanwhile, the makeup artist had pulled out a huge brush and was covering my whole forehead with some creamy substance. I felt hair twirling past my ears simultaneously. She drew lines across my eyelids and then frantically began swashing liquid across the bottom half of my face.

Final touches were made and then I was ushered out of the chair and over to Anthony, who was much warmer in conversation and assistance.

"Janie! Wow, they did some great work. Here's your body suit," he said as he guided me behind a small curtain. I thanked the heavens it didn't have mesh down the middle and instead was sort of like a dance leotard with cutouts on the shoulders. I put it on and came out for layer two, which was a corset like Shay's, except mine was violet.

Anthony was appraising my progress and thinking, "You're going to get a nice little scarf. It's tighter and an infinity so I shouldn't wiggle too much during your routine. And since we're on theme here, a gas mask for you as well. Single filter style for you, to even out your space buns," he said, gesturing at my hair.

"What is the theme?" I asked him. "What would you even call this style?"

"I think of it as a sort of dystopian survivor or wasteland combatant," he lowered his voice and drew nearer, "It's Mr. Kyte's theme. He requested it, which really means it was mandatory in order to do the gig. It's not my favorite of looks but I do like it. Wait til you see what I have in mind for Alex."

Before I could blush, Anthony said he was sorry that he had to rush me out and get on to the next one. I clunked out in my thick black combat boots and stalked toward Shay and Alex.

"Whoa," said Alex. "You look good... Like a space ranger meets chemical spill. "

"Thanks," I said flatly.

"In an attractive way. It's cool," he rebounded as he scratched behind his ear.

I looked down at my boots and was happy I had the gas mask on to cover any expression that may have resulted in him saying I was attractive. "Why don't you head on in? Let's see what Anthony's got in store for you."

"I guess I may as well," he said with a half grin before he sauntered off.

Shay had her arms crossed and was smirking when he got out of sight. She bounced her eyebrows at me, and I rolled my eyes at her.

"We look good," she said. "I dig this style. You've got the space buns. You're really pulling them off."

"You think? I kind of like them too."

"Yeah, I do! I just hope we can move enough in these corsets," she said as she bent down to touch her toes. I followed suit in experimentation. "We should be alright," she said.

"How much time do we have?" I said rhetorically as I looked toward the clock above the entry to the theater. "Two hours?"

"Something like that," Shay replied.

We watched the tight ropers transform into Victorian burlesque girls and dapper dans, fire breathers into something futuristic and supernatural. Strong man Kai wore boots, pants and suspenders, no shirt at all, some interesting goggles with scope cross hairs on each lens, and an enormous top hat. His dark skin rippled over giant rounded muscles and the thick braids of his hair hung down his back as usual. In lace and pearls with her hair done up like a flapper, Big Bertha basically wore cream-colored lingerie, with fringe on the hips and draped across the shoulders, and some chunky belts and swooping gold chains.

Finally, Alex came out of costume and makeup... and it was horrifying. By the time he was done, Ava had joined our group to spectate and wait on showtime. The three of us had no idea it was him until Ava jumped at the sight of him and we realized he was coming our way. From the neck down, his outfit was much like strong man Kai's; yet obviously several sizes smaller. The pale skin of his chest was visible, only blocked by the straps of his suspenders. He wore high-waisted pants and lacing combat boots that rose to mid shin. They had hennaed his arms and hands with tribal markings.

What was scary about him was his appearance from the neck up. His face was completely occluded by a sixteenth century style plague doctor mask that had been zhuzhed up to theme. It still had the long bird-like beak and goggled eyes, but this mask was metal and had air filters on the side, where Alex's cheeks would be, and duct tubing that ran from the filters to beneath the beak. His hair was straightened, stiffly sprayed, and pieced between the straps that held the mask securely on his head.

Muffled through the mask we heard him say, "What do you think?" as he gesticulated with his forearms.

"Well, it sure is a sight to behold. I'll tell ya that," said Ava.

"Creepy as hell if you ask me," I chimed in. "Do you have to wear it until show time? Take it off."

Shay was laughing as she watched the looks on mine and Ava's faces.

Alex slid the mask up. The beak looked like it was coming out of his forehead. He laughed, "No, I can peek out and breathe until show time. I think it's gonna look pretty sick while I'm on the coaster though."

"I like the suspenders though," said Ava, as my stomach knotted. It lurched again when she said, "What do you think, Janie?"

"Uh, well, I think it will be hard to notice anything other than the mask, but yeah, the rest is alright," I said coolly.

Chapter 12

Unprecedented Actions

From inside the theater's lobby window, I could see that the sun was lingering in the western portion of the vista, still bright at the moment but on its way down for the day. It was Friday, and the electric buzz of the emerging weekend was almost tangible.

Fifteen minutes before the show began, people were congregating around the front of the theater to watch the first acts, which took place outside. They swarmed all around the scrap metal sculptures. Some children had climbed up parts of them for a better view. Parents sat on benches and propped up against the raised flower beds that contained magenta winter heather and blue pansies along the pathways through Mr. Kyte's grounds. During their waiting, they put quarters into kaleidoscope viewers to watch psychedelic colors shifting or warmed themselves with cups of cocoa and hot apple cider. The smell of it permeated the air.

The hot air balloons were tethered and ready. A line between the two of them parallel to the ground, though it was fifty feet higher than ground level. Behind it, in the backdrop, the mountain was ablaze in golden sunlight. There was no snowfall, and the air was clear and crisp. Eagles were being spotted in games of I spy, by a crowd waiting for the show to begin.

A modest sized circus tent had been erected to the left of the theater entrance. It was wonderfully whimsical in appearance. Swooping up to a high point in striped canvas. Its colors teal, hot pink, and tangerine yellow, contrasting nicely against the purple theater. We outside performers were to wait inside it and emerge when it was time for our act. Unfortunately, as quaint as the tent was, it was still freezing inside it. Several performers were just running circles along the perimeter of the tent to keep their bodies warm. Some jumped in place, others rubbed their arms and legs quickly up and down for some welcome friction.

Outside was a tall, elaborate platform that was crafted to look like it was being held up by a blue dragon. Its eyes flickered and glowed with green light and dry ice was smoking out of its mouth, like it had just woken from sleep. Music echoed off the metal sculptures and mountain tops, and from a crack in the tent I could see Mr. Kyte was climbing up the stair of the blue dragon platform. The crowd went nuts at the sight of him, like he was a celebrity.

"My loves! My loves! Welcome to Kaleidoscope Kyte's!" He lifted his top hat and swung it up ceremoniously. His white hair was perfectly styled and slicked back, and his eyes were shielded by circular framed glasses with rose-colored lenses.

He gave the crowd a brief moment to continue their roar, to relish the praise, and then set his hat back atop his head and flicked the lenses of the glasses up so that he could see his fans eye to eye.

"So kind you are! So kind! To the glorious first time viewers of our show, I am Mr. Kyte. Now then. As you may have noticed by the white hair beneath this hat, I've been around for a while," he warmed the crowd. I heard soft chuckles in approval of the relatable self deprecating humor. He continued, "And I have spent most of my days producing shows unlike any other, seeking talent like you've never seen, and upping the circus ante to every other show I come up against." Everyone in the crowd, regardless of age, grew wide-eyed.

"Tonight I have allowed an old friend to join me in entertaining you fine people. Mr. Mandeville come on out here, won't you?" his voiced boomed through the microphone.

Reg strode arm in arm with Caroline from out of nowhere in full circus attire. He wore a puffy white shirt with a black and gold filigree vest and pinstriped pants. His hair was styled more wavy than curly so that it looked longer than usual. And above it was a top hat that housed extravagant feathers around the band.

Caroline wore a partially transparent body suit that completely covered her feet and gloved her hands. It was lined, of course, to cover important parts of her body but transparent at other random sections. There were gears of different sizes all over it, even on the fingers of its gloves. Only her head of flowing blonde hair was free of the nylon. She usually wore her hair up for shows, but for this ensemble it was half up in interesting braided knobs along the top of her head while the rest fell naturally at length to her lower back. Both of them wore black eye liner with an added streak down the check, on Caroline's right eye and Reginald's left. They complimented each other thanks to Anthony's handiwork.

"Oh Reginald, I didn't say bring your wife along. She is beautiful though," Mr. Kyte continued. This circus was Caroline's as much as it was Reginald's, but evidently Kyte believed otherwise.

Reg really had no choice but to play along. Through their mics, they introduced themselves to the crowd. Reg first and then Caroline. And then they gave a slight bow and their faces swung up to the platform where Mr. Kyte still towered.

"I can barely see you down there, Reginald," Kyte said, as he made exaggerated gestures toward the ground below him, like he was searching for a dropped coin that might have rolled away. The audience was smiling and laughing like it was a comedy show. Kyte continued, "I'd let you up, but I don't have the room for you."

I didn't feel sorry for him, but I knew Reg would not be enjoying this kind of banter. He didn't really know how to because usually it was his way or nothing. Part of me rooted for Mr. Kyte, to get back at Reg for all that he'd put our troupe through, my best friends through. But then I remembered that Mr. Kyte could be a loose cannon and had a history of potentially axing performers. Not to mention his hints of misogyny.

"Alright, Mr. Kyte. Are we going to do this show or what?" Reg said as he held up his performance facade. Extended posture, a toothy wide grin, and bright eyes, though I knew there were flames licking behind them.

Mr. Kyte clicked his tongue on his teeth a few times and spoke as if he was talking to a pair of children, "Patience, patience. I'll tell you when it's time. We're in my world now. Beside the people seem to enjoy a little wise cracking to warm up on. Are you in a mood because you're nervous, Reggie?"

When the chuckles subsided Reginald replied, "I guess I'm just excited for the people to see the amazing acts The Marvelous Marvels have in store for them tonight." A wise retort, I thought.

"Right you are," Mr. Kyte said and finally gave him a rest. He turned back to the crowd. "Ladies and gentlemen, you are in for a spectacular treat. Are you ready for the show?"

The crowd screamed yes.

"I can't hear you? Are you ready?" Mr. Kyte asked emphatically.

The screams intensified with stomping feet, clapping and waving hands.

"Welcome to Kaleidoscope Kyte's circus night!" His voiced boomed as he stretch out his hands like he was on the bow of a great ship.

Big Bertha stepped out of the tent and walked to center stage under the hot air balloons. Strong man Kai and the snake charmer followed in succession.

Big Bertha was working her costume, or lack their of, with some simple dance choreography. A strand of pearls around her neck and her dark hair in pinned swirls. She pranced in her cream-colored lingerie and its fringes at the hips and shoulders wiggled as she did. She shook her shoulders and spun, flicked a foot with pointed toe out to the side. All while the side show acts were initiating their acts as well.

Though he was only two-thirds her size, Kai was still enormous in an entirely different aesthetic. Whereas Bertha's skin was almost as ivory as the snow blanketing the mountain behind them, Kai's was a dark, chocolaty tone. And in further contrast, though Bertha's body looked soft as a pillow, Kai's looked like actual stone boulders. You may break your finger if you poked it too hard.

Strong man Kai's lack of a shirt made him appear massive and his suspenders had the effect of making his torso look longer. He wore odd looking leather bands that rose from wrist to forearm full of rivets and tacks and peculiar little vials across the top of his arm, as if they might house the elixir that gave strength to his gargantuan biceps and shoulders. Finally, the fact that you couldn't really see his eyes behind those odd cross hair goggles made him all the more intimidating.

He posed to show off his body, as intricate and defined as a marble statue. He lifted huge round-ended barbells while the snake charmer played for her cobra. Big Bertha had danced her way over to the snake charmer and was pretending to sneakily dig through the baskets set up behind her. She lifted the top of a basket and without noise jumped back and threw her hands up like she was in shock, but then appeared very happy at what she discovered. She glanced at the charmer, who was busy with her cobra, and leaned into the basket and withdrew a large banana colored boa constrictor. She made kissy faces at his flicking tongue and then laid him across her shoulders and continued to feign surreptitious retreat towards Kai and away from the charmer who pretended she was oblivious to the whole charade.

Kai had performed several feats by now and Bertha batted her eyelashes at him as if to say, "Check out what I've done." Kai crossed his enormous arms and nodded like it impressed him. He gestured Bertha to come toward him. The crowd was eating it up and cheering them on.

Kai then laid his back flat on the ground and put his hands palm up just above his shoulders. Bertha took bouncy steps over him, straddling his enormous quadriceps, his waist, and expansive chest, and waving coyly down at him. He returned the little wave and then Berta stepped one foot up on his open palm.

There was a pregnant pause and the audience seem to hold their breath, filled with excitement and expectation. Wondering how on Earth this would end. Little boys elbowed their fathers to be sure they were paying attention.

Bertha slowly balanced and stepped the other foot up to his open palm. She extended her arms cautiously balancing. The snake comfortably laid his head on her ivory arm as if he were bored. Steadily, Kai contracted his bulging pectorals and pushed Bertha higher in the sky. Bertha beckoned the crowd by gesture, to count the coming repetitions. He bench pressed her five times to a roar of applause.

Up until then, the snake charmer had taken a back seat. Now she led the cobra, by the sound of her horn, up over Kai's chest where it sat drunkenly swaying. She continued to honk the pungi with one hand as she reached up with the other to grasp Bertha's. As the cobra swayed, the yellow boa constrictor seemed to have understood the call home and slithered across the ladies' arms until it sat across the snake charmer's shoulder.

The audience applauded the snake's obedient journey, and the charmer beckoned the cobra forward. It slithered off Kai's neck and beside his ear until it was back to its original performance zone. Then Bertha carefully stepped down and blew a kiss at Kai.

"Weren't these guys great?" Mr. Kyte had resumed post on the dragon platform and announced the transition loudly. "If it weren't for my wife, I'd ask Miss Bertha on a date."

Bertha played along with a curtsey, despite the fact that the comment was at her and Mrs. Kyte's expense, and the crowd applauded. The three acts followed suit and made their way back to the tent. The sun had sank a little, but was still pretty high, and the snow on the mountain was sparkling. A few people in the crowd squinted or lidded their eyes with their hand.

"Let's get right to it, ladies and gentleman. The Sky Wire!" Mr. Kyte's voice rang as he swung an arm up to the hot air balloon. And just as he did so, a rope ladder tumbled out from the bottom of each of them. Our roustabouts scurried to position the safety net below the balloons.

The music changed to a very interesting version of an old eighties song. I recognized it from living with my rock-and-roll father when I was in high school. But the words had been changed to Sky Wire, and the instrumentation was replaced with electronic music and sped up to intensify its effect.

Our troupe's tight rope walking duo, Cynthia and Patrick, whipped back the tent flaps ceremoniously and strutted out towards the bottom of the ladders. With flair they climbed, stopping at the twenty-five foot point, and forty foot point to wave at the audience below. They climbed all the way up through the bottom of the baskets and positioned themselves with one foot up on the wire. In synchrony, they contracted their leg muscles and lifted up to stand on the wire, fifty feet above ground level, in a slow and graceful ascension.

They stepped across slowly, facing each other. When they met in the middle of the wire, Cynthia took Patrick's hands and slowly lifted one leg behind her. Once she was balanced, he did the same. He placed his foot back on the wire and leaned back slightly. Cynthia slowly swung her leg over one hundred and eighty degrees until her foot rested on Patrick's shoulder in a graceful split.

They continued a variety of balancing poses and tricks and were gearing up for their more dangerous stuff. Tricks where Cynthia would balance on Patrick's shoulders as he walked. It was an old hat for them, but a good twenty feet higher than usual.

Everyone, the crowd and those of us in the tent waiting, were craning their necks up to watch in suspense when the music faded down and a smooth voice resounded on the microphone.

"These guys are so good. I don't think we need a safety net. Ladies and gentlemen, what do you think?" Mr. Kyte was smooth and had subdued his charisma to feign his concern for distracting the walkers mid act. He knew that was all he needed to do. The crowd gasped and awed and were eager to see the safety net removed. Some of them started chanting, "Move the net. Move the net."

Our roustabouts were looking frantic, nervous as cats and unsure of what to do. Reg emerged from the tent and put one hand palm down in front of his chest as if to say, "Stay put."

"Let's give it a whirl. What do you say?" Mr. Kyte egged the crowd on. He looked at Reg, "Oh, come on, Reggie. You trust them, don't you?"

He had put Reginald in a bad spot in front of a live crowd. And Reg was kind of frozen.

"Move the nets," Mr. Kyte said firmly to the roustabouts.

They looked to Reg again, who gave a small exhausted nod. He appeared genuinely apprehensive.

The roustabouts obeyed and Cynthia and Patrick continued their act, no doubt trying to ignore what they were hearing below. I had never held my breath so hard in my life, and I prayed Whisper would hold them up there. Everyone was silent.

Cynthia had successfully transitioned up to stand on Patrick's shoulders as he walked with a balancing pole. He walked all the way to her balloon basket. There was a pause, and she flexed completely forward and moved into a handstand position on his shoulders. Then Cynthia executed a split and bent her knees, making her legs look like a wave. Now Patrick walked backwards to his balloon basket.

Our troupe watched in horror. Everyone's eyes alternately flicking down at the empty space beneath them, the hard cement below them, and back up again. The sun still sinking and the mountain still glistening, unyielding to their usual routines.

Cynthia came back down to the wire very carefully. She and Patrick, hand in hand, stepped back to the middle of the wire where their act first began. In an unprecedented action, they leaned forward and kissed each other on the mouth, to which the crowd went nuts. Then they slowly pivoted on the wire and stepped back to their baskets. Finally, on the edge of the hot air balloon, they waved and blew their kisses down to the crowd. We all started exhaling again once they were descending from the rope ladders.

"I knew they could do it! Didn't I tell you guys?" Mr. Kyte shouted emphatically. The crowd roared and applauded passionately.

Reg had gone back inside the tent in defeat. And I grew increasingly horrified at what might happen during Shay and mine's act. We were up next, and Mr. Kyte was a sick man for putting performers at risk for his own twisted amusement. If Reg no longer had the reins, we had just stepped into unpredictable territory.

Chapter 13

Feeling The Burn

I thought I was going to hyperventilate. Shay spun me around to face her, her warm hands firmly on my shoulders. "Breathe. Breathe. We're going to be fine. But if you feel unsafe at any point, stop." She paused until she had my eye contact. "Stop. Don't do the move. It's not worth dying for."

I nodded rapidly and tried to listen to her continued mantras of encouragement while simultaneously seeking any input from Whisper. After catching my breath, I started jumping in place to get my blood moving again. There was no time left to flounder. We were about to be announced. Shay and I both slapped our gas masks on and double checked to make sure the straps were tightened.

It was getting close to sunset. A few scattered clouds were starting to cast crepuscular rays. Native birds were actively sweeping across the vista, searching for their dinner. And the temperature drop was a bit more noticeable.

"Look at that beautiful backdrop, folks! Breath taking, isn't it? We're about to add a bit more excitement to the aesthetic."

The intro music faded in and my stomach started flipping somersaults. But it was now or never. I was grateful that the gas mask covered half of my face. At least I wouldn't have to fake a smile the whole time.

I followed Shay out of the tent, shoulders back and chest high. Stepping confidently, even if it was an act in my case, toward the hot air balloons which had just released the silks from the rigging in the basket. The crowd was watching them tumble and swing through the chilly air, so we approached mostly unnoticed. It felt like slow motion, and like I was outside of my body for a moment.

When we reached our own silk, we gave them a hearty tug as an extra check, and began a steady climb. Violins, drums, and horns began pleasantly mixing in an upbeat tempo just under the surface of some trippy verses about tomorrow being unknown. It seemed to evoke a sense of determination for the task ahead.

Once we were about twenty-five feet up, we started transitioning through our poses, holding them for a good slow count of eight before moving on to the next one.

The crowded roared for the double foot knot splits. They always do. Spectators seem to think splits are quite impressive. Herein lies the frustrations with aerial silks routines. That there is so much effort and strength involved in the setup of a fabulous drop, but the crowd never realizes that because you are smiling your head off throughout like it's nothing. Then you execute the drop and it gets some claps, sure. But do a simple split and they go bananas. I digress.

A candy cane pose and into a cross back straddle. We were now upside down yet elegant butterflies flapping our silky wings through the cold air. I imagined it would look especially magical against the beautiful view behind us. From there we went into our creature pose, an impressive sort of back bend where your legs end up over your head.

As we held the position, I scanned the audience. They were oohing and awing, especially the little girls, which made my heart swell. To inspire anyone was great, but there was always something a little more special about how they watched us. I tried to spot those happy faces in the crowd, to fuel me on to the coming more dangerous moves. The ones I was apprehensive about from the start, that Reg had demanded. As I looked for them in the crowd, I noticed a familiar person under the grizzly bear. Ironically, where I had last noticed Gray Cloud. This time, Felicity stood there.

Felicity's outfit, mask, and lustrous hair made her stick out like a sore thumb. She appeared to be there to see the show, leaned back against the sculpture, her arms crossed comfortably. I was immediately excited at the potential opportunity to speak to her again post show, but I had to refocus quickly.

We continued our choreography. The neck hang, the long graceful set up that led to the angel drop. The crowd still appear enthralled and attentive and the music raged on. Now we were almost to the end. Only Reginald's prescribed star drop and bullet were left.

For the star drop, we climbed all the way up to about forty feet above ground level, which was incredibly daunting. I tried not to think about it or look at anything other than parts of my own body, so that maybe I wouldn't realize how high it was. However, my adrenaline was off the charts at this point because I just wanted to get it done, get it over with. And I wasn't very worried about this drop because you were very secure. Even if you tumbled like the unrolling of gift wrapping paper through the sky toward the earth below. At the end of the unrolling, you came to a jolting halt via a securely wrapped waist, like a harness.

I wrapped furiously and awaited the cue from Shay to drop. We hung just under the balloons. Quite high. Very high. I saw her signal and then shut my eyes and willed myself to release my toe, which was all that held me in place. Down we spiraled simultaneously like leaves off an autumn maple tree. We were caught by our wrapping at the end range, which was back in the comfortable territory of twenty feet above ground.

The crowd cheered and applauded, but now it was time for the most dreadful of all, the ten-foot bullet drop. Again we climbed, and I silently prayed for Whisper to catch me. The sun was down enough to cast pink and orange hues across the skyline, the swipes of the artist's paintbrush. I concentrated on its grandness as I climbed back to a height of forty feet and set up with a simple catcher's hang. We were positioned like a deer mid leap, only upside down. I pulled enough slack to drop me as much as Reg's standard, and I stared off at the fuchsia and peach painted sky. The music was about to crescendo as we held the pose and I watched for the cue once more. A subtle flick of Shay's foot and I knew it was time.

I let go of my top hand and whooshed straight down toward the ground below. The baby hairs around my crown startled and swiftly waving as the cold air intensified with my acceleration. The friction of the silk on my thigh grew hot quickly as I shot down. I never opened my eyes until my body jerked to a stop. But I thanked Whisper when I did, even though my tights were now ripped from the friction and a nasty red burn had made its debut.

We descended gracefully and raised our hands toward the crowd before bowing. They rallied, shouting and whistling.

"What a drop! You folks want to see some more aerial action?" Mr. Kyte boomed. He quickly moved on to the next bit of entertainment. His voiced trailed as we exited.

I led our walk back to the tent, trying to step as serenely as possible. When we were behind the flaps I inspected my leg.

"Oh, dang. Yours is way worse than mine," said Shay. She too had a rip in her hosiery and the beginning marks of a burn.

"That's gonna be a bitch for tomorrow's show," said strong man Kai before continuing his dumbbell workout.

"He's not wrong," said Shay under her breath, pulling the fabric of my tights to the side to get a better look. "I've got some ointment back in our room. That'll help some. Both of us will have to be bandaged tomorrow or we'll have to use the other leg," she huffed frustratedly to herself. "But then we'll be walking around bow legged for the whole next week."

"It burns something awful. But at least Kyte didn't do anything insane while we were performing," I breathed.

The show must go on. I heard outside that Mr. Kyte had not skipped a beat.

"Next up, we have some high flyers!" Mr. Kyte boomed.

Safety nets reappeared below, and trapeze stands erected to the sides of the hot air balloons. The lengthy silks pulled up now and replaced by a hanging silvery bar. Our troupe's flyers, Wentworth and Artem, ascended the stand followed by two assistants to edge the trapeze platform on each side of them. They would hold the bar and assist in pulling their flyer up all the way if the momentum grew shy on his return to the stand. What's called a noodle, which looked like a shepherd's hook, was extended by a member of the trapeze team to pull the dangling bar to the stand.

Our view of the sun was teetering above the edge of the earth, threatening its withdrawal of light. But the crowd was still amped, full of electricity and seeming to bobble where they stood. Munching down wads of cotton candy procured by gloved hands. Since it was quite cold by this point. Nevertheless, the music again began to resound across the mountain, a deep house remix of a pop song.

Wentworth began the first swing from the left stand. He flowed through the air in a simple arc before tucking his legs to his chest and wrapping his knees around the bar. The momentum of the timed release of his hands, and the arch of his back, projected him a bit higher in the arc. On the right side trapeze, Artem was swinging and alternating hand positions to perform a turnaround. First, he swung facing Wentworth, turned at end range to face his assistants at the stand, and then back again. Next, he extended a hand toward his partner in an impressive one arm swing.

Wentworth set up in the catch trap position. At the center point of the two arcs, Artem engaged in a catcher's lock and released his knees from his bar. Held by Wentworth's grasp, he swung to the left side and then back to the right where he caught his own bar once again.

Again he did the same, except Wentworth caught his ankles rather than his wrists, and the two continued into more challenging tricks. Mid air rotations or three-sixty flips. Their agility amazed the crowd, floating through the air like feathers on a breeze. Timing perfectly and working in harmony and unity.

"Ladies and gentleman, wouldn't this look spectacular in a soft falling snow?" Mr. Kyte, again on his platform, appeared in awe of the act. The crowd responded with applause and cheers. They were privy to what Mr. Kyte may have in store next, but our troupe was not.

"Shall I summon Gray Cloud?" he continued to his audience. Again they cheered. Kyte extracted a ram's horn from within his platform, raised it high and blew it. It rang in one resounding tone, and I worried this insensitive gimmick would distract the flyers above.

A few seconds later, Gray Cloud appeared on his horse from behind the theater. But this time he looked much different. He wasn't wearing his usual handy man looking outfit, and instead was clothed in a new set of garb.

On his chest was what looked like the inner workings of a computer. Circuit boards, hard drives, ports, connectors, and power supplies. The same materials wrapped around his forearms. Like a futuristic armor. His dark shoulders were left bare and around his neck was an actual bear claw pendant. His jet black hair was separated down the middle and braided on each side, but the most magnificent accoutrement was on top of his head.

On his crown sat an extraordinary headdress. Clock dials and gear trains wrapped around the base of it. Rising up from that were thin plates of copper scrap, which were topped with carefully cut CDs. The compact discs appeared as what would have been the feathers in an original headdress. He looked like a dystopian postmodern version of the first Native American chief.

"Chief Gray Cloud, we ask you to call water from the sky," Mr. Kyte said, in what I perceived was irreverently.

He bowed toward Gray Cloud as if he respected him. The faces in the audience were all wide-eyed and mouths gaping.

Gray Cloud's face was as unchanging and blank as I had ever seen it. He slowly flexed his elbows until his open subservient palms were near his ears. Snow began to float down in little soft flakes. Sparse but noticeable.

We all looked up to find Wentworth and Artem still going through their routine amongst the soft flurries.

"Isn't it beautiful?" Mr. Kyte continued to guide the crowd on this self-seeking journey for the most whimsical and amazing aesthetics. Even if they were at the expense of the performers' safety.

"It needs to be a bit brighter. Add some more, Gray Cloud," he said.

Gray Cloud slowly looked up at the performers and then back at Mr. Kyte, flat-faced.

"Oh, come on. They have a net under them," Mr. Kyte whined, and the crowd looked greedy and eager.

Gray Cloud closed his eyes and let his chin fall. As he did so, the snow picked up a little.

The act was nearly finished, but during the last return to the free bar, Artem seemed to slip a little. There were small gasps from the few of us below who noticed. He spent the rest of the time performing small tricks on his own bar, and appeared to signal something to Wentworth, who did the same. About thirty seconds later, they swung back to their stands, waved at the crowd emphatically, and descended.

"Not the ending I envisioned, but beautiful none the less thanks to Chief Gray Cloud. Ladies and gentlemen, let's give him a hand," said Mr. Kyte. The audience diverted their attention from the trapeze artists to Gray Cloud and cheered. But Gray Cloud's face remained solemn as stone.

Wentworth and Artem entered the tent and immediately washed their countenances clean of the counterfeit smiles. Exhaling and becoming visibly irritable.

"Screw that. I'm not doing the full act in conditions that could end my career," Artem huffed. The troupe patted him on the back and offered words of encouragement, but we all knew that Reg was going to flip.

Outside the tent, the jugglers and fire breathers began their drills and choreography. Ava would make her debut on the walking globe soon.

"If this is any indication of the rest of the show. Of the rest of tomorrow's and next week's..." I said to Shay apprehensively.

"It's going to be a wild ride. Mr. Kyte is living up to the reputation that preceded him," she replied.

"He makes Reg look like a piece of cake."

"Somewhat," Shay said wearily.

I could hear the music, and applause heightened outside the tent. We peaked out and saw that Ava was now center stage atop her globe, amongst the fire breathers and jugglers. Her assistant was tossing her hoops to spin across every joint on her body. It comforted us that Ava was incredibly skilled at her act and that it did not take place dangerously floating above us. It was a welcome chance to slacken our tensed muscles and diaphragms, even if only slightly.

I turned back to Shay. "Felicity is here. I saw her in the crowd during our performance. We've got to catch her before she leaves. Geez, I wonder what she thinks of Kyte's exploitation of her uncle."

"Not too highly, I'd imagine," said Shay. "How are we going to catch her during a show?"

"I'm thinking when every one transitions to go inside the theater."

Shay's eyes grew big and stern, "Janie, if we get caught they'll do who knows what."

"You just cover for me. I'll catch her before she goes to a seat. In that nook beside the entry."

Ava's act was going smoothly, thank goodness. Her feet delicately patting the top of the globe, alternating to make it roll forwards or backwards or to the side. It was like driving a car to her.

She was adorable, seductive, and charismatic all at once, as usual. The boys in the audience were staring with unwavering attention. Grown men were trying to appear only slightly impressed as they simultaneously attempted to conceal any blatant stares, or looks that lasted too long on one body part, from their wives or dates.

All the ruffles on her costume served as accentuation marks for her body shape. And of course, no man could resist her blonde locks. I tried to think of another girl in the show that men looked at the way they did Ava. And interestingly, one did come to mind, one that I never paid much attention to. I guess because she wasn't directly in my group of frequently seen people. That person was Caroline. I wondered how on Earth Reg could tolerate that. He was so possessive.

"Folks, give it up for the lovely lady!" Mr. Kyte exclaimed as he gestured to Ava. "She will be your guide to the theater for the second act. Don't worry, she has plenty more up her sleeve for tonight." He gave the crowd a very animated wink. "Lead the way, Miss Ava!"

I peaked outside at the red glowing sunset that cast its color over the mountain face and shined on the scrap metal sculptures where the crowd was excitedly waiting to go into the theater.

"How are we going to do this? We're supposed to wait in the tent?" Shay asked.

"Out the backside of the tent. We'll go along the edge of the garden beds and in the side door of the theater. Everyone will be watching the girl on the giant red ball rolling in the front door. We'll be fine, come on!"

I tugged Shay's arm and winded my way around Bertha and Kai's dumbbells to the back of the tent. Peaking outside of it, I could see Ava was atop the globe walking it backwards and beckoning the crowd forward. The people we trailing towards her like zombies. I skirted out of the tent toward the farthest opposite side direction of the crowd and swiftly made for the side door. Shay followed.

Once inside, we made our way to the nook by the entry and waited as far back as possible to avoid being seen. I took off my gas mask. We scanned those entering for long dark hair and leathery face mask.

Face after face passed by until there was a fizzled out pause in action. "Did we miss her?"

Our troupe was lingering in. The jugglers, the fire breathers, Bertha, and Kai. We tucked back further in the nook. As the aerialist made their way inside, the sound of hasty stomping came from the within the theater toward the doors. Reg had stopped them mid entry.

"You two," he said, pointing at Wentworth and Artem, "What the hell was that? You only did half of the damned act!"

"The bars were icing. There was no way…" Wentworth tried for Artem's sake.

"You're the catcher. You were fine. You, on the other hand, lost your nerve and bowed out," Reg hissed at Artem, who tried to respond but was halted by Patrick's interjection.

"Come on Mr. Mandeville, we can't do our acts full out with no safety, or with added hazards," Patrick pleaded.

"Hey! I wasn't talking to you, now was I?" His tempered flared and his face was turning pink, and then there was a noticeable shift and attempt to pull it back down.

The entry door opened and Felicity stepped through. Reg nodded at her like everything was just swell. With a very inauthentic smile, he said, "This way ma'am. Enjoy the show."

Her dark eyes jumped around to each face, but she nodded politely and continued inside.

"Where are the damn girls?" Reg spat. Shay and I tried to shrink our bodies.

"They must already be inside," Artem replied. "Reg, I know you're angry, but Kyte is a bit out of control. We can't..."

"I know that rabid little weasel is looney, but we've got shows to do. Don't let it happen again," Reg thundered, with a final poke of his thick calloused finger in Artem's chest before turning back inside.

"Oh my gosh. I think I almost passed out," I said. "And all that for nothing. We missed her."

Shay softened. "We've got to get back with the troupe. We'll look for her inside."

Inside the theater, the crowd was nearly seated, though a few were still at concessions. The adults hauled boxes of popcorn while the children ran amuck with large swirling lollipops in their hands.

We shuffled in cautiously and made for the backstage area. No time to search for Felicity with the chance of us being on Reg's immediate radar. Not that anyone noticed us, but we must've looked funny clutching gas masks and trying to walk swiftly and surreptitiously—though bow legged from silk burns.

Chapter 14

Theater Lights

Kastle Theater was aglow and buzzing with energy. Most spectators were seated, and Mr. Kyte was now on the stage under the scrap metal goddess. He waved animatedly and blew kisses to his adoring audience. His eyebrows bouncing above a warm smile, and the audience eating out of the palm of his hand.

From a discreet corner where we were obscured from sight, Shay and I watched the second set of acts. The lights faded on and off to notify everyone that the show would start soon. The smell of concessions wafted through the air though the room grew steadily quiet. The music began with tones of suspense as the start of the second act was beginning.

Everything went dark and the excitement in the seats was palpable. A spotlight swirled around the edges of the room in search for a landing. In the constructed ring, at the very center of the room, the spotlight halted to reveal Reginald and Caroline Mandeville in full circus attire. Their arms extended in grandeur.

"Ladies and gentlemen, we are the Mandevilles and tonight we continue to bring you a series of Marvelous Marvels!" Reginald bellowed while Caroline curtsied.

He swung his hand behind him and the lights increased in a variety of color to reveal our beloved pachyderm, Eloise, standing behind him in the center ring. She was standing on top of a small platform with her right foot posed in the air in front of her.

Daniel stood gleefully just below her on the ground, his smile wide under a top hat that had a pocket watch strung up and pinned on it. He led Eloise down the platform and through a sequence of tricks in the middle ring. After a few minutes had passed, he led Eloise to another platform that was shadowed and unlit. She raised up until she was standing on her hind legs and then stretched her trunk up to it.

When Eloise's trunk was seen again, it held Ava, who sat perched on its curve with her dainty legs crossed. One hand wrapped around Eloise's trunk and the other gracefully waving to the audience. Eloise slowly lowered her front legs back to the ground. She raised her trunk up for Ava to crawl up over her head to the saddle on her back. There, Ava balanced on one foot between Eloise's thick shoulders and lifted the other leg up and over her head, holding it there gracefully with both arms as Eloise began to walk around the ring. Ava repositioned out of the split and into a standing bow pose.

The audience was bursting with applause at every move she made. Ava continued through a few more bendy looking poses and then executed a back bend atop the curve of Eloise's spine. After holding for a few seconds, she kicked her legs over and balanced into a full handstand as the elephant continued to step, splitting her legs to aid in balance. From there, she transitioned to a very poised final position of a lady like seat. Her legs draped across Eloise's forehead and crossed at the ankles as she waved to the crowd. They responded with passionate encouragement and praise.

Daniel led them out of the center ring, and the big cats and lion tamer were ready in their cage. In between watching the cats, I continued scanning the crowd.

"Look, there she is!" I tugged Shay's arm and pointed to the row where I had spotted Felicity sitting with her arms crossed.

"I wonder what she's here for. She looks miffed," Shay said.

"What's the best way to catch her, you think?"

"We need to get to the other side of the room without being noticed."

After the big cats finished with their jumps, rolls, and growls, they got rubbed on their heads and dismissed back to their corresponding cages with the flick of a flexible cane that looked more like a riding crop.

Zeke and Tombo were up next. As the music changed and the lights turned back up, the two of them strode out into the center ring in a blur of forest green hues. Both of them smiling brightly. Tombo took off his top hat and bowed to the audience before placing it back on his fuzzy head.

"Good evening, ladies and gentlemen! I'm Zeke and this is my dear friend Tombo."

The crowd clapped and cheered for the adorable coat wearing chimpanzee, eager to see how he would entertain them tonight.

"Hello ladies," the English voice rang as Zeke's Adam's apple bobbed slightly. Tombo was bouncing his eyebrow ridge up and down while the women in the audience cooed.

"Hey fellas," came the English accent again, this time quick and sharp, as Tombo suddenly appeared unenthusiastic. Zeke rolled his eyes ostentatiously.

"Always checking out the ladies. Trying to impress the ladies," said Zeke.

Tombo replied with incredulous look, "Yeah, so. I'm an impressive bloke."

I could see children asking their parents how the monkey was talking. I watched as their parents responded by pointing to Zeke. I felt relieved that Zeke was continuing to pull it off, since that was the first time I had watched his ventriloquy act knowing the truth of it.

"Alright. Have you planned an exhibition of your impressive skills for tonight?" Zeke asked.

"No need to plan. I'm always ready." Tombo's lips moved as Zeke's twitched. After Tombo's every line, there was a pause strategically placed to allow the audience time for a laugh or giggle.

"Next to you, it's easy to impress the ladies," said Tombo. Zeke frowned. "How bout a competition?"

"You're on," said Zeke animatedly.

"Right-o, I bet I can hula hoop longer than you," said Tombo.

"You just want that pretty girl to bring you the hoops."

Tombo shrugged and his frock coat raised up as its shoulder pieces glistened in the light. Ava appeared, a sparkling smile plastered across her face like a game show assistant, carrying two hula hoops to the stage. She handed one to Zeke. Then she placed the second hoop over Tombo's head. When he grasped it around his body, she kissed him on the top of his head and then pranced away. Tombo pretended to faint, falling to the ground hoop and all. Spectators gushed and giggled as Zeke feigned genuine concern and rushed to Tombo's side.

"Are you alright?"

"That's the most action I've had in a month," the accent blurted.

Zeke helped him back up and smugly said, "I hope this doesn't affect your competition."

"Nope, it has fueled the fire. Ready?" Tombo bounced up and down, holding the hoop as if trying to get his blood flowing again after being lightheaded.

Ava re-emerged to play assistant with a squeezable air horn in hand. When she blew it, Tombo and Zeke began hooping. It lasted about a minute before Zeke's hoop fell to the floor as Tombo kept rocking his hips. Ava extended her long, slender arms to Tombo as the audience clapped.

"Alright, alright. Let's see who can run the fastest?" Zeke said.

The two positioned at a starting line, the horn blew, and Zeke just barely beat Tombo. The adorable chimp hung his head as the crowd awed.

"Oy. Flip contest," said Tombo resolutely.

Zeke executed a front flip, tucked and rolled over the ground, and then a back flip. When Tombo's turn came, he performed a double back tuck and a cork screw forward, which easily beat Zeke, to the delight of the spectators.

"Alright. Dance off," said Zeke.

Tombo began with a simple sort of two step that lead to a couple of break dancing spins. Zeke followed with advanced ballet moves and spins with the utmost gracefulness, body isolation moves that jerked and stuck like a robot, and pop and locks that looked humanly impossible. The audience roared as Zeke moved.

"Who can climb the best and highest?" Tombo seemed to snort irritatedly.

Zeke didn't even attempt any climbing. But Tombo was up a column and swinging off rafters in a matter of seconds. When he returned, Zeke applauded him.

"How about a swimming contest?" Zeke said sarcastically.

"There's no pool here. And I'm not stepping foot near that river," came Tombo's voice. His eyebrows raised to the audience showing trepidation.

I felt my pulse increase and shot a glance at Shay, who also looked surprised.

Zeke was caught off guard, but had to maintain the appearance that he had actually made Tombo say that. He quickly attempted to deflect with a joke.

"Hey, what's the best exercise for swimmers? Mind you, I know I could do more of these than you?"

"What?"

"Pool-ups."

"This is why you don't have any friends," Tombo spouted. The audience had recovered and laughed at the curt retort.

"Well, that's very obviously not true. I've got you. And you've got me. Let's end this thing on a good note. A truce maybe."

Music began to play, and Zeke prepped to sing. He began a verse and Tombo visibly softened up. They harmonized intermittently, which greatly impressed the spectators who believed it was only one man actually singing. When the music faded, the man and chimpanzee gave the audience a bow.

"Thank you, ladies and gentlemen. Enjoy the rest of the show!" Zeke said before they gave another bow and turned to briskly exit the ring.

Reg gave Zeke and Tombo a nasty look as they crossed paths, thankfully walking hastily in opposite directions. A look that conveyed the feeling that there was imminent battering punishment ahead.

Reginald and Caroline reappeared in their themed garb, compliments of Anthony. For their acts, a round end table had been set up adjacent center stage. It was covered with a crocheted doile and on it was a large antique phonograph. Its brassy flaring horn gleamed in the show lights.

Caroline tip toed, in a serene yet coy manner, to the phonograph and moved the needle. It began to play and she flurried back to Reg, who caught her and spun her around in a preliminary dance number. As they began to move, so did the ground they were standing on. It was a hidden rotating platform. When the dance was complete, increasingly energetic music kicked in and they began their contortion and sword swallowing acts.

Reg swished a sword back and forth like he was fencing an invisible opponent. He inspected the gilded handle and spun it in his hand before lifting it high, tilting his head back, and swallowing the shiny blade. Its handle sat on the corners of his mouth as Reg extended his hands to his side and slowly began a three hundred and sixty degree turn. The audience roared, and he slowly pulled the sword out of his abdomen.

Caroline transitioned through a number of bending poses as Reg returned to his props. An assistant brought out a very large birdcage and sat it down center stage, its door open. Caroline traveled across the ring by a series of overturning backbends until she was at the birdcage. She contorted her body so that each limb slowly flicked and then inserted into the cage until she was completely inside. The assistant shut the door and through a set of small movements she moved position in the tiny space, like an exotic coiling boa constrictor.

A small light was under the scrap metal goddess where Mr. Kyte was positioned to commentate. Though he was miked, he had thus far been quiet.

"Impressive!" Mr. Kyte's husky voice rang out. "But wouldn't it be all the more if she was doing the sword swallowing and he was trapped in a cage?" Mr. Kyte bounced his eyebrows creepily. He was pushing the limits of Reginald's nerves. The audience cheered and momentarily laughed at the innuendo.

Reg was working hard to mask his feelings of appall and rage. Caroline flickered her eyes to check on him as the two of them continued with their stunts.

I jerked Shay's wrist. "She's coming out of the stands," I said, pointing at Felicity. I had noticed her movement, which was in view just past Caroline's direction. "Maybe she's going to concessions or the bathroom."

"What are you doing?" Shay said as I pulled her.

"We're going now. To catch her. We may not get another chance."

"You're just going to interrogate her on the spot?" Shay asked.

"I guess. I'm tired of running around for Caroline's favor. We need to get it over with."

"My my, Janie Morgan has come a long way. Remember when you were scared as a kitten of the Mandevilles?" Shay poked with a grin.

"I don't know about all that. But let's go," I said.

We snuck around the dressing rooms in the back, to the other side of the hall, and out towards concessions. I saw the back of Felicity's thick hair as she went into the ladies' room.

We followed her in, hopeful that the rest of the room would be otherwise empty. A few women washing their hands tried to hide funny looks at us from the mirror's reflection. We were in body suits and corsets after all. I bent over to look for feet under the stalls and was relieved that there was only one set.

Felicity came out, looking to the sink to wash her hands, and spotted us instead, but she more or less rolled her eyes.

"Ladies," she said as she turned on the sink, "good to see you again."

"Hi Felicity. Look, I'm just gonna cut to the chase," I began. She didn't look up from her hygiene routine.

"The doctor I asked you about. Is he in the mountains? With your people?" I asked carefully.

"What makes you think the fertility doctor is a he?" she smarted off.

I processed her statement for a second. "So the doctor is there? It's a woman?"

She didn't respond, just looked at me with her deep brown eyes. I continued, "Felicity, we really need your help. My job sort of depends on it. See, I'm due Mrs. Mandeville a favor and she's been trying to have a baby for so long. She asked us to try to find the doctor."

"Why should I help her?"

I didn't really have a convincing answer, so I stuttered, "I'm sure they would be willing to pay whatever the cost."

Shay spoke up, "I know her husband has been causing chaos since they arrived at the peaks, but..."

Felicity paused for a moment, looking at Shay as if she were surprised to hear her actually speak. "I've heard enough about it, and I'm not so sure we can help them," she said, crossing her arms after drying her hands.

"Why not?"

"We don't consort with people like Reginald Mandeville."

"Understandable," I mumbled. "What if it was just Mrs. Mandeville? She's not to Reginald's level. And we could bring her instead."

"I don't know. I'd have to speak to the elders."

Felicity's eyes were unsearchable and wide. I didn't feel very hopeful that we had a deal. "Can I tell her you're going to?" I asked hesitantly.

Felicity turned to appraise Shay once again. When she answered, she didn't bother to turn and speak to me, but continued peering into Shay's eyes scrutinizingly.

"I'll notify you if the doctor is willing," she said and then walked out.

We dropped our shoulders and relaxed for a moment after she left and then snuck back to the performer's side of the theater. Reg and Caroline's act was ending, and they were bowing at an applauding and whistling crowd.

"This, folks, is why we have such a great circus tonight. Give it up for the Mandevilles!" Mr. Kyte exclaimed over the mic. "Without them there would be no Marvelous Marvels!"

The crowd roared and Reg seemed to exude genuine pride in his show and in the fact that Kyte seemed momentarily in approval.

"I'm very intrigued by this last act, very eager to see it. Folks, get ready for the flying drummer!"

Darkness fell throughout the whole theater and I knew Alex would be undergoing the final checks of the platform in the dark. After the audience endured two minutes of vision occluded suspense, he began a soft rapid trill on a high tom mixed with cymbal tings. The red and blue lights slowly scanned the floor of the theater and across the room to reveal the drum set platform that was paused on the track at about five feet off the ground. More lights shot beams outside the platform and throughout the coaster track, showing spectators the intended path. Gasps of excitement were audible.

A purple spotlight now rested on Alex and everyone was now processing the strange looking creature causing the drums to ring out. In the dark plague doctor's mask, his face was completely covered. His dark hair spilling around its edges. I wondered if the mask's long birdlike beak would interfere with his ability to play.

His arms were already taut and glistening as he continued playing, revealed by a tank undershirt and dark suspenders. I thought overall he looked ghastly and sinister, but I always admired how his arms became toned and veiny as he played. As did most every other female.

The platform began to rise again, slowly and steadily as he wailed. A string of beats resounded on top of intermittent bass pedal booming. His arms were flying in synchronous and rotating motions. At the top, the peak of the first wave, the platform rotated forward. As his arms crossed and crashed, he turned three hundred and sixty degrees. The audience went nuts, screaming and whistling. When he was upside down, he really let loose. Picking up speed, engaging in double bass pedaling, vigorous slamming of drum heads. His arms extended down toward spectators below him. They raised their arms as if reaching for his, pumping them to the beats he created.

The beaked mask remained secure to his head, and he looked like an otherworldly musical creature on a rampage. Upright once more, he rode on to the second wave and into another rotation, this time backwards. When reclined at forty-five degrees, he executed fast trills as if he was bored, his head back and his arms rapidly alternating but close to his lap. Upside down for the second wave, he shattered cymbals like a madman.

On the third and final wave, he went full throttle, giving the audience everything he had. His most challenging sequences, beats, trills, and bass pedaling. Intensity and volume was dialed up to its maximum. And the light show intensified for dramatic effect. The beams of it reflecting off of his arms which glistened with sweat.

As he descended down to the other side of the track to end the act, the audience raged. Assistants rushed out to unbuckle him and he execute a perfect back flip off the platform, beaked mask and all. He hurtled a single excited fist punch in the air as the crowd extolled his feat.

"I've never seen such an inventive display of musical artistry! Bravo!" Kyte spoke over the mic. "Ladies and gentlemen, the Mandeville's Marvelous Marvels! Have a beautiful night!"

The audience cheered and seemed to want to stay in the theater even though the show was over. The troupe was buzzing around the dressing rooms and backstage area. Another show completed. I changed out of my show attire and hung them on Anthony's racks. The friction burn was incredibly tender and though my leg was relieved to be out of tights, my worn in jeans still agitated the wound. I sat down and positioned my leg as best I could to avoid irritating it.

"How's the leg?" Alex said. He had redressed in his own clothes and was, thankfully, unmasked. He sat down next to me and seemed to unravel his long legs and arms in exhaustion.

"Uh, well, hurts pretty freaking bad," I answered, as even toned as possible.

"Hey guys! Great show, huh?" Ava said as she bounced over to us. "Such a thrill doing a new act," she sighed.

"You were great with Eloise," Alex said to her.

"Thanks," she propped a hand on her hip and flipped her hair, "your act was amazing as usual, even with that crazy mask."

I fought to keep my eyes from rolling.

"Janie, is your leg okay?" Ava asked.

"I guess I'll live. Shay's got some ointment back in our room."

"Yours looks worse than hers. You need first at showers."

"Thanks."

"Looks like you need first at showers, too. You're sweating like a sinner in church," Ava flirted with Alex.

"Stinks too," I said laconically. He elbowed me in return.

I watched Shay crossing the room to join our circle and then saw a chair fly behind her path. It landed with a loud crash outside the dressing rooms, and she ducked reflexively at the sound.

Everyone turned their face toward the sound to see what happened. Their eyes were led to Zeke and Tombo near the wall and Reg barreling toward them like a freight train through the middle of the room.

Tombo jumped up on Zeke, gripping his shoulders. The chimp looked like a hairy backpack. Reg didn't say a word until his own nose was inches from Zeke's.

"Who do you think you are?" Reg growled through gritted teeth. "Think you're really something trying to humiliate me through a monkey. I'm right here. Why don't you use your own voice this time if you want to cause trouble."

"Sir, I didn't mean it to sound like that. About the town." Zeke stuttered a bit. "I meant we all know most apes and monkeys can't swim and avoid bodies of water," he tried, but Reg wasn't anywhere close to buying it.

Tombo carefully positioned his head just behind Zeke's, trying to stay hidden.

"Really. That's what you stupidly thought when you wrote this act? That's the best you can come up with," Reg sneered.

"I'm sorry. It's common knowledge where I'm from," Zeke tried.

"Listen here. You're wearing thin on my nerves. You step out of line again, and you're out. I will kick you to the streets and make sure you never perform in a circus again," Reg slowly enunciated every syllable for emphasis.

They stared at each other silently for what seemed like hours. Finally, Reg backed away, maintaining fiery eye contact. He shouted for the entire room to hear, "That goes for each one of you!"

Reginald was extra inflamed, and his presence exuded more contention than usual. Mr. Kyte had nerved him up and he was clawing his way to keep control.

We all watched as Zeke held his breath until Reg exited. Zeke's body seemed to shrink, like a balloon when the air is let out, exhausted and limp from keeping such a tight shape. He couldn't admonish Tombo here, so he kept quiet.

We all gathered our things and made our way out of the theater. Just in front of the doors to leave stood Mr. Kyte, a smile as long and smooth as a crescent moon.

The first of those leaving were Reginald and Caroline. I could see Reg was fighting to be calm, and all the more challenging, to feign genuine appreciation for Kyte.

As the troupe slowly filtered out, Mr. Kyte appeared to be encouraging them and praising their contribution with phrases like, "bravo," and "excellent act, m'boy." I watched his face and though he was clearly quite animated, his words felt empty.

Ahead of us, Ava nodded to Mr. Kyte. He responded by asking, "Miss Ava, isn't it? Beautiful job tonight! Thank you for filling our vacancy, my dear."

"My pleasure," she grinned as she did a little curtesy on her way out.

Mr. Kyte merely tipped his hat to us as we passed him by. But I was fine with that. If I never spoke to him, or him to me, that would be the best scenario.

The ride back to the lodge was a mixture of excited conversation and hushing by those fatigued and ready to end the day. After quick snacking in the lobby, the troupe bid each other goodnight and dispersed. In the sanctuary of our room at last, a warm shower soothed my aching muscles and cleaned the wound on my leg. I could only imagine how bad it would feel during the performance that would relentlessly come tomorrow.

Chapter 15

Sparkles & Euphoria

During breakfast, the group of us sat at a table with added chairs to facilitate our huddle. In a cautious whisper, Zeke recounted for us the reprimand he had given Tombo for going rogue in the middle of their act.

"I cannot believe he did that. I don't know what came over him. He says it just slipped out. But he's never popped off a snide remark during a performance before," Zeke huffed in a whisper.

"Maybe he did it because his feelings were h-h-hurt from what happened at p-practice," Daniel offered.

"That was more at me. Maybe he's trying to take up for me," said Zeke.

"We walked in at the end of it. What happened?" Shay asked.

"Well, Reg flew in and went straight backstage like he was on a mission. When he came back through, I think he was heading out, but decided to chastise a few of us on his way," Zeke answered animatedly.

"He lit into me for no reason," Ava added under her breath. She crossed her arms, and there was a slight drop in her lower lip.

"We were just going through our choreography and he freaked out over our dance routine. Starting in saying we did that in Merdwick and need new material for this show. Saying things like, 'Can't you come up with any more than that? I thought you were a trainer. You can't train that monkey to do anything else?'" Zeke imitated Reg's voice in low tones and a vocal rhythm that made him sound stupid.

"Should've told him to swallow a tire iron," Alex spat.

"What's a tire iron?" Ava asked.

"Or maybe an umbrella. And then open it," Alex continued after being egged on by snickering and chortle.

Anthony looked as if the appalling comment woke him from exhausted stupor.

"Anyway," Zeke said, as if disturbed and trying to steer the ship back on course. "I told him I was more than capable of further training but thought the act was received so well in Merdwick... and then he went off. It was like he went from sixty to a hundred miles per hour in a second. It flipped his switch."

"What did Tombo say when you reprimanded him?" I asked.

"Don't let him fool you," Anthony said, jerking his chin toward Zeke. "He wasn't as hard on him as he makes it sound. Besides, Tombo is like his child. You think Tombo blindly follows everything he says? Do children always listen to their parents? Negative."

"I l-l-listened to my parents," said Daniel.

"That's cause you're an angel on earth," Anthony said, patting Daniel's shoulder.

We took the trolley to the park as usual, and at first it seemed it was going to be the typical day of pre-show practices, rehearsals, and prep. But around noon, as the troupe was about to break for lunch, there was an extraordinary commotion in the dressing rooms backstage of Kastle theater.

After a variety of noises were heard, including yelling, several thunderous bangs, and a sharp crack of glass, Reg stomped into the main theater room. He was coated with green glitter from head to toe and screaming for Zeke who was breaking with Anthony by the costumes. Everyone's jaws dropped at the sight of this livid man sparkling like a fairy.

"That damn monkey! Where is he?"

"What? I don't know. Why?" Zeke stammered. He was unprepared to deal with this unforeseen situation.

"You can see why! I saw him run out the door, guilty and grinning!"

Zeke was frowning and about to defend Tombo relentlessly, whether the accusation was true or not, but then the fire was stoked. Mr. Kyte was making his rounds to check on the theater and monitor our preparations. Gray Cloud followed silently beside him.

"Ello Marvels! What on earth is going on here?" Mr. Kyte asked, looking very intrigued and almost gleeful. He appraised Reginald from top to bottom a couple of times, his mustache twitching and attempting to hide a smile. "What have you done, Mr. Mandeville?"

"What I haven't done is kill a monkey and I'm bound to do it yet!" Despite Mr. Kyte's entry, Reg remained steamed.

"Ho, ho. Slow down. You wouldn't want to do that," Mr. Kyte frowned, almost matching Zeke. Now it was two against one.

"That monkey did this. The vengeful barbaric thing that he is. I've done nothing but caudal the thing since you've joined this circus," he huffed at Zeke.

"I do love your act, son. Lots of personality that monkey has," Mr. Kyte said, more or less ignoring Reg and giving Zeke accolades over admonishment.

Reginald had a bate with Mr. Kyte's commentary. His parting words before his brisk exit were, "You best not let me catch him before this show."

When he left, Mr. Kyte simply watched him go and shrugged his shoulders. Gray Cloud stood silent. He turned back to face Zeke, like a father would console a son after his mother reprimanded him for something he thought petty.

"Where did you find Tombo?" Mr. Kyte asked.

"I inherited him from a retiring circus from back home," Zeke lied. "My apologies, Mr. Kyte. For all the kerfuffle."

"Alright, son. Have a great show tonight."

Mr. Kyte patted Zeke's shoulder and left. Just before Gray Cloud moved to follow his path, he turned and extended his hand towards me. I looked down at a small piece of paper he was handing me wordlessly. I took it and looked to his lined face, his dark eyes like an endless vortex. He turned and followed Mr. Kyte, and I quickly shoved the note in my jacket pocket.

Anthony approached. "Good grief. Shows how he listens to you," he said to Zeke of Tombo. "Good play on your answer. Something odd about Kyte's sudden peak in interest."

"I can't believe him! I may kill him myself. Now I've got to go hunt him down," Zeke said exasperatedly.

Shay and I excused ourselves to the empty dressing rooms, and I pulled out the small note, unfolded it, and read the message before handing it to Shay. All that it read was, "tomorrow. dusk. mountain's base. women only."

"We're doing this?" Shay asked.

"I guess so."

Since Reg had left to de-glitter himself, Shay and I went looking for Caroline. We scoured the park and finally found her in the cafe, coffee at the table, cigarette in hand, a book laid open in front of her. A couple men at the table continuously glanced at her long blonde waves, particularly unable to hide their gawking when she put the cigarette to her lips for a drag. We approached the table and when she looked up, she invited us to sit.

We huddled forward and spoke quietly, "She's in the mountains," I said, "the doctor."

Caroline's eyes grew wider, but she said nothing.

"We've been granted the opportunity to go in tomorrow at dusk. I don't know all the details, but we'll be led in from the base of the mountain by the park. And there's one more thing." I looked at Shay for moral support.

"You can only go in if we escort you," Shay said gently and tactfully.

"And Reginald," she said, as if there was no other option.

"No," I said slowly. "Just the three of us."

"I don't understand, how would this work without Reg," Caroline whispered.

"I don't know. But our entry is contingent on the three of us."

"What will I tell him, though?" Caroline looked incredulous and nervous.

Shay and I looked at each other, neither of us having anything more to offer. We all sat quietly for a moment.

"Alright. I'll handle it. You girls get back to practice," she said.

We pushed our chairs back and made to stand. Caroline extended an ivory hand across the table, her nails perfectly polished in brilliant red.

"Thank you," she whispered. And it sounded genuine, though her face was almost as flat at stoic as Gray Cloud's.

We nodded and left the cafe, the door bell rattling as we walked out and the cold air smacking our faces.

"What have we gotten ourselves into?" I muttered under my breath as we walked back to the theater.

Shay answered, "I can't decide. I think Caroline is being vulnerable with us. Which is something I haven't seen since I joined this troupe. She's usually so elusive. But I guess I haven't often been close enough to get a feel for what she's thinking. She's genuinely grateful, but I still can't tell where her allegiances lie."

"Why do you think Felicity decided to help us?"

"Her thoughts were guarded. It was hard to tell," Shay said. "We've done our civic duty for the day. Let's just worry about the show now. How's your leg?"

"It feels like someone rubbed honey on it and then dropped a bunch of fire ants on the honey. Then the ants lapped it all up, got mad that the honey was gone, and revolted against the territory."

"That's extremely vivid," Shay laughed.

"What about yours?"

"Mine stings, but not that intensely. We're going to have to use the other leg tonight."

"I'll be bow legged!" I laughed and winced at the thought.

"We'll see if Anthony has some extra padding."

When we got back to the theater and walked inside, the first thing I laid my eyes on was Alex and Ava. He had a hoop around his waist and she was trying to show him how to hula hoop. Every time it hit the ground they laughed and she bent down to pick it up for him. I did not like how close the two of them were.

Shay pulled me out of their view, where we had hid waiting for Felicity. She gave me her serious maternal expression, "Look, I know that sight probably makes you want to scream. But we've got enough to worry about today and tomorrow. Maybe we should practice elsewhere. I'm sure it's harmless"

"I don't get it. I thought she was pushing me to confess whether or not I like Alex. She's really nice to me and seems genuine, but I don't know what to make of this," I said.

"First off, that's how she is with every guy she sees. Second, she doesn't know you have feelings for him. You keep telling her you don't."

"You're saying I should tell her I do?" I asked anxiously.

"I'm saying Ava is just being Ava. If you don't like it, you're going to have to do something about it, but not today. It will have to wait."

"I'll wait, but I want to see what goes on," I said in a surly tone as I pulled her back toward the theater. Shay rolled her eyes in defeat and followed.

"Hey guys! Check it out!" Alex greeted our entry as he hula hooped about four rotations before it fell to the floor.

"Don't quit your day job," I scoffed.

"Wanna have a contest?" he said cheerily.

"I've got better things to do."

Alex's face sagged, "What's your problem today?"

I didn't respond. I felt Shay's hand push me forward. "Her leg's just smarting," Shay said excusably to Alex. Then turned to me, "Let's go see Anthony."

We were almost to the dressing rooms when Shay huffed, "Exactly what I'm talking about, Janie. Let it go today."

Anthony inspected the wound area and assured us he'd sew on a little padding in our tights. I simmered down as we practiced choreography and stretched. It took my mind off of things, thankfully. For the rest of the day, we tried to keep mostly to ourselves.

The night came quickly, and Saturday's crowd seemed bigger. At times I thought I saw familiar faces in the crowd, back again after seeing last night's show, which was encouraging. Mr. Kyte eased up on his surprise attacks mid show and our troupe seemed a bit more calm knowing what to expect for the most part.

When Shay and I performed the bullet, we hooked our unburned leg and, thankfully, the friction didn't break the skin. The added padding helped prevent injury to the other leg. My unsaved leg still burned like the dickens, but at least I had finished the first weekend of shows and hopefully could heal up by the next.

Ava did great, as usual. The sweetheart of the show. I felt terrible for wanting her to mess up a little. To stop being so perfect.

Zeke and Tombo seemed cautious when entering the ring, but their show was superb. They even added a few more lines and tricks. Mr. Kyte went on and on over the microphone, praising their additions and prompting the crowd. Shay and I watched as he commentated from the dragon stand. He looked genuinely enthralled.

And of course, Alex was amazing. Though he wasn't getting any praise from me afterwards. I was determined to stay flat. I rather hoped to avoid him altogether, though I knew that would be unlikely. When we got back to the lodge that night, he cornered me.

We had all arrived back to Frigid Ridge and semi-dispersed for the night. It was the usual. Some were celebrating as if they were off their nine to five job and ready for drinks. Some were retiring for self care and sleep. I was about to go in my room when he caught me in the hall way.

"Hey, got a minute?"

"I'm just heading in for the night," I tried.

"Well, I want to talk to you first."

"You can't get everything you want," I shot at him.

He looked at me like I had three heads and said, "What is wrong? Are you mad at me? Because if you are that is ridiculous. I haven't done anything."

"No, I'm fine. We'll talk," I sharply turned to him, waiting to be led.

He didn't move at first, just processed while staring at me. "Can we go sit down?"

"Of course."

He slowly turned and walked down the hallway. I followed, looking at the back of his dark head of hair and telling myself to calm down. Twice he shook his head as if someone had said something appalling to him.

We sat near the piano. There was some music playing in the background, and troupe members were shuffling back and forth with drinks. They were boisterous enough to render us inconspicuous. Alex and I were still considered somewhat outsiders, or newbies, to them. So it wasn't like they were going to invite us to partake with their group. They barely acknowledged us. As Alex plopped down he rolled his eyes, and I didn't know if he was exasperated by them, me, or both.

"So," he began slowly, "Is there something we should talk about? Air out maybe?"

"I don't think so."

He enunciated every word to me like I didn't understand the English language. "It seemed like you were upset about something when you first came in the theater today."

I sighed and flopped my arms on my lap. "I'm just a little stressed with the show and the project."

"Janie. I've known you for a few years now. That's not what you look like when you're stressed, not to me anyway. So, if it's about Ava,"

"It's not about Ava!" I interjected and lied.

Alex looked smug, like he was doing an experiment and elicited a reaction he was pleased with.

"Okay, moving on then. Your task as little helper. How's that going?"

I relaxed slightly. "We're going in the mountains tomorrow night. Caroline, Shay, and I."

"You guys? Not Reg?"

"Apparently, the people in the mountain don't like people like Reginald Mandeville. I can't imagine why," I said sarcastically. "The deal was it had to be us instead."

"So you just show up in the mountains tomorrow?"

"I don't know, the note said meet at the base."

"The note from who?" Alex said, confused.

"Felicity. Well, I assume Felicity."

"How did Caroline seem about it?"

"Uh, apprehensive but grateful," I thought. "I don't really know what to make of her right now. She seems honest, but I don't know whether or not I can trust her for sure."

"So that's it then. You're going in tomorrow. No protection, just being led into the wilderness blindly."

"I guess." I hadn't really thought of it that way until now and consequently started to feel more anxious. I made a mental note to talk to Whisper about this later.

"How are you going to protect yourself?" Alex asked incredulously.

"Uh," I thought, "I don't know. I'm sure it'll be fine."

Alex replied a little too stern for my liking. "Well, that's not a smart move at all. Just go in hanging on hopes and dreams. I hate when you say, 'it'll be fine.' You need more than that," he said.

"Like what?" I snorted.

"I don't know, but something. I've got a knife you can borrow," he tried.

"What in the world can I do with a knife?"

"Well, you need something to defend yourself. And you need an escort. Maybe I could come with you guys."

"No. The note said women only. Beside how are you going to defend us. You're not exactly trained in combat or big enough to fend off a bear."

"I fight bears all the time. Moose too. I had to beat up three of them after you left the woods the other night," he charmed.

"Oh, that's what took you so long to get back," I played along. Happy to feel a bit more relaxed, getting back to the normal banter. I changed subjects. "How's Zeke and Tombo? I guess you heard about that whole spectacle, right?"

"Yeah. They're alright, laying kinda low. I thought it was great, Tombo getting him back like that. All he did was put glitter on top of the ceiling fan. Reg flipped it on and turned into a disco ball."

"Oh my gosh. That's pretty smart actually," I laughed.

"Zeke was livid though. That he pulled that little stunt."

"I figured. Sounds pretty harmless all in all, but I guess we don't need any extra ammo against us. That was the pact we made."

"Tombo didn't make the pact though," Alex grinned.

"I gotta go to bed. Are you satisfied now?" I asked.

"That you're acting normal? Yes."

We got up and passed the wandering jugglers and acrobats, now drunk and slightly more friendly, as we headed back to the hallway.

"You need to be careful tomorrow night. You're still my partner in crime," he said over his shoulder as we walked down the hallway.

"I'll be fine, relax. Shay is a superhero."

"True," he replied.

We reached my room door and he turned to face me. "I'm serious though. You need to be careful."

"I will, I will," I said. He stood there looking at me for a few seconds and seemed to be trying to work up more words to say.

I looked at him a little confused. "Goodnight?" I said with an upward inflection.

"Yeah, goodnight," he said and turned to go further down the hall to his room.

I turned and reached for the doorknob, but felt a hand grasp above my elbow and pull me back around.

I was spun. For a second I saw Alex's eyes, determined and focused, and then I felt his lips press against mine. I was rigid, frozen in place from the shock of it for a second. But his arms wrapped around my waist and my body seemed to melt. Almost involuntarily, I wrapped my arms around his shoulders. I felt his lips more firmly as they changed positions, pressure points changing to my top lip, then bottom lip. I felt like it was happening fast and slow at the same time.

He pulled away slowly and released his arms, and after a quick look in my shocked eyes, he turned and went down the hallway without a word.

I couldn't completely process what had just happened, but my whole being felt a sense of euphoria. Finally, I realized I was alone in the hallway and needed to go inside. The last thing I wanted was Ava to see my face or Shay to read my mind. I needed a minute to myself. So I entered the room, shouted, "gotta pee," and ran into the bathroom.

I heard chuckles from Shay and Ava, who were sorting through their suitcases on the other side of the door. I leaned against the wall for a minute, my arms like limp noodles. Trying to make sense of what had just happened. It took no time until I started over analyzing. A quick thought, what on earth did I look like? I put my face close to the mirror and inspected it, then tried to smell my own breath by cupping my hand over my mouth. Eh, hopefully it wasn't noticeable.

"What is happening?" I asked Whisper in my mind.

"Oh hello dear, it's good to hear your voice."

I felt guilty for not having connected today. Lost in the rush of finding Caroline, the show, and everything else. Then again, I don't think they would hold it against me. But certainly, when important things were happening, I needed their involvement and direction.

"It's been a crazy day. No burns, so that's good. But the plan is to traipse through the wilderness tomorrow. And now Alex has my mind completely boggled."

"The wilderness you say?" They seemed to reply as if they didn't already know.

"I'm a little nervous about it. But oddly, not as much as I thought I would be."

"There's strength in numbers."

"Shay is going of course," I thought. "I'll need your guidance for all that."

"Are you asking me for help?" Whisper countered.

"Yes."

"Well, then ask me."

"I need your help, Whisper. Will you help me?" I knew I certainly needed their help. Why does it still feel like a struggle to ask for it?

"Alright then, done. You need to work on that a bit more."

"Yeah, yeah, I know," I said in my mind. "And what about Alex?"

"What about him?"

"You know. Can you show me what it means?"

"Well, of course not. That wouldn't be any fun anyway," Whisper answered. I felt like I could imagine them sitting back and grinning.

"I thought he liked Ava," I tried.

"Why don't you just prepare for your journey. Get some sleep."

"I won't sleep a wink after that!" I said. I was met with no answer. Like someone on the other end of the phone line had stopped engaging in conversation, but they were still there listening.

I closed my eyes and tried to reimagine the whole thing again. The way Alex spun me around, the way his lips felt on mine, the way my body relaxed in his grasp. Electricity seemed to rush up and down my body, not completely unlike the incident with Ceto. But this electricity wasn't painful. It felt incredibly good.

I snapped back into reality at the thought of having to face him tomorrow. What would he say? What could I possibly say? Would it be awkward? Would we keep it a secret?

There was one person that I knew I would be completely unable to keep this a secret from. I might as well prepare for it.

I showered, trying to calm and refocus as the warm water hit my tired body. Standing in front of the bathroom door, I tried to clear my mind. When I opened the door and walked out, I went straight to my suitcase, trying to shield my face from Ava. She didn't seem to notice a thing.

A few glimpses up at Shay, I tried to inconspicuously gauge the amount of attention she was paying me. She had been reading a book until she suddenly stopped, staring just above the top edge of the pages. Her eyes grew wide, and she glanced at me. I shot her a tiny shrugged expression. She looked back at her book, raising her eyebrows as she pretended to read, but I saw the little grin.

"Well," Shay said, as she shut the book in her lap and turned off her lamp. "Goodnight, girls."

"Night," Ava chimed, as she thankfully did the same.

"Night," I echoed.

Grateful for the dark and quiet, I laid there replaying what had happened. Thinking about the years of struggle with Alex beside me. Crap jobs, dusty and grimy lodgings, sharing costs of meals, working the same shifts at the restaurant back in Espíritu Del Mar, hearing him play drums for the first time. Meeting him in the woods a few nights before this one, how he held me in his jacket when I was shaking in the cold. I knew I was in for it, and it felt like ages before I fell asleep.

At least I felt completely at peace about going into the mountains. Thanks to Whisper, of course.

Chapter 16

Foothill Clan

It was clear as crystal by morning, the sun casting its early rays across the snowy mountain. And the troupe was in an especially jovial mood because that crisp Sunday morning brought our first bit of compensation from the Mandeville payroll since the Merdwick gigs. Anthony had handed out of envelopes to eager hands that morning at breakfast. It wasn't like we were all going to be rich. Maybe we were just relieved to have it, but everyone was more upbeat nonetheless.

I felt extremely awkward when the girls and I walked into the lounges and saw Alex and his roommates at a table eating breakfast. The two of us were trying to figure out where to rest our eyes. It felt strange to look at each other and pretend nothing happened, but we couldn't completely ignore each other either. That would be obvious and cause questioning from the rest of the group.

"That looks great. I'm starved," I said, gesturing at the plates and then eagerly walking past them to the counter of food. I tried to take as long as possible choosing breakfast, Shay rolling her eyes at me all the while. I was actually kind of thankful that Ava plopped down next to the boys and started her usual jabbering. An unknowing diversion.

"So you're just going to ignore him now," Shay smirked. "I mean, you have to say something."

"Oh gah, it's going to be a long wait till dusk. What are we doing all day anyway?"

"It's a free day. No shows. No practices. Money to blow."

"Great. Perfect timing. Well, then. I guess I'm going to spend the day psyching myself up to go in the mountains. That and picking out weather appropriate gear for our little adventure tonight," I said.

"I think a lot of people are going into town. You can buy some gear there," Shay replied with a laugh.

"I'm not buying gear."

"Well, what on earth do you have that would be appropriate for tonight, then?"

I looked at her through my eyebrows, pleading for mercy. "I just want to stay here." I nodded toward the table where Ava was excitedly talking about going shopping in town with Zeke, and Alex seemed to nod in agreement to go too.

"They'll all go to town. We'll stay here. We'll have time to plan for Caroline. And we can leave less conspicuously."

We took our plates to the table and joined them. Small talked our way through breakfast. Gave lame excuses for why were staying at Frigid Ridge instead of going to town. Alex knew I had a lot to plan for, so he didn't flinch. The rest of them tried to encourage us, but when we didn't budge, they went on with their planning.

After breakfast, everyone shuffled to their rooms in prep to catch the trolley. Being that she understood, Shay went to our room when the rest left. I was trying to hang back, finishing my pancakes slowly so that if Alex lingered we could speak alone for a minute.

When they left, Alex started with, "You all set for tonight?"

"I think so," I said, pretending to be really interested in the syrup pooled on my plate.

"Hey, I hope... you know. I hope I didn't... make you feel," Alex struggled.

"I'm fine," I said sincerely, looking at him for the first time and fighting the muscles in my mouth that were trying to grin. A corner of it surrendered.

"Oh... good," he said, relaxing slightly. "Anyway, you're not coming to town?"

"Nah, I'm going to," I looked for the right word, "prep."

"Do you need me to get anything for you?"

"No, I can't think of anything that would make a difference. You should get yourself something. Our first circus check, ya know," I replied.

"Have you looked at it? I made more waiting tables some nights."

"Figures," I said, thinking of Reg withholding our last check.

"Alright—well." Alex ran his hand through the side of his dark hair as he stood, "I guess I'm going to go catch the rickety hunk a tin... You'll be super careful, right?"

"Yes. I promise."

He looked at me for a minute, processing and in thought, then half way smiled before walking off.

People were clearing out after dining. I had the table to myself and a tiny shred of pancake remaining. Through the window, rays of sun now heated the black and white checkered flooring. I could see dust floating in a ray beside the piano.

"That wasn't so bad," I thought in my head. "He was pretty normal. Everything's cool. Whisper, everything is okay, right?"

"Of course it is. Now, focus on the next task at hand," Whisper seemed to answer.

Around four o'clock, Shay and I heard a knock on the door to our room. Caroline was on the other side of it. We were a little surprised to see her so early, and more so when she asked if she could come in.

She looked around as if she was confused by our shabby personal effects. Her room was probably spotless and held finer things. I pictured gowns and fur shawls hanging in a wardrobe and fancy makeup containers sitting neatly across a vanity.

Her blonde hair was modestly pulled back in a low ponytail that fell down her back in waves. She donned an expensive looking jacket, the type that was thermally insulated, and high lacing mountain boots that obviously came from a store in White Cap Peaks because they looked like the Victorian garb everyone around here wore.

"I'm early, I know. But Reg didn't take his ban from the mountain very well, so… I decided to get a move on," she said. Shay and I just stared at her. "We can go ahead and take the trolley in a few hours," she offered.

Shay empathetically wondered how Caroline must have been handling the whole situation and asked her, "How are you feeling?"

Caroline's answers were guarded, yet she also seemed to want to keep the dialogue going. It made me wonder who she talked to besides Reg. She never came around the troupe much, unless it was to spy on us. Make sure we were staying in line. Hitting our marks. Perfecting our acts. But did she have a confidant to vent to?

It was as dicey for us to answer her as it was for her to engage in conversation with us. Everyone had a reputation to uphold. And we still felt we could trust no employers. Caroline, Reg, or Kyte. They were the bad guys. Us performers were the good guys. The mistreated and unappreciated. And those most at risk for danger, injury, and now that Mr. Kyte was involved, death. I had to keep my head on straight. My nature is to care for others, to have compassion, but it had gotten me burned many times and I couldn't afford for it to do so now.

Caroline answered Shay's question, "Don't really know what to expect. So I don't really know how to feel."

"You'll be fine," I tried to be encouraging.

"So, what were you guys doing before I interrupted?"

"Eh, just trying to find our warmest ensemble," I said.

Caroline looked at our clothes, which were scattered across our beds. "I brought some extra jackets," she said, opening a case. She held them up and extended them out to us. "You can wear these, if you like."

I didn't know what to think. I took one look at the jacket and could feel the warmth of it. But taking something from Caroline might mean I owe her... again. Then again, she owes me for finding this dang doctor.

"Oh. Well, those are... really warm looking. Are you sure?" I asked hesitantly.

"Yes, yes. I brought them for you two," Caroline said, seemingly genuine.

I looked at Shay. Her face was relaxed and she was moving to take one, so I followed suit.

"That was really kind of you, Mrs. Mandeville," said Shay.

"It's nothing," she replied. "I might just go do a little reading by the piano. Keep my mind occupied," she was turning to leave as we stared at her. "Oh and—girls, I really appreciate what you've done for me."

"You're welcome," we said.

Caroline gave a little nod before heading out our door. When she was gone, I turned to Shay, "What do you make of all that?"

"I think it's for real. I mean, I was pretty close to her. I didn't hear any other thoughts."

"You think we can trust her now?" I asked.

"No, I didn't say that. But maybe we can relax a little for the next few hours."

"This is so weird."

"The Mandevilles have always been weird. This is just a little more extra. Trying to cook up a baby and all," Shay said, making a face.

At about five-thirty, we met Caroline at the piano. Everyone was still in town for the day and the only person around, other than us, was the receptionist. Walking to the station, we all sort of matched in big, warm, puffy jackets. I kept trying to stop myself from thinking we were friends. Of course Shay and I, but not Caroline Mandeville. Onto the trolley we went, and the conversation was minimal. All parties involved were feeling unsure.

We arrived at the parking area in front of Kaleidoscope Kyte's as the sun was beginning to set, casting its final orange rays across the grounds at an angle. As we clambered off the trolley, flurries sparsely floated on the cold breeze and occasionally landed in our hair, contrasting with Shay's and mine, but blending in with Caroline's. It was freezing and I, for one, was quite grateful that Caroline had lent us weather appropriate coats. Regardless of the motivations behind it.

The park was closed and desolate, so we wondered which way to start towards. Hesitantly scanning the area, I spotted Gray Cloud silently waiting atop his dark colored horse. He was wearing an impressive fur coat, which looked to be the skin of a bear. Maybe a grizzly. And a gray beaver felt hat on top of his long and straight black hair. He looked majestic.

We approached him and he extended his arm toward the back edge of the park where three horses were tied onto tree limbs. They were beautiful creatures. A brown and white Appaloosa, a Buckskin, and a three color paint with big brown and white spots, but a long black mane and tail.

Caroline looked apprehensive, but Shay and I were eager to pick. I approached the buckskin and slowly moved a hand toward his nose so that he could explore my scent. He was calm, maybe even bored. I gestured at Gray Cloud, seeking permission to mount. When I had positioned myself up on the saddle, I looked down at the girls. They seemed vaguely impressed, but I had ridden horses growing up. Plus, I figured the horses would follow the leader regardless of how good or bad we rode. Caroline climbed up the Appaloosa and Shay the paint. All the while, Gray Cloud simply watched us.

After reaching over to untie the reins and hand them to us, Gray Cloud pointed to our horses and told us their names. Caroline's horse's name was Gola, Shay's was Koda, and mine was Adohi. Gray Cloud pointed to his horse, "Night Sky."

Being that women, in particular, usually have an affinity for horses, we sat in awe for a moment. Contemplating their names and meanings. And then Gray

Cloud led Night Sky past us, leading the way along a very indistinct trail.

The sun was fading and the temperature dropped ferociously. As we followed in a line, I found the time riding Adohi quite therapeutic, even calming. But then I noticed the forest coming alive as we continued. A bullfrog croaking amongst singing crickets, a limb snapping somewhere in the distance, rustling up in the spiny tree branches heavily blanketed in snow. Some of the sounds were disconcerting to one not used to the noise of the wilderness. But our leader was unfazed, which helped us all to remain at ease.

Gray Cloud seemed to float on top of Night Sky. Relaxed and very one with his animal companion. Behind him, Caroline's upper body jostled left and right awkwardly. Maybe she had never ridden a horse before. And conversely, Shay rode beautifully.

I heard another cracking sound behind me. I noticed Gray Cloud slightly turned his head, as if lending an ear, but he did nothing more than that. So I patted Adohi's shoulder as we went on lightly swaying.

Our travel took ten or fifteen minutes, and during that time it grew very dim. The fireflies started slowly presenting themselves. They intermittently glowed and always seemed to float upwards. We were nearing a widening of the path that opened to a clearing nestled between the giant rocks. As I bounced along, leaning to see around the party in front of me, the view of a soft glowing fire lay ahead in the distance.

As we drew nearer, I could see that it was a very small population living there. Four buildings arced in a half moon perimeter which must have housed the people, a pen for horses, and the fire in the center. It was quiet and solemn and the aesthetic oozed of nature's essence.

Gray Cloud led us to the pen of horses, dismounted, and tied Night Sky to the fencing. Night Sky seemed to greet the other horses who approached the edge of the pen, looking and sniffing to see what was going on. We waited our turn as Gray Cloud gestured at each of us to come down and tied our horses as well.

"We go inside," Gray Cloud's grave voice said, and he led us towards one of the buildings.

It had a tapered ceiling and was constructed completely from wood. On each side of the entry stood totem poles, and on top of each of them were eagles with wings outstretched at least five feet wide. When Gray Cloud reached the entry, the door was opened by his brother, Felix; Felicity's father who owned the clock shop in town.

I followed Caroline and Shay in succession to the inside of the building. There was another fire in an ornately designed pit in the middle of the room. The rising smoke of it exited in gray plumes through a hole in the ceiling, which was trimmed by a geometrically designed circle of sizable wooden logs; like a woven basket with a hole left in the bottom. The floors were tiled stone and across it laid a bear skin rug, a black bear.

The room itself was unexpectedly furnished. There was a wooden table, hand carved in painstakingly intricate detail with precious coral and turquoise stone inlay winding in patterns across it. Painted instruments, hunting bows, and tapestry of bold colors hung on the walls. This building was like an exquisite hunting lodge, but the hunters weren't in it for sport and accolades. They honored all things living and dead with art and song and warm, genuine respect.

Fine leather chairs were positioned around the fire, and in them sat dark skinned and dark haired people. A full grown timber wolf sleepily rose up from the ground on the other side of the room and came to place his head under Gray Cloud's callused hand. He petted the animal as if it was a small child.

Felicity stood from one of the leather chairs and began introductions. "Janie, Shay, Caroline. Welcome to the Foothill Clan's meeting chambers." Her voice was still softened by the leather face mask I had always seen her wearing. She extended her hand towards one of the leather chairs. "I will introduce you to Dr. Cheveyo, spirit warrior."

She led us a bit further in to a seated lady with gray and black hair, straight as an arrow and falling down to her lap. A leather band wrapped around her crown, and off of it, strings of cord with beads and feathers flowed down with her hair. Her faced was lined with happy wrinkles, and she seemed to exude wisdom and command reverence.

Felicity introduced us, and we all exchanged greetings. Dr. Cheveyo nodded and got right to it, "Which one of you is troubled?"

"I am," said Caroline. "My husband and I have been trying to conceive for years."

"So, what is the trouble?" Dr. Cheveyo's voice was slow and calm as a streaming river, despite our obvious unexpectedness of the question.

"I want to be a mother. I want to have a baby," Caroline said, trying not to look confused.

"Maybe your natural essence does not match your husband's."

Caroline was calculating, trying to make sense of what that statement might mean. "He's a good man deep down."

Dr. Cheveyo looked so serenely at her, I thought perhaps she too could read minds. Whatever the case, she didn't seem sold on Reg's character witness.

"Your blood and your husband's blood will intertwine to make up every part of this child's being."

"Yes—I guess it will," Caroline answered.

Dr. Cheveyo looked at her with a little more scrutiny and gave pause, so that her words might ruminate. Then she stood and said, "It will require the completion of ancient rituals for me to help you."

Caroline's eyes were becoming a little darty. "What must I do?"

"You must surrender your spirit to truth. You must sacrifice time and energy. You must bear the heaviness of the burden of joy."

Caroline was in a daze. Her eyes resting on the flicking flames ahead as she tried to translate the idea. "Will you show me how?"

"If you wish," Dr. Cheveyo said quietly. Caroline nodded.

"Come with me," the doctor said as she wrapped a skinny arm around Caroline's mid back, and she led her past a curtain. Shay and I were trying not to gawk, but the rest of the people in that room remained calm and quiet.

"She will initiate the first ritual now," said Felicity. "We will all gather by the fire outside when Dr. Cheveyo is ready. To witness and encourage."

Now Shay and I were confused and trying to decipher. We stood there looking at her blankly and wondering what we would do in the meantime.

"I've done you a favor, you know?" Felicity said calmly. Her dark eyes glowing with the reflection of the fire.

"Of course, and thank you again," I said.

"Now I need a favor repaid in return," she said, turning to look at Shay. "I know you hear thoughts. I knew it for certain when the two of you approached me at the circus."

I thought back to the bathroom during our first show.

"I suspected it before, but I knew as soon as you spoke about Reginald Mandeville causing trouble that you heard my thoughts," Felicity said. Her eyes looked convinced and resolute.

"Yes, you're right," Shay replied.

"You can hear mine now then, can't you?"

"Yes."

I looked back and forth rapidly, from one face to the next.

"My husband was in an accident about two years ago. He cannot speak," Felicity said for me to hear. "He is in a bad state. His consciousness wavers and he is very weak."

"I'm sorry," Shay gave condolences.

"He's still my husband. He's still the love of my life. I just wish I could talk to him again. Your gift can help me," Felicity said. Her voice cracked as a plump tear welled out of her left eye and rolled down her face mask.

"I'll do all that I can for you," Shay said genuinely as the air grew heavy at the revelation of Felicity's pain. The heart break was almost tangible, and we were all momentarily frozen in time.

Felicity brushed the tears off her mask and the tops of her cheeks. "I just want him to know how much I love him. I just want to hear his words again, even if they come by your voice." The tears continued to roll, but she stayed straight as a board in posture, trying to hold everything together. "I'll take you to him. Hopefully, he is still awake."

Felicity signaled to the other members of the clan that we were leaving the meeting chamber. When we stepped outside, the fire was still high in the night sky, crackling as we walked past it to a small cabin on the other side of the arced buildings. It too was beautifully crafted, and when we walked through the doors, we saw several dream catchers hanging from the braces of the ceiling. They led through a sitting room and down the length of a hallway.

A curtain of strung beads and owl feathers hung in a doorway at the end of the hall. We followed Felicity through them and found a man lying in a bed. The sheet was just past his navel and we could see intense scarring all over his torso. He had long straight hair, black as night, just like the rest of the clan, but four huge scar lines across one side of his head.

I watched Shay look from the man to Felicity and back again. Already reading Felicity's mind. Felicity sat on the edge of the bed and stroked the man's head.

"This is Kitchi," she said to us. "Awake, my love," she whispered in his ear, "it's me." His eyes opened slightly, and he barely turned his neck towards her. His movements were slow and labored.

Looking at the two of them was heartbreaking. We could see, despite his current state, he was a handsome man. Underneath puckering scars, curved muscles still showed his strength.

"We were fishing the river early in the morning. A mother grizzly was trying to pass and found us between her and her cubs. She went for me first, and I cried out. Kitchi got between us. He didn't want to kill her. A mother only thinks of protecting her young. So he fought her instead, and it lasted until she had the cubs in her sight again," Felicity soft quietly. "He is so brave, so strong." We watched as he slowly moved a hand to hers.

With slow honoring posture, Shay knelt on the floor beside them. "He says he would do anything for you, that he would do it all again. He would change nothing."

Felicity started to cry. It was unnerving for me to watch. She was so guarded, snappy, and tough on main street; a firecracker. This was a totally different view of her.

Felicity answered, "I wish we could go fishing again. I wish we could dance by the fire every dusk."

"He says that the two of you will do this again one day, in another world. He says it hurts him most to see you so lonely and heartbroken," Shay relayed.

"You are my everything. Of course I am broken," Felicity said, stroking his hair and holding his hand.

"He says he wishes you to find happiness and joy again. To dance again. Even without him," Shay paused, and we saw the unsteadiness in her eyes. "He says you should find another. Another who can give you children. Who can dance with you."

Felicity's tears grew bigger, and she hung her head in pain. She slowly removed her hand from his and unfastened the mask we had always seen her wearing. The mask that covered her nose and mouth, that accentuated her strong entrancing eyes. Shay and I watched the covering fall to her lap, her dark hair released with it now hung around her tilted face like a curtain.

Her shoulders were jumping as she cried, and she turned her head to him. When she lifted her face, we saw three deep scar lines starting at her left ear and flowing diagonally like a river across the edge of her nose, her lips, and down to the right side of her neck. They were so similar to the ones on the side of Kitchi's head.

Felicity looked at her husband and spoke to him with her eyes before ever saying a word. When she could muster words she said, "You are the only dancer for me. We are one. We are bound and tied together by the fabric of our souls. I will be by your side always." She spoke steadily, with passion. "I need you to know that I chose you. Past, present, and future. I chose you then. I choose you now. I would choose you in a hundred different lifetimes."

I was crying now, watching this all unfold. I looked at Shay, who was pouring tears as well. Above Kitchi's sharp cheekbones, a small drop welled.

"He says, 'but I wasn't even that good of a dancer'," Shay smiled.

Felicity laughed as the tears lightened, "True." She looked at him with awe and love. "Do you know of a way that would help you to speak?" She was careful with her words.

"He says no," said Shay. "But my grandmother, who taught me, was a healer. I could try."

"Please, please," Felicity said eagerly, and stood up from the bed.

Shay rose a little higher on her knees and placed her flat palms on Kitchi's scarred chest. She bowed her head and from the side I could see her lips move.

"Whisper," I prayed in my head, "Oh, if you could heal Kitchi. If he could only speak."

Shay looked up and carefully lifted her hands. There were no voices, no words. Nothing had changed.

Felicity looked disheartened, but thanked her for the attempt appreciatively.

"Put your hand on his head," I felt I heard Whisper speak.

"Whisper, is that you? Are you sure? Felicity has been through so much."

"Trust me," they said.

I asked Felicity, "May I touch him?"

She looked at me quite confused, but went along with it. I placed my hand softly on his head and prayed, "Okay. Do your stuff. We wish for Kitchi to be blessed."

I stood there with my eyes closed, scared to look at the others, embarrassed to look at Kitchi. And then I heard a sigh, and the slow syllables, "Ah... yo... ka."

Felicity gasped and hurried to kneel beside her husband.

"Ah... yo... ka," came Kitchi's labored voice.

"Yes, my love. Yes," Felicity said, "Ahyoka." Kitchi slowly smiled, and again tears flowed throughout the house.

"How did you?" Shay and Felicity seemed to say at the same time.

"I didn't," I said. "Whisper did."

"Whisper? I didn't hear it," said Shay, confused.

"Whisper is in my soul, more than my mind," I pondered with her.

"Will it last?" Shay asked.

"I don't know."

"Thank you," Felicity said earnestly to me.

"I didn't do it. It was only done through me."

Everyone, including me, was a bit bamboozled, surprised, and joyful all the same. We had nearly forgotten completely about Caroline. I finally noticed the sound of drums outside.

"Oh! The ceremony!" Felicity jumped. She bent down to kiss her husband and told him she would be back as soon as she could. "We need to join them at the fire," she said.

Chapter 17

The Ceremony

While we were meeting Kitchi, Dr. Cheveyo had been prepping Caroline for the sacred fertility ritual. She anointed her with oils and burned incense to cleanse, purify, and protect her, according to the custom. They led Caroline out of the warm and inviting meeting chambers into the sharp, cold night.

When Shay, Felicity, and I left Kitchi, we found the clan and Caroline standing in front of the large outside fire in the middle of the Foothill clan's arc of lodgings. Caroline held her hands clasped together in front of her stomach subserviently. As reverent as a churchgoer in a cathedral.

Dr. Cheveyo stood in front of her holding a small bowl of burning herbs in one hand. With the other hand she held a falcon feather, which she used to waft the smoke of the burning herbs. The beautiful feather was striped like a tiger and glowing in the firelight as it spun dark vapors to curl and dance around Caroline's body. And the light flurries of snow continued to float down to us, uninhibited by the excitement.

One member of the clan beat a drum with a goat skin head, deep and timely its tones resonated against the cold rock of the mountains. It echoed off of them and alerted all the woodland creatures that something was going on tonight. Another member played a flute. Ee-oo, ee-oo, it rang emphasizing the backbeat. Lulling us all into a serene sort of meditation.

Dr. Cheveyo, wrapped in furry animal skins to protect her aged bones from the cold, placed her fragile hands on Caroline's shoulders and began to chant in native tongue. Caroline remained in position, and it was then that I realized she might be holding something. The doctor continued on, her words riding the waves of the drums and flute notes like a song. The rest of the Foothill clan stood quietly and dutifully, witnessing the ceremony. We followed suit.

This lasted for about ten minutes. Then, the doctor's chanting faded, the drum quieted, and we were left with the soft calling of the flute. It danced on the night air a minute more and then faded out as well.

Caroline looked at Dr. Cheveyo expectantly, who kindly led her gaze to Gray Cloud. It was finished and our visit had ended.

Gray Cloud helped Caroline onto her horse, for she had no hands to pull up with. They were still clasped, palms domed, containing something to be handled with care.

Shay and I said goodbye to Felicity and climbed atop our horses. For this ride, Gray Cloud remained beside

Caroline unless the path grew too narrow, then he would give way to her. We assumed this was because her hands were still occupied, and she couldn't hold the reins.

The dark purple sky was calm and solemn, dotted with what looked like hundreds of white sparkles, but again the woods were alive. A hooting owl, rustling noises on the ground. The path wound through thick pine forests until we were back towards the edge on the mountain. We were almost out and into the clearing by the park when Caroline said, "Stop."

Our horses all followed the cue from Night Sky and there we were, surrounded by snow clumped pine limbs. The only light present was reflecting off of its white sheen. It was eerily quiet.

We watched Caroline with curiosity and scrutiny as she raised her clasped hands up towards her face. She opened them over her mouth and jerked her head back to swallow. As her hands rested back on her lap, she gave a little shudder.

Silently, Gray Cloud led us back to the park because he understood the action Caroline had completed. We dismounted at the location where our journey began, rubbing our horses' noses to show them our appreciation.

When Gray Cloud took the reins on Adohi from me, he squinted at me and said, "Boy is dedicated."

I was so confused and taken off guard that I didn't respond. And I didn't have a chance to because he immediately walked back to Night Sky, our horses in a line behind him. Maybe it meant Caroline would have a boy.

It was an hour from midnight, and everything was still and quiet. We watched him hike a leg up and over his dark beauty. Night Sky carried him and the other horses back into the mountains. We waited as he vanished in the night like a ghost.

"Are you alright?" I scanned Caroline up and down. She looked sort of dazed.

"I suppose."

"What just happened?" I asked, though when I looked at Shay she seemed to know already.

"I swallowed Palli... in the form of a dead grasshopper," Caroline said as I tried not to grimace. "I was instructed to hold him carefully until I no longer felt him hopping around in my hands. Apparently, Palli is a symbol of fertility." She clicked her tongue, "I wish I had a smooth vanilla chai."

"Alright. Well... good then. I guess," I stammered awkwardly. "What's next?"

Caroline looked sort of embarrassed.

Shay answered for her, "The ritual is complete. Dr. Cheveyo says the next consummation will yield a child."

"Oh. Right. Well, let's get out of the cold then. Get to the trolley."

Caroline lowered her head and led the way, eager to end one of the most awkard nights of her life.

We crossed the empty parking lot and sat on the bench at the park's trolley stop, all of us being pretty quiet and growing sleepy. When it finally arrived, we climbed aboard and dismissed the conductor's nosy remarks of, "You girls are out late."

No one was on board, so we spread out in seats of our own and put our legs up. The ratcheting noise that continued as we moved on the track was like a metronome. There would be two more stops before we reached Frigid ridge.

At the first stop, which was near the town's main street, there was one passenger waiting to board. They clambered in and removed their hood. My eyes grew as wide as tea saucers.

Caroline was immediately suspicious. "What are you doing out?"

"Platform lever needed repair. The guys at the smithery work magic," Alex said as he held up an odd looking piece of metal.

"This late?" Caroline pressed sarcastically. He replied with a shrug.

None of us said another word the whole ride home. When we reached the warm and cozy entry way of the lodge, Caroline must have been worried about her reputation because she didn't say goodnight or thank you or anything else to Shay and I. Just walked quietly to her room.

The three of us had been dawdling slowly in her wake and when she was gone I smacked Alex in the arm, "What are you doing?"

"Ow," he rubbed his arm as Shay rolled her eyes. "I couldn't let you two go into the woods alone with Mr. Kyte's rumored hit man," Alex said.

Shay gasped at the thought, "Gray Cloud is not a hit man."

"I know, I know. I'm kidding. I just wanted to make sure you guys were okay."

"Ummhmm," Shay sounded through pursed lips, "Well, tomorrow is Monday and we all have a full week of strenuous practice and likely drama. So I am going to the room while you two duke it out."

"Oh gah, she's right," I said exhaustedly. She bounced her eyebrows at me as she left.

"Yeah, I guess we should all hit the hay…" Alex said, watching Shay turn the corner.

When he turned back to look at me, something happened and I lost control of my body. I don't know what came over me. I grabbed Alex's head with both hands and kissed him like I may die tomorrow and never have the chance to do it again. I felt him reciprocate the action. Neither of us knew where our hands should land, so we both were grabbing each other's arms and backs and the fabric of our jackets, almost like we were fighting each other.

I knew he had followed us into the woods. I knew that he was the cracking branches I heard behind us. I knew he did it because he really was worried and wanted to make sure I was safe. And I suddenly realized that Gray Cloud was talking about him.

Gray Cloud knew he was following, knew it was no danger, and understood why he followed. And Alex must have ran like mad to make it to the next trolley stop in town, in order to get back home.

I was immersed in all the feelings when I heard someone clear their throat. We stopped abruptly and saw the lodge receptionist shuffling papers awkwardly.

"Alright, goodnight then," I said to Alex, as if we were onstage acting out a play and then straighten my jacket before walking off towards my room in a manner as dignified as I could manage.

When I entered our room, it was dark except for the small reading light Shay held. She smirked at me as Ava snored. I bit my lip to slow down all the grinning and went into the bathroom to wash my face and change.

"What a night," I thought as I smiled at my reflection in the mirror, knowing that yet again I would struggle to sleep. But I was getting used to it.

Chapter 18

The Devil You Know

Morning dawned relentlessly, and I struggled to make it on time to grab breakfast and get on the trolley. Exhaustedly running on five hours of sleep made it difficult to tolerate bright lights and loud chatting. The troupe arrived at the park by eight o'clock in the morning and I trudged behind them all the way to the theater. Even the frosty morning air did little to alert me.

Inside the theater, Mr. Kyte and the Mandevilles were already waiting for us. Caroline was poised as ever, but I could see in her eyes that she too was more tired than usual. Reginald was deferentially listening to Mr. Kyte blabber on while simultaneously eyeballing him with fastidious disdain. It made no difference to Kyte. He seemed not to notice.

"Ah, they have arrived. Good morning, Marvels!" Mr. Kyte seemed to beam. "You folks proved yourselves famously this past weekend."

The troupe looked unsure, but smiled placatingly and politely.

Mr. Kyte continued, "Bravo! Truly, I am impressed with your performances." He clapped and gave a little bow towards our congregation. "That is why I'm going to sit in on your practice. I want to see the behind the scenes. You folks just pretend I'm not even here. Carry on as usual."

There it was. Looking at the faces of the performers, I noticed all the lightbulbs turning on. They looked apprehensive and awkward. I was sure my face looked the same, if not worse. Mr. Kyte had a way of perpetuating grandiosity right before delivering a potential blow.

We had no choice in the matter, obviously, so we did just as he asked. We tiptoed through our usual routine of practice, frequently glancing toward where he sat to see who he was watching. And when it came time for the flyers and aerialist to practice on our rigged apparatuses outside, we thought he may follow us. But he didn't. He stayed inside the theater the whole day.

"Who is he watching?" I asked Shay, after we had climbed down from the silks attached to the hot air balloons outside, adjacent to the theater of doom.

"I don't know. Could be that he wants to keep tabs on Reg and how he manages the troupe. He could be watching your boy. He seems intrigued by the drum coaster."

"Why would he do that?"

"To steal the idea. Or... I don't want to scare you, but maybe to steal the performer," Shay said cautiously. "I could see Kyte offering his price, or blackmail. Just like

Reg did when he started this troupe. We were all taken away from a dying circus."

"Our circus isn't dying, is it?"

"No, but it's the nature of the occupation."

"If he's got it in mind to steal acts, what if he's watching Ava? He's in the market for an acrobat. Now she's proven herself," I speculated.

"It's possible. I hope he's just in there to intimidate Reg. To keep up this whole alfa male challenge they've got going on."

We took a break for lunch and then went back to the theater for our usual stretching and flexibility routine. Mr. Kyte was still there, seated on one side of the stage next to Reginald. They seemed more cordial now, and sat comfortably in their chairs as if they were watching a game of sports.

There were several groups of performers practicing at the time. The balancing acts, Zeke and Tombo, and Ava. Alex couldn't have been who they were watching because he had to practice drums in a back room in order to decrease the noise. "Oh gosh," I thought, "Maybe it is Ava he's after."

I had my issues with Ava, but she was part of our little family. She was kind and a good person. The feelings I had toward her weren't her fault. I never communicated a need for her to refrain from pursuing Alex, and she had asked me about it, hinting questions loads of times. All of which I shrugged off like I was Alex's sister or something. There were still so many performers who looked down on

Alex and me, and she was not one of them. She, like Shay, welcomed us into the fold. They didn't hold their years of seniority with the Marvelous Marvels over our heads.

I watched her balance on the walking globe as she spun eight hoops around her arms, legs, and body. Then I shifted my view to Kyte, who seemed to appraise her while talking to Reg.

"She'll be fine," Shay said, patting my knee. "She can't take the weather out here, or stay in one place. And there aren't enough boys. That's probably half the reason she has stayed in the troupe. It's a revolving door of boys, a new crop for every stop we make."

Alex came in on break and sat down next to us. As usual, he slouched against the wall, as we sat on the floor trying to keep perfect posture while stretching to each side of our straddle.

"What did I miss?" He asked, breathing heavily and guzzling down water from a bottle, damp with sweat from slamming drum heads.

"We're just trying to figure out who he's watching," I whispered, nodding my head toward Kyte. "Don't think it's us. He never came outside during the flyers' practice."

"Guess he didn't care to see our 'behind the scenes'," Shay said with gusto, though she remained as poised in the face as a royal matriarch.

"He's been in this room all day. He ain't watching me," Alex added. "Maybe he's just trying to give Reg hell."

"That's what I said," said Shay.

"Yeah, and then you said he could be stealing acts," I huffed at her quietly.

We all watched the room again, hypothesizing. Ava still on the globe at center, with jugglers and balancers scattered in groups all around her. Kai and Bertha in one corner, pumping iron and flipping through a magazine, respectively.

Zeke was talking to Anthony by the dressing racks, Tombo beside them. Tombo was probably still leery of being too close to Reg, but Zeke looked happy, and Anthony had more color in his face than usual. He must have been getting more sleep. Seeing him with Zeke, I remembered Anthony was indeed a handsome guy. Rest and happiness make everyone more beautiful.

Daniel, absent of Eloise, was hanging out watching acts too. He would praise them and tell them what a great job they were doing or clap when they finished a trick. Caroline walked through the room on her way to the cafe. She patted Daniel on the back of the shoulder as she passed by. He beamed and smiled at her, and Caroline returned the sentiment.

"What do you guys say to a smorgasbord at Frigid Ridge tonight?" I asked. "I'm running on no sleep, but this is the first time in a while where all I have to worry about is not falling off a silk for the next few days."

"Didn't you sleep?" Shay said with a bit of sass. I tried to keep my face from Alex's view, so he wouldn't see if I blushed. I didn't say a word and neither did he.

"I just want to take the night off from worrying."

"Can't turn down a smorgasbord," Alex chimed, as he popped up from the bench and walked back to his practice room.

The day finished smoothly and that night the whole dysfunctional lot of us sat in the lounge of Frigid Ridge, amongst the rest of the performers, whether they welcomed us or not. Shay and Ava, Zeke and Anthony, Daniel and Tombo, Alex and me. Eating, drinking, storytelling, and laughing. It was comfortable and cozy, like the movies, the ones I watched where friends were more like family. Plus a monkey. And that night I slept like a rock, a peaceful dreamless sleep.

After that, the week steadily rocked on. Mr. Kyte wasn't spending the full day watching us, but was intermittently in and out fairly often. However... by Thursday, the night before show day, things got a bit strange. It just felt like things were off during the packed trolley ride back to the lodge.

When we reached the lobby area of the lodge, I saw Anthony briskly walking to his room. Zeke and Tombo trailing behind him. Usually they wanted to hang out a while before ending the night.

Ava sat down at the piano and the rest of us plopped down in chairs to listen to her melodies. Her fingers rolled across the ivories and I let my head drop back against my chair. It had been a strenuous week of practice. We had the two shows left and then we would leave White Cap Peaks for the next location, which was yet to be disclosed to us.

The piano melody was a pleasing mix of punchy jazz and soft echoing. We were all enjoying it when Zeke quickly approached. The keys were interrupted when Ava jumped and turned. Zeke's face looked stricken, and he asked her to keep playing. He said that he needed the noise cover. Ava turned back on the bench and obliged him as he told Shay, Alex, and I what was happening. His voice quiet and careful, hidden under the string of piano notes Ava continued to play.

"He knows. Kyte knows." Zeke was nearing panic.

"Knows what?" Alex asked.

"About Tombo," Shay said quietly as she leaned in closer to the huddle. We all shrank in our chairs. We were so close to getting out of this place unscathed, and now this.

"He ambushed Anthony while he was in the back rooms using the steamer. He asked him about Tombo and Anthony said, 'I don't know what you're talking about.' Kyte pulled a knife out and held it to his throat, threatened to end him right there. And Anthony had to tell him Tombo speaks," Zeke continued as tears started pouring out of his eyes. "He is wrecked. Anthony is wrecked over it. And I can't lose Tombo. I can't lose either of them."

"What did Kyte say after that?" Alex asked.

"He didn't say anything. Just let Anthony go and left. I think he's going to try to take Tombo."

Alex thought for a minute. "He will have to involve Reginald. Maybe he's going to try to make a trade, undercut him. And Reg could go for it depending on what the trade is because he doesn't know what a rarity Tombo is. He doesn't know how unique his own act is. Plus, Tombo recently pissed him off."

"Then we have to tell the Mandevilles about Tombo. They need to want to keep him," I added.

"That may protect us from Kyte, but not from Reginald," Zeke said.

"If you don't tell Reg, you and Tombo may wind up stuck here in White Cap Peaks. Without Anthony," said Shay calmly. "I don't think we have much of a choice."

"Yeah… I guess you're right," Zeke said hesitantly as his eyes went blank in thought. "I don't like it, but I guess I have to tell him."

"Where's Tombo now?" I asked.

"He's with Anthony, he's safe. Right now. He's been raving like an old Londoner, irate that someone would dare intrude on his autonomy." He took a deep breath. "I'll talk to Reginald in the morning."

"Tread lightly, bro. It will be a show day," Alex added.

"Yeah, yeah. I will. Thanks for being there, guys," Zeke said. We all leaned in for a hug ball as Zeke wiped at his eyes. When Zeke stood up, he went to kiss Ava on top of her head. She looked at him nervously while continuing to play.

"So, we're banking on Reginald Mandeville now? That's a first," Alex said when Zeke had left.

"Better the devil you know than the devil you don't," Shay replied.

It was going to be a hard test of faith to put our trust in the likes of Reginald Mandeville. The man who had threatened to leave us abandoned in who knows where if he saw fit. The man that held back our pay. Threatened us over lack of absolute perfection. He had a history of explosiveness that Alex and I had already witnessed in our short time traveling with the Marvelous Marvels. But Shay was right. What choice did we really have? It was that or Zeke and Tombo could be taken away.

Our night time routines were gloomy and slow as we anxiously moved about our bedsides and shared the bathroom. Sleep was a struggle, though not in a good way. It replaced the usual giddiness about the recent interactions with Alex, with bad dreams and fearful visions. Everything that would come in the morning, on a show day, laid heavy on the mind.

Chapter 19

Caught In The Web

The general pace of the troupe, as they had breakfast near the piano and gathered their equipment, was more up tempo. It wasn't out of eagerness or excitement, but the desire to get another show over with. I heard the flyers and tight ropers verbalizing their disdain and anxiety over the potential sabotaging Mr. Kyte might do, since he had ambushed the last set of shows.

At least the weather was going to play fair. Predicted cold without snow would keep every one dry, which was less chance of an icy demise for acts that depended on hand grip to support their entire body weight while swinging in the air.

In the hectic activity of practice, stretching, choreography, hair, makeup, and costuming, we all went through the day without a safe opportunity to get with Zeke for an update. I hoped Reg received the information well, and that maybe he was in a Dr. Jekyll mood when Zeke caught him.

By six o'clock, we had donned all the accoutrements of a dystopian steam working barbarian. We watched the crowd pour in and thicken along the outside area where the first half of the show would begin. As we peeped our viewers, I realized I had almost gotten used to wearing the gas mask, and I felt pretty cool wearing it. I wondered if Anthony would let me have it as a keepsake—if we survived the last two shows that is.

On the dot of the following hour, it was surprisingly Reginald and Caroline who introduced the start of the show. They were hand in hand with pearly smiles, like the beginning of a Vegas residency. The crowd cheered with suspenseful glee, and then Kai, Bertha, and the snake charmer debuted a third time for a White Cap Peaks audience. Things went smoothly and as usual, without Mr. Kyte making an appearance.

Next up were the tight rope walkers. Trepidation and precaution laid just under the surface of their forced smiles. They were rightfully worried about what Kyte had in store for them, but again he never appeared. They made it through the entire act with no demands for change or threat to their balance. And when they descended from the rope ladder of the hot air balloons, they looked relieved.

Shay and I hoped for the same luck. The man in the hot air balloon switched out the rope ladder for our red silks and dropped them down. We gave them the standard pull, posed, and then initiated our choreography. As we were setting up the cross back straddle, the one that looked like a butterfly, a voice came over the microphone.

"How spectacular is this, folks? I mean, these girls are talented," Mr. Kyte said.

The crowd roared at his appearance, which further egged him on. "Oh well hello there, you beautiful people. You thought I was missing, did you?" He grew vivacious and dismissively played. "Oh, you all just want to see if I'm going to spice things up around here." Again, spectators clapped and hollered for him, as panic and fear punched me in the gut over and over again.

We were upside down flapping the tails of the silk like butterfly wings when Kyte said, "Butterflies are certainly very resilient creatures, but have you ever seen a butterfly in a strong wind? Gray Cloud, give us some wind."

From upside down, I could see the top of Gray Cloud's head. He was just staring at Mr. Kyte.

"Go on, bring us a little gust. I think they can take it," said Kyte, unrelenting.

I could see that Gray Cloud didn't want to do it, to risk hurting us, but he was obligated to comply. I held my silks tightly and braced. A swift wind shot into me and swung me toward the mountains. I was squeezing my eyes shut, but had to check on Shay. She was still hanging there, in the same position as me.

"Hit 'em again!"

The second blow rocked us and I felt the balloon seem to move with us. The audience rallied and the sound of their greed disgusted me and filled me with anger. I grew so mad adrenaline shot through my body and made me feel like I could hold strong in a tornado.

"One more!" Kyte bellowed.

There was a longer pause. Gray Cloud was trying to give us a second to get our best grip. Doing all he felt he could do.

The third blow was a great prolonged gust, and the tails of my silk went flying. They wrapped all around my legs and waist. Shay was in the same predicament and it left us like insects in a spider web. It destroyed the whole flow of our act and as our music and cues continued on without us, we had no choice but to carefully try detangling ourselves from thirty feet in the air and upside down. The crowd guffawed as we struggled.

It took us the time allotted for the rest of our act to untangle and safely get back down. When our feet finally touched the concrete, the anger slightly subsided to make room for the feelings of humiliation to set in.

"Nice jobs, ladies," Mr. Kyte said tauntingly as we walked back to the tent.

Shay ripped open the tent flap. "I don't think I've ever been so embarrassed in my life," she said, starting to shake.

Outside, I could hear Mr. Kyte beckoning the trapeze flyers to the performance area and promising them he would give them a break tonight. Inside the tent, I saw the back flap fly open and Alex came barreling in, dressed in costume but thankfully minus the plague doctor mask.

"Are you guys okay?" Alex's eyes were scanning Shay and I for injury.

"I guess," Shay said hotly.

"Good," he relaxed a little. "Listen, Zeke told me he talked to Reg."

"How'd it go?"

"He said it sent Reg in a tizzy. He was furious that they had kept him in the dark about it at first, but then he was irate at the thought of Kyte messing with his show. He said Reg kept going on and on about how sick and tired he was of Kyte mocking and belittling him. Said he wasn't letting him have his acts for damn sure."

"Okay. Well, that's good."

"Yeah. Apparently, he said he didn't care if Kyte offered him the moon at this point. Which is good. But he starting saying things like, 'that's my monkey,' which didn't really sit well with Zeke."

"Understandably. He pretty much predicted that," said Shay.

"But now that he's told Reg, it will fulfill our purposes. For now. Hopefully," I interjected. "Now Reg will fight to keep him."

"I think Reg has already confronted Mr. Kyte. I think that's why he wasn't around to introduce the show. And why he's taking out frustration on our performers," said Alex.

We stopped and listened to the commentary outside. The trapeze act had survived. We heard Mr. Kyte talking about the fire breathers and jugglers. It seemed innocuous at the moment.

"So, what do we do?" I asked.

"I don't know what we can do. Other than be on guard. Keep a close watch for the rest of the performers," Shay replied.

I heard Ava's bubbly voice greet the crowd outside. We took turns peaking outside the tent and found her beginning her hooping act as the fire breathers exited and the jugglers flanked her. I saw Mr. Kyte on his dragon platform watching her kind of creepily. Reg and Caroline were nowhere to be seen.

"I've got to get back in the theater," said Alex. "Just keep your heads down and be careful."

We nodded as he ran back out of the tent, high-fiving Kai as he went. We peaked out again. Ava was getting ready to walk on the globe, to lead the crowd in.

"It's she beautiful, folks?" Mr. Kyte said. It looked like he was going to leave her alone, too.

"Let's get a head start to the theater," I said to Shay, and we snuck out the back flap same as Alex. When we had made it inside and into the side stage area, I watched Ava walk the globe through the doors, the masses trailing into the theater. The big cats were lounging in their personal cages near their chain link ring, and Eloise was already at her marker with Daniel. The cats yawned audibly as the crowd poured inside. Little children became exuberant as they eyed the animals. Some of them lugged in boxes of popcorn or big clouds of cotton candy, which were absentmindedly smacked against dirty railings as their parents herded them to a seat.

When everyone settled, Reg and Caroline entered the center of the ring, and I was thankful to lay eyes on them. Mr. Kyte was side stage on the dragon platform, with a nice view of all that took place ahead of him.

"Ladies and Gentlemen, we present to you Dapper Daniel and Elegant Eloise!" Caroline's introduction rang out. A melody of drums and horns resounded, cueing Eloise to start her choreography. She executed each pose beautifully as Daniel grinned and extended his arm. He pet her lovingly after each successful move.

"This is great! Really great, ain't it folks? But wouldn't you like to a see a little more pizzazz?" Mr. Kyte boomed over the music. "Don't you think we should get that pretty lady out here once again? I mean, if she can balance on the ball, an elephant should be no problem."

The crowd hollered and whistled, beckoning Ava to present herself once again. When she stepped into the spotlight, the crowd's cheers and applause grew louder.

"There she is! Come, come, my dear!" Mr. Kyte bellowed.

Ava kissed Eloise, aiming for the front of her face but landing on her trunk due to lack of height. Daniel crossed his arms disappointedly and Ava gestured to ask what was wrong. Daniel enacted their choreography by pointing and tapping his cheek. He extended his short neck towards her. Ava pretended to smack her head like the lightbulb had flipped on, and then kissed Daniel on the cheek. He grinned and twisted at the torso jubilantly. Their act was going perfectly.

Ava gingerly stepped up on Eloise's curling trunk, which hoisted her all the way up and over her head so that Ava could sit on top of her back. From there, she began her acrobatic act full of impressive back bends, complex yoga poses, and balancing single leg stance poses as Eloise walked.

"How about a hand stand?" Mr. Kyte feigned request; it was truly a demand. Ava would not be immune to his control of the show tonight.

Ava complied and executed a perfect hand stand, straight as an arrow, atop Eloise's mid back.

"A single hand stand?" Kyte pressed.

Ava tried but could only lift one hand up momentarily. When she was seated again, Eloise shook her head from side to side and trumpeted.

"What do you think, ladies and gentleman?" Mr. Kyte shouted triumphantly, and the crowd cheered. "She couldn't possible do anymore, could she?" Kyte pretended to kick back in deep thought. "How about balancing on top of this great elephant's head? Do you folks think she could do a handstand from there?"

The people gesticulated encouragingly. Ava looked a little nervous. Kyte's banter had already elongated the time of their act, and Eloise was getting confused by the unrehearsed extension. Despite her reluctancy, Ava moved to try it. She achieved a handstand on top of Eloise's head and the spectators roared in delight. She held the position a good eight seconds before Mr. Kyte demanded she try maintaining the pose one handed.

She lifted one hand for a moment and then quickly tried to regain her balance. Shay and I watched in horror. She wasn't able to get back to a normal handstand. Instead, she tried to counter correct, and slid down Eloise's trunk. This startled the elephant, who jerked, but ended up halfway catching Ava around the torso.

Unfortunately, Eloise couldn't catch her before she slammed her right leg into the ground below. I could see Ava wincing. Eloise tried to release her near the ground, but Ava obviously couldn't bear weight on the right leg because she grasped at Eloise and Daniel, who had rushed up beside her, for support.

"Don't be alarmed, folks! She's a tough one. I bet..." Mr. Kyte's voice was halted over the microphone. Reginald had stormed over to the dragon and was yelling up at him as the show music continued to play. I watched him swipe his arm through the air angrily, and then glanced back to Ava, who was hopping off stage with her arm across Daniel's shoulders to keep from falling.

"You broke her damn leg, you son of a bitch!" I saw Reg's lips mouthing the words up at Mr. Kyte, who seemed worried that Reg's voice might carry to the crowd over the mic. He blocked it with his hand and yelled back down at him. This went on another minute, confusing the big cat tamer, who was way behind schedule at this point. And the crowd was grossly amused at the genuine drama.

No one heard from Kyte during the acts of the big cats or the domestic animals because he was missing from the platform. During that time, Shay and I snuck backstage to find Ava.

She was in one of the back rooms, seated with her leg up, and looked like she had been crying. Caroline and Alex were hovering around her. When we entered, she looked up at us with anxiety and urgency on her face.

She said, "It's broken. My leg. I know it's broken."

"She's probably right," Caroline said with a sort of disgust at the situation.

We all stopped talking and breathing, jolted to attention at the sound of men yelling and items slamming down the hallway.

"I've got to get Reg. Don't let her move," Caroline said exhaustedly before walking out.

"We've called a doctor. Supposed to be on the way," Alex said.

The echo of yelling stopped abruptly, and we heard stomping footsteps coming nearer.

Reginald flew into the room, Caroline following behind him. He took one look at Ava's leg, which was already turning red, and let out a string of curse words.

"We're taking care of this. It's going to be fine," Caroline tried to assuage him.

"Where's Zeke? Where is that damn monkey? If this is any indication, I can't let them out of my sight," Reg shouted. He was cherry red and his eyes were glassy. He looked like he might literally explode. "This was a mistake coming here," he fumed and vigorously pointed a finger at Caroline.

"Don't blame this on me! Go handle it!" She shouted back at him, her blonde hair jostled as she quaked. The rest of us wanted to disappear, fearful of being impaled by the shrapnel of their argument. Reginald was biting his lip, attempting self control, before he stomped out.

Consequently, the Mandevilles didn't perform their acts at all. There was no contortion or sword swallowing for this greedy audience. And because of that, only Zeke and Alex's acts were left. And Zeke was up.

Chapter 20

Pegged

Shay and I rushed back to the main theater and found that all players were present. Zeke and Tombo were trying to start their choreography and dialogue as usual. Reg was in one corner surveying the situation like a hawk, and Mr. Kyte was back on the dragon platform.

We watched helplessly, but were, for once, thankful to have Reginald around. And things were pretty smooth the first two minutes of the act, but two alpha males usually can't cohabit for very long.

Zeke was performing the ventriloquy act, where he pretended to switch voices or to take Tombo's voice away from him. Tombo was silently and animatedly playing along, moving his lips without audible noise as if he couldn't speak. Zeke explained to the audience that whether Tombo liked him or not, Tombo needs him in order to have a voice.

"But that's not true, now is it?" Mr. Kyte interjected over the microphone. It seemed like the heads of every member of the audience snapped over to watch Kyte. I watched Reginald's eyes grow huge and face turn crimson.

"Oh come on now, Reggie. You need to show how truly great an act you have. Otherwise, this marvelous act would be better suited in the hands of someone who appreciated it."

The audience cheered Mr. Kyte on. Reg tried to fake smile at the lot of them. Zeke looked worried and Tombo stood on his platform mouth agape, stopped in his tracks.

"Let him speak. Let him speak," Mr. Kyte initiated a chant, and the crowd was fueled to join in. They didn't even know what Kyte was talking about but on they went following his cult of personality. When their demands weren't readily met, Kyte encouraged revolt with his gestures. Slowly popcorn and jelly beans started soaring towards Tombo's platform.

Reg was now in front of the dragon podium again, arms waving resentfully. Spectators raged on as Shay and I watched helplessly. Zeke moved closer to Tombo, who was now getting pegged with candy, and asked the crowd to please stop. They wouldn't listen, so Zeke and Tombo were just about to make efforts to exit the arena. At that time, an entire tray of nachos was thrown. It missed Tombo, but landed all down Zeke's shoulder and front of his costume.

"STOPPP!" Tombo shouted, baring his teeth and jumping with pulsating energy.

Everyone paused, quieted, and stared.

After what seemed like minutes Mr. Kyte said, "What did I tell you folks? I would not lie to you."

They cheered and clapped and hoo-rayed as Zeke and Tombo hastily got the heck out of dodge. Reginald was scathing, but retreated to follow Zeke and Tombo's every move. And Mr. Kyte acted as if completely unperturbed. Actually, he might have been emboldened.

Shay and I stayed put to make sure Kyte didn't try anything funny during Alex's act, and I sent inaudible praises to Whisper when he completed the whole set uninjured. At the end of the circus, Mr. Kyte made encouraging and endorsing statements regarding the ridicule he had incited from his adoring fans. About what a fun and exciting night this crowd had gotten to witness because of his own superior skill, particularly coercion, and grandiose generosity.

Finally, after what felt like hours, the crowd dispersed and left. The theater floor was a disarrayed mess from confused performers and acts who scrambled to go along with the sudden changes to the sequence of the show. Plus, it was littered with thrown edibles.

I found it odd that the roustabouts seemed extra busy that night, and after a while, I realized they were breaking down Alex's coaster and moving it out. We went looking for him to see if something was wrong with it, or if he knew why.

We found him in the back with Ava. Apparently, in the time since we had last seen her, a doctor had come and reset her leg. It was now encased in an odd looking metal contraption with gears and knobs and locks; undoubtedly the typical, albeit unusual, work of the people of White Cap Peaks. She would have to be rolled in a chair for transport.

From that room, through very thin walls, we could hear the conversations taking place in the room beside us. Reginald's voice echoed like a train horn, "We're done. That's it!"

"You are not. You've got another show!"

"Not anymore! You broke my performer's leg. Made a mockery out of my whole circus, and most of all, of me!" Reg screamed the last bit so loud I think the walls vibrated. It gave us all a shudder.

"If you neglect to provide me a final show, then you owe for the advanced pay. But… tell you what. I'll take the monkey and we'll call it settled."

"You owe me that money in damages! And you're not getting anything else from me."

In the room behind us, Mr. Kyte lowered his chin to look Reginald eye to eye over his spectacles. His response came calm, steady, and smooth as a sneaking snake. "Reggie, Reggie, Reggie. Have you forgotten who you're talking to? You may be good at what you do, and you may have some hidden gems up your sleeve, but mark my words, if you skip town tonight, if you cannot honor our agreement and leave me empty handed, I'll make it my mission to find you. To collect. By whatever means necessary."

"Don't you dare threaten me. You'll do nothing, old man. And I won't be intimidated by some con artist low life such as you," Reginald answered through gritted teeth.

My whole body was tense as we all listened bug-eyed. Alex, trying to voice reason and avoid catastrophe, said, "I think we need to get a move on."

We took a quick glance around to take an inventory of any things we couldn't leave behind; potentially forever. Ava sat there helplessly, so Alex picked her up like an infant and we headed for the trolley. Though it was a false sense of security, it felt like a good plan to get as far away from Mr. Kyte as possible.

When we got on the trolley, to our thankful relief, Zeke, Tombo, and Anthony were already seated. Alex placed Ava in the seat in front of them and we all huddled together, our little circus family, around our wounded and vulnerable.

"Gah, can this thing go already? I smell like cheese." Zeke tried at comedic relief, but his face was fraught with worry.

"Oy, well, you ain't sore from being pegged with beans, are you?" Tombo added. Zeke's eyes looked shocked at the unapologetic volume with which Tombo finally amplified his voice. Tombo continued, "Cat's out of the bag now, mate. Don't see no harm in using my larynx at this point." A couple of performers tried to glance nonchalantly over their shoulder towards the intrigue of Tombo's words.

Slowly the trolley filled and finally we started moving, but the Mandevilles never got on. That wasn't entirely unusual, but considering all that had happened that night, I found myself actually a little reluctant about leaving them behind. Particularly Caroline.

We didn't know the true range of what Mr. Kyte was capable of. Would he strike now on impulse? Certainly that's what Reg would have done. Or would he wait till we were unsuspecting? Would he really follow us? None of us knew where we were even going.

When we reached Frigid Ridge, there was still no sign of the Mandevilles and everyone went straight to their rooms. The girls and I tried to focus on our normal nightly routines. Poor Ava had a time trying to bathe with one leg propped outside the tub. I sat on the lidded toilet and handed her soap or shampoo or washcloths from the other side of the curtain while Shay used the sink.

"Everything's been so chaotic and busy. We haven't had a chance to all be together. And I guess this is as good a time as any to bring up the recent changes in personal relationship statuses…," Ava said from behind the shower curtain as she tried to scrub her foot with a washcloth.

"You have a change?" Shay asked.

"Not me. Janie," Ava said emphatically.

I twitched at the unexpected turn of discussion. "Me?"

"Yes, you!"

I looked at Shay with furrowed brows, who returned a slight shrug.

"I know there's been a development with you and Alex."

"You do?" I was perplexed, "How do you know that?"

"I've been talking to him for weeks about finally telling you how he feels," Ava answered.

"What? But… I thought…" My mind was confused. She had been talking to him about me? I thought she took a liking to him herself. I thought she was going to take him from me. There were certainly times I felt like she would take him from me. Like when she jumped at the opportunity to get him alone on the Ferris wheel.

"Thought what?" Ava sounded confused. She paused a minute then gasped aloud. "You thought I was after him!"

Shay softly smiled as she continued combing out her hair, relieved at my revelation. "You do flirt with everyone you come in contact with," Shay said to Ava. "It would've been an honest mistake."

"Well, honestly, I may have played with the idea for a second. But you can't blame me. You said there was nothing there," Ava confided.

"Well, I… I just…" I tried, but Ava stopped me.

"But he told me he wanted to be with someone else. He was very upfront and honest about it. Of course, I knew it was you. From then on I was trying to encourage him to be a man. Teach him the chivalry of a romantic. Get him to quit that bad attitude and risk calculating he incessantly does."

"And you knew too?" I asked Shay.

"I told you. You've got to find out on your own. Remember? I'm not the thought messenger unless it's life or death. Ignorance can be bliss and knowledge comes when the time is right. I don't need to tamper with it," said Shay.

"Anyway… I heard there's been some smooching going on," Ava chirped. Then she swiftly pulled the shower curtain around the edge of her face to peek at me blushing. "That good, huh?" She giggled.

"Well, yeah! Probably three years worth of pent up emotion." I felt myself turning pink and sweaty with confession.

"Well, I'm thrilled! You know, I knew this all along. I could tell immediately. The way your eyes darted around, guilty as can be, when I asked you if you ever had feelings for him," Ava bubbled.

"Alright, alright. You may have been on to me before I was on to me."

"I know these things," Ava swept back behind the shower curtain with confidence.

"You better get on with bathing, lady one leg. We've got to hoist you out of there and pack to leave this frozen tundra. Before Mr. Kyte's fury catches us all," Shay steered the conversation to the more pressing issue.

That was all we could do. Pack our things and lie in agonizing wait until the morning. Wondering where we were going, how we would get there, and what would become of us if Mr. Kyte made good on his promise. It was a foreboding night, dark and heavy. The air in the room seemed stagnant and there was an electric pulse lingering in my body that wouldn't let me drop my guard. It didn't want to allow myself to drift to sleep.

All of us struggled. Ava must have been uncomfortable in the boot, because I heard her wiggling all night. And as

I intermittently woke from short spells of unconsciousness,
I found Shay up with her reading light.

255

Chapter 21

Viajero Salvaje

Each of us woke up groggy and moved at sloth-like speed getting ready. However, the smell of breakfast, salty bacon and hot pancakes, was encouraging and the tangy orange juice perked us up. Alex, Zeke and Tombo, Anthony, and Daniel joined us. They looked haggard, too. But despite feeling zombified, we all had jumpy nerves and felt uneasy, anxious to see what the day would hold. Ordinarily this would be a show day and everyone would be frantic, but now we were in some type of White Cap Peaks purgatory. We had no purpose there if we weren't bringing a circus.

The Mandevilles finally showed their faces and I have to admit, I was happy to see they weren't acting any different than usual. It made the situation feel a bit more routine.

"Alright, troupe," Reginald said from the middle of the room, which was packed with our colorful crew of characters. "As you know, last night was a total disaster, and therefore we are breaking our little contract with Kyte and moving on." We could all see that he was trying to maintain his volatile temper as he continued to speak about Kyte. "He's caused us loads of damages, and you should know that he has made threats to take punitive measures. My advice to you is to keep an eye out for your own wellbeing, and should you notice anything awry, immediately bring it to our attention." He couldn't help growling out the bit of instruction. "Obviously, we are now securing our own transportation out of this infernal place. So, you'll need to have all your things packed and be on the trolley within the next hour. We're taking it past the town and to the harbor. There we'll board a ship, animals and all. Make way before noon." He was resolute and matter of fact as he spoke, and I noticed he kept eyeing Zeke and Tombo. His parting words were, "I suggest you be timely."

We hurriedly downed our last bits of breakfast and went to get our things, return the room key, and get on the trolley. The three of us girls got on well before the hour just to be safe, and the boys seemed to follow suit.

When we made our departure, it was a solemn but beautiful ride away from Frigid Ridge. The sun was high and stray cumulus clouds appeared across the azure atmosphere. No snow fell to cloud our view of the vista as we wound around the snaking track near the lodge, into town and across Main Street.

Shay and I sat together and watched as we passed all the little shops on the street that we had tried to do reconnaissance on while searching for Dr. Cheveyo. We looked more eagerly when we were nearing Felix's clock shop, and when we were passing it, of course, Felicity was there to wave and bid us goodbye. She no doubt had more intel on our situation than we did.

Rolling past the Victorian style houses and oddly dressed locals, I could feel a true sense of leaving. It was a relief.

On the other side of town, there was more rugged landscape to mediate on as we journeyed out. A breathtaking bridge made of stone led over a vein of water and into the side of the mountain. It was pitch black inside except for the tiny overhead light in the middle of each car. Once through the mountain, the harbor was only a short stretch further.

It was a humble sort of boatyard, quite small, and there was only one ship docked there, which meant it must have been the one we would travel on. Initially, I had my doubts about fitting all of us, plus an elephant, the big cats, and the domestic animals. Light Catcher had been quite large, lavish, and spacious. Fitting us all on her was a cinch. But everything I'd seen around White Cap Peaks was antiquated and normally sized.

This ship, however, was enormous. It put my dubious attitude to rest pretty quickly, though I felt for the roustabouts that would have to figure out how to load it. It looked like a giant pirate ship, and maybe it was. Constructed completely of wood, dark and aged by sea water. Its sails were dark red under stain and wear. And there was nothing lavish about this vessel. It would be dirty, damp, and rustic.

When we had gotten off the trolley and were waiting to board, I saw the figurehead. It was a skeleton holding a chalice and had undergone significant saltwater erosion. My eyes travelled along the length of the ship and toward the stern. Barnacles coated the underbelly. As water lapped up on the side of the hull, I saw the name she had been dubbed with. Viajero Salvaje. The exotic name seemed very out of place in this cold climate.

"We're evading Kyte by pirate ship. Guess it's appropriate," said Alex.

"Dreams do come true," I answered. And I wasn't be facetious because I had always loved stories of old sailors and pictures of old ships.

Shay and I bore Ava's arms around our shoulders so that she could, fittingly, hobble on board one legged.

Ava's face looked like she had smelled something foul. "It's filthy," she whined.

A roustabout who heard her was passing by carrying a large piece of stage equipment and interjected, "Wait till you see the sleeping quarters." Ava's eyes grew wider at the thought.

"You'll do just fine, princess," Shay goaded.

"I'm sure Anthony can redecorate even the most hopeless of lost causes in interior design. Can't you, babe?" Zeke patted Anthony as they followed us.

"E's got iz work cut out for him today then," Tombo said cautiously quiet.

We saw the Mandevilles in the middle of the deck, Reg barking orders, and Caroline looking much like Ava.

Behind us, Daniel was now coaxing a semi reluctant Eloise up the ramp and on board. The horses behind them and the big cats, looking bored in their cages, next in line to be rolled on. It must've taken the roustabouts all night to transport our animals over the mountain to this small harbour. And if Kyte was paying attention to this, then he knew we were trying to leave and where we were disembarking from.

When everyone had boarded, we realized how tight this ride would be. Near the stern, under captain's and important persons' quarters, were some inner stalls that held the animals; Eloise just barely fitting. Daniel would worry constantly.

Toward the bow side were some very humble sleeping quarters for the rest of us, performers and roustabouts alike. We would definitely get to know each other because it comprised small bunks stacked in one big room; if you could even call it a room. Forget bathing. That wasn't really much of an option, so we all hoped this would be a trip of short duration.

We threw ours, and Ava's, bags in a tiered set of bunks. Ava would take bottom since she currently had one useless leg, Shay middle, and I would climb to the top. Directly adjacent to us, the boys would do the same. Then a row of jugglers and fire breathers, another of aerialists, and so on. Kai and Bertha would struggle, being the largest people on board, so they would have to use the hammocks in the middle. Even if the hammocks sagged to the floor under their weight. We were utterly jam packed. And no one would want to spend their time in these quarters for anything other than sleeping.

Once we meandered around each other and back out to the deck, most of the circus was settled. The Mandevilles were accompanied by a man, very broad in stature, who I assumed was the captain. He wore what was once a pristine and impressive frock with tasseled shoulder pads and numerous buttons in a straight vertical line, but was now aged and stained as the ship's sails from years of seafaring. His skin was the color of cinnamon and his eyes dark as night. His hair, matching his eyes in color, was fine combed and slicked back, tied at the nape of his neck and hanging down between his shoulder blades. He had thick eyebrows and side burns that went well past his ears, but the rest of his face was shaved smooth, which highlighted his chiseled jaw.

Reginald whistled loudly through his fingers to get everyone's attention. "Troupe, let me introduce you to our captain."

"Bienvenidos a bordo. I am Capitán Jiménez. I will take you to Mezul." The captain's words rolled off his tongue in an alluring accent. He gave a happy nod at the end of his greeting, as if to indicate that was all he had to say.

"Mezul is our next stop, troupe. It'll take us three days to get there if we keep strong winds, but you can look forward to higher temperatures there," Reginald boomed. "You will do whatever Capitán Jiménez or his comrades tell you to do, and that will likely include helping crew the ship. No one is exempt."

And with that, we were on our own. Reg turned to continue his discussion with the captain and followed him up to the fanciest, if you could call it that, quarters of the ship.

Within the next twenty minutes, the captain's comrades had us pulling lines and aiding them to set sail. In the bitter cold of White Cap Peaks, we pulled rough rope until our hands were red, and frequently bumped into each other as we unwittingly attempted to do whatever the comrades asked of us. There was a lot of bumbling and repeated instruction since none of us knew anything about ships in general, much less one of this size, or how on earth to get it to move.

However, when I finally saw progressive movement out of the harbor, I felt a sense of accomplishment. There was a sense of peace to being back on water and we were all comforted at the thought of going to a warmer climate. Since there was no affinity for White Cap Peaks in me, I was quite happy to be getting away from it.

Soon we had sailed far enough that the harbor was a speck in the distance. Once we were sailing, the chores of crewing Viajero Salvaje lessened. We could amble around, viewing the starboard or port sides alternately, and talk amongst ourselves.

Moving over water in cold temperatures was tough. The wind is relentless and seems to cut you to the core. Heaven forbid you get sea sprayed enough to dampen your clothes. Some of us had more difficulty bearing it than others, one of which was Tombo. Tombo didn't have any clothes on and, being indigenous to the tropics, was quite uncomfortable. He rattled off a list of swear words that would make Reginald Mandeville proud. The only difference was that his came out with a cockney jargon and an accent to it.

"Go to the quarters then," said Zeke.

"And risk getting snatched? I'm a valuable commodity around 'ere now," Tombo answered.

"Two minutes with you and they'd send you right back to me," Zeke said playfully.

"Why don't you just hand me off to Reginald now, then?"

"Oh come on, Tombo. You know Zeke would never do that. He'd be lost without you. And we would all be far less entertained," Anthony interjected. "I can pin you up a jacket though. Come with me." After puckering his lips and sticking his tongue out at Zeke, Tombo agreed and followed Anthony.

"At least he can move around and keep his blood flowing. I'm going to be stiff as a board after all this down time. I doubt I'll be able to do any acrobatics or globe walking for the next gig," Ava said. She pouted from a perched position on a bench that was far too unkept for her based on her countenance.

"How and when are we gonna get that thing off of you anyway?" I asked.

"That oddball doctor created it to have settings. It will unlock and open on its own in five weeks," Ava said, defeated.

"Five weeks!?"

"Yep. It's supposedly some state-of-the-art contraption that makes healing time less than usual. But depending on when we do our next gig, my act may have to be cut."

Ava looked genuinely disappointed. This would definitely be hard for her. Especially since she was used to so much attention during our shows. Not to mention the fact that, knowing Reg, she most likely wouldn't get paid.

"We'll take care of you," Shay said to her in a mocking tone that a babysitter would use to engage with an infant. Ava rolled her eyes.

"M-m-maybe you can still ride Eloise. Sh-she could carry you in her trunk and you can p-p-parade during our act," Daniel said encouragingly.

"Hey! That's a good idea, Daniel!" Ava replied, causing Daniel to glow, even in the most dreary environment.

There was no dining room or piano lounge or really anywhere to sit and socialize, so everyone ate humble meals at sporadic times while scrunched on their bunks or propped against the ship to keep from wobbling so much. When night fell, we shivered harder. We were making good time, but still had much to go before we could expect any relief from the bitter cold.

As expected, from years of travel and our personal nature, Alex and I found ourselves leaned on the side of a gliding vessel, watching the water move and the stars begin to flicker in between streaking clouds. A vast horizon dimmed to moonlight as we quietly cut across the surface of the sea.

"You think there's mer-folk in this area?" Alex asked somewhat sarcastically, but with newfound merit acknowledged in the question.

"Who knows?" I said, feigning exhaustion at the unpredictability of our current possibilities. "I'm not sure anything would surprise me at this point. But we have enough to deal with, so I hope these waters are too cold for them. It's certainly too cold above it."

Alex moved his arm around my shoulders, trying to warm me. He was pretending there was nothing unusual about such behavior and continued the conversation. "Maybe they're cold blooded. Maybe they followed us and they're still after Reg, like everyone else."

"Don't remind me." I didn't want to think about anything negative for a moment, especially while I was in his arms. "Remember that time we were in Espíritu Del Mar and went to the beach every off day we had, and tried to surf on those crappy plastic boards."

"Yeah," he laughed. "You had that huge bruise on your arm from the cord for weeks."

"It was so humid and hot. And I complained at the time. But man, I wish we were there now," I said.

"Same."

I felt a little apprehensive about it, but I let the words out anyway. In a rush like ripping off a bandaid. "I think I knew then," I said.

"Knew what?"

I gave him a look to say that I knew he knew exactly what.

"Oh, you mean you kinda liked me?" Alex said playfully. "Well, it was way after that for me. I mean, you had all that seaweed in your hair…"

Nudging him semi-roughly, "gimme a break." I looked him in the eyes, squinting as if angry. His half smile, crooked grin, was staring back at me. His eyes changed. We looked at each other for a moment as if pleasantly surprised at our own revelations.

"Okaaay," Zeke said through half of his mouth as he walked past behind us. Demonstrating approval and the giddiness of a friend who had long awaited this happening. I acknowledged him with a blushing face.

"Guess we're not being very secret right now," I whispered to Alex.

"I guess not," he whispered and leaned in.

My stomach turned somersaults, and I felt the hairs on my arms trying to stand up under layers of sleeves. His lips found mine and that same melty feeling seemed to warm my whole body.

I pulled back and slowly opened my eyes, trying to savor every sensation. I was taking in the aesthetics of his chiseled face when I noticed some movement to the left of his ear. I jerked backwards.

"I'm sorry," Alex said hurriedly. "Are you…"

I fought to catch my breath and wake up from my daydreams. "No no. I saw… What is that?"

"What?" Alex asked, as he turned towards the direction I was staring.

In the distance, low in the skyline, I could see a big dark spot shielding stars from our view and floating slowly nearer. Its movement subtle but steady.

"Go tell the others. I'll go to Reg and the captain," Alex said calmly but urgently.

I watched for a second as he bolted across the deck. Skipping stairs, he climbed up a level and ran toward the captain's quarters. I turned the opposite direction and ran to the cramped sleeping quarters where several members of the troupe were milling about or trying to get comfortable.

"Listen," I shouted, "There's something nearing us. Everyone needs to get focused and prepared for whatever it may be!" It was abrupt and therefore sent out somewhat of a panic as the troupe tried guessing what it might mean. A dull roar steadily rose in the barracks as the people grew steadily worrisome.

I moved toward Shay and Ava to warn them. "I think we're being followed. And it's airborne." The girls' responses were disheartened rather than surprised.

"Buggar," Tombo's voice rang as Zeke anxiously snapped to from his bunk. "E's 'ere to haul me back, ain't 'e," Tombo said worriedly.

"What do we do?" Ava asked the group of us.

"Just stay put for now," answered Shay.

I went back out to find sprinkles of rain splattering on the wooden deck and the dark spot now larger and nearer, maybe two hundred yards out. Capitán Jiménez was outside his quarters, squinting through a spyglass, taking inventory of the aggressor. Reginald was beside him, hands bracing on the rail to keep from exploding.

Minutes later, the rain had increased in volume and pressure and the outline of the dark spot took shape. A large oval silhouette, that of a zeppelin.

Alex had made his way back towards the quarters. "What are they going to do?" I asked.

"I don't know. But I hope this thing has cannons on board."

Chapter 22

Clash

It was still dreadfully cold, and we were becoming soaked by the increasing rain. It felt like a thousand needles. The troupe huddled in the entry of the barracks, trying to stay dry but taking turns at having a look at what was happening outside. I saw Caroline was now doing the same on the other side of the ship, near Reg and the captain.

By the time the zeppelin was next to us, the rain was so heavy we could no longer make out the stars. Clouds were encasing us in the dark sky. Up on the gondola, I could see two familiar figures. A tall dark skinned figure and a menacing man almost glowing white in face and beard.

"Ahoy Marvels! Why are you trying to get so far away from me?" Mr. Kyte shouted to us from above.

"We're done, Kyte!" Reginald shouted back.

"Last chance to turn around!" The reply came with delight at the forecasted battle that would soon ensue.

Reg spent the next minute talking animatedly to the captain and then ran down to the main deck, where he shouted at the roustabouts and comrades and anyone else nearby to bring out the cannons.

I had never been in a situation where there could potentially be deliberate murder, and watching them roll around cannons made my stomach sick. Alex and I moved near the rest of the troupe, trying to get out of the way. Looking up at the zeppelin, I realized that Mr. Kyte was forcing Gray Cloud to make the torrential downpour.

I slowly began hypothesizing what he aimed to do. What I settled at was that he planned to sink us. That way, he could evade blame. If anyone heard our story, it could be chalked up to a tragic mishap in a storm.

"Do I take that as a refusal?" Mr. Kyte shouted. The sneer of his tone could be perceived even through rain and atmosphere. He placed a hand to one ear as if listening for a reply.

Reginald stared at Kyte without verbal response. He looked to the helm where Capitán Jiménez was readied. The crew and roustabouts stood waiting.

"Then let it be known to all those around you that you are to blame for their demise!" Mr. Kyte looked at Gray Cloud and sternly growled, "Wind."

Gray Cloud, with despondence, silently carried out the command. He lightly flicked his worn and knobby hands and a great gust blew across the deck. It was so strong that it pulled a rolling cannon out of a crew member's grasp, which then slammed into Reginald, who had been looking up at Kyte at the time. His foot was pinned underneath it. Kyte laughed and demanded more wind relentlessly.

The roustabouts were having lots of trouble freeing Reg's foot. Every time they rolled or pushed it Reg hollered out in pain. They'd have to lift it instead and before I could grab him, Alex ran out to help them. Rain pelted them at an angle and water was slinging off their hair and bodies as they hurriedly moved to lift the cannon.

Caroline, who had overseen all of this from the upper deck, moved to come down the stairs to aid her husband. On her way, she slipped in the water accumulation and was knocked backwards by the wind gusts, which sent her over the ship's low railing. She grasped at anything she could on her descent and landed one hand on a wet line, to which she clung with all her might. The line was rigged at a slant and she couldn't get her other hand up to grab the tattered rope. Rain obstructed her vision, and she didn't have enough strength. Before a roustabout could get to her, she lost her grasp and fell in the choppy sea.

I rushed to the railing and looked over to find her bobbing in the water. It was such an odd sight to see her hair void of volume and flat against her head, no jewelry, no cigarette. She looked helpless and fearful.

Shay came running with a lifeline and dingy white buoy. She slung it over and tied the end around her waist.

Caroline was gulping for air and grasping in all directions, trying to get to the buoy. Above us, Mr. Kyte yelled, "Again!" But this time, no gusts came. I glanced quickly between Caroline and the zeppelin. Positioning myself between Shay and the railing, I held the line, ready to help Shay pull Caroline up. Above us, Gray Cloud was refusing to comply. Fearfulness was on his face as he looked at Caroline struggling in the water.

"Go on, man!" Mr. Kyte shouted. He struck Gray Cloud in the arm so that it slung forward from the momentum. Gray Cloud turned his stoic face to Kyte, but didn't respond. "If you don't obey me, you know what happens to the Foothill clan!" Kyte raved.

But Gray Cloud stood there, unmoving. He looked at Caroline and I thought it must have been the first time Mr. Kyte had made him directly responsible for someone's harm. He couldn't go through with any more instruction if it meant harming others. That was not Gray Cloud's nature. He was a protector.

"Fine, I'll do it!" Mr. Kyte screamed in aggravation and disappeared momentarily. When he came back, he held an odd looking metal contraption with knobs and triggers. It was two feet long and a strange capsule within it glowed.

Mr. Kyte aimed the tool at the fore boom, and a loud blast resounded. It splintered the wood of the railing beside Shay and me as we covered our faces. Thankfully, Reginald was unpinned and standing upright just before the blast. He ran to the rail and we all looked over the edge for Caroline.

Her body was still and floating lifelessly on top of the water, wood from the railing bobbing next to her. It appeared she must have been hit by the debris. At the sight of this, Reginald utterly lost it.

This rocket launcher would require response by cannon fire. Reg ran to the cannon and aimed it at the zeppelin as he yelled at the others to pull her out of the water. Our life line was now useless, and the crew pushed past us to lower themselves down in a dingy and bring Caroline back.

While Reg stopped at nothing to ready for fire, Kyte launched another blast into the hull of Viajero Salvaje which destroyed several of the bunks in our sleeping quarters and just barely missed Ava, who was sitting helplessly inside. Screams resounded from our performers. The gunpowder was too wet to ignite and Reginald was a madman at the disappointment of the cannons.

"Whisper, help! What should we do?" I prayed in my head.

"Move," they answered.

"What?" I thought, confused at the answer I perceived. Immediately I felt an unseen force throw Shay and I out from under the fore boom. It was seconds within a third blast from Kyte, which caused that boom to fall to the deck in a heavy crash that destroyed everything beneath it.

"What was that?" Shay said, dazed.

I got up quickly and rushed to pull Shay to her feet and toward the side of the ship. "Thank you, Whisper," I thought quickly. "Now what?"

"Stay focused."

I looked around haphazardly, wondering what I was supposed to be focused on. Scanning up the ship, I saw movement in the crow's nest. A slender, currently wet, black hairy arm was rotating like a baseball pitcher and hurtling juggling balls of bright primary colors.

Tombo looked like the angry alpha male you see in nature shows. Teeth bared with energy coursing so heavily through his body that he trembled between every jump and throw. He meant business and aimed to do his part in protecting the troupe. He finally hit his target with a bright red ball the size of those you'd find on a billiard table. It smacked Kyte in the bicep of his shooting arm, which thankfully caused him to misfire. But the misfire went more toward Capitán Jiménez, whizzing past his head and blowing a hole in the side of the captain's quarters.

"Caray!" He shouted huffily after regaining his stance from ducking. His hand still on the wheel of the ship, he pointed enthusiastically at his comrades and rolled off new instructions to them in Spanish.

On deck, the cannons were now deemed pretty useless and people were running about grabbing harpoons or whatever looked weapon-like. One juggler chucked a harpoon like a spear toward the zeppelin's hull, but he didn't make the height.

Over to the ship's side, where the dingy was rigged, roustabouts were pulling up the small boat that they had retrieved Caroline in. When it was up, two men jumped out of it and carefully removed her unconscious body. Reg ran over and knelt beside her. He shook her to no avail and then began CPR.

Above us, Mr. Kyte had been trying to reload the rocket launcher when Gray Cloud decided that he couldn't stand by any longer. The two men were in a tussle, as Gray Cloud was trying to wrestle the gun away. Mr. Kyte screamed in his face and made all manner of threats against Gray Cloud's family, the Foothill clan, their territory in the mountains, and their lively hood in the town of White Cap Peaks. But nevertheless, Gray Cloud would not stop or unhand the launcher.

When he felt he had enough hold in once hand, Mr. Kyte reared back and hit him with a good punch in the jaw, but it barely rattled him. He was tough and hardened by far worse pain than that which was physical. And strangely enough, Gray Cloud made no efforts to hit him back. He just kept his grip on the gun.

I heard a sputter and cough near me and looked toward the huddle on deck. It was a small relief amidst chaos to see that Reginald was pulling his wife to sit up. Caroline looked dazed and disoriented, but her eyes were open and she was breathing again. Reg held her in his arms and kissed her forcefully on the cheek in his elation.

Overhead, the tussle continued, and Gray Cloud must have been growing more aggrieved and tempestuous in his thoughts because he was slinging Mr. Kyte by the hold of the launcher with increasing power. Shay and I were still watching from our retreat beside the broken and fallen boom, when Mr. Kyte somehow slung Gray Cloud from his hold which flung him by momentum in the opposite direction and to the floor. Mr. Kyte laughed in celebration and then ran to the side opening in the gondola and aimed the launcher directly at the Mandevilles.

Kyte's eye was settled at the scope and he was exhaling his breath in preparation to pull the trigger.

"Move!" Shay and I desperately screamed at the group of people that included the Mandevilles. They all looked up in reaction at the pointed launcher and tried to scramble. I knew they wouldn't be able to move quick enough. It felt like the entire journey of my time with Marvels was whizzing past my eyes in a vision, and my heart was breaking at its impending end.

Mr. Kyte was at the ready and prepared to end them when he jolted forward, lost his balance, and fell out of the gondola. Unfree from the laws of gravity, he flailed during his descent, grasping at holds that weren't there to save him. In shock, he let go of the launcher, which fell through the atmosphere somewhere along side him. He descended roughly forty feet and smacked the icy water.

In the open space of the zeppelin's gondola stood Gray Cloud, bracing both hands on the doorway, breathing heavily, and looking down at the sea. We all ran to the starboard side railing of the ship and looked over. Eyes scanning with haste. It was like checking to see if the spider you smashed was actually dead. Is it over?

We all finally laid eyes on a white dot that bobbled at the frigid and unfriendly surface of the water. Mr. Kyte was alive but undoubtedly had the wind knocked out of him and was therefore struggling to keep his head up in the chops. The rain picked up again, and I looked up and found Gray Cloud's hands slightly extended.

Reginald left Caroline with the roustabouts and came to the starboard side to see for himself. His face was flat, exhausted from the terrifying concern that Caroline would not breathe again. We watched him look at Mr. Kyte unfazed and calmly gesture to Capitán Jiménez to sail onward. He turned his chin up to the sky and stared at Gray Cloud for a moment. When their eyes met, Reginald gave him a brief nod.

The ship began to move in a new direction, and I watched as Gray Cloud disappeared inside the gondola. The zeppelin started to head back in the direction it came. And with our movement, slowly the white dot that bobbed in the water grew smaller and smaller until it disappeared.

As the zeppelin flew away the rain let up, which was a slight comfort though we all remained soaked and feeling frozen to the bone. The soggy crew slowly shuffled back to our quarters to change into dry clothes and take an inventory of the new hole that was blasted into the side of it. After changing, we huddled in the barracks, wrapped in our humble scraps of cloth the crew referred to as blankets. Our first night on board would be even colder.

Chapter 23

Caroline's Secret

"How are we supposed to sleep now?" Ava said between chattering teeth.

"What with having watched Mr. Kyte drown, half the troupe nearly die, and with only the comfort of an already dilapidated and now war torn pirate ship to rest our heads in," Zeke said sarcastically. "Should be a cinch."

"I'm just happy to be 'ere," added Tombo, as he made himself comfortable in the corner of one of the top bunks.

Anthony poked jokingly, "Zeke was about to hand you over, had it not been for Gray Cloud."

"I've known Zeke a lot longer than you. He's all talk. You'll learn, baby. You'll learn," Tombo answered light heartedly from under a cover.

"He knows I'm stuck to him," Zeke replied.

"Cause I'm so lovable."

"Valiant, too," added Alex. "I saw you chuck those juggling balls. You should have played fast pitch."

"What do you think really happened? You know, to Mr. Kyte?" Ava said quietly.

"The freezing cold. The fatigue. You can imagine," Alex replied as he sat down next to Daniel, who looked quite sorrowful and had not said a word. Daniel wanted happiness, peace, and kindness for all people. His tender heart was clearly shook and it pained me to see the light in him dimmed.

"Maybe the merpeople took him," Anthony whispered.

"Maybe he's still lost at sea," Shay said, and everyone grew quiet at the eery thought of that.

I tried to process all that I had just witnessed, and it didn't sit well with me either. To abandon Kyte in the water like that. Even if he was trying to kill us and inherently evil. I knew Gray Cloud must have felt something similar, the way he valued all things of the earth. In contrast, I figured Reginald was in a celebratory mood.

"Look, everyone is overwhelmed right now. Maybe we should all just try to get some sleep," Shay encouraged. "We'll have several days to ponder all these things. Let's give ourselves a break."

"Yeah, I think she's right," Zeke said, climbing up to the top bunk with Tombo.

Each of us clambered into our tiny rectangular holes, dirty, cold, and apprehensive about what insects or crustaceans might be suctioned to the wooden separators. There was a lot of creaking and cracking from all the people in the quarters tossing and turning, but somehow I fell asleep.

I dreamt a bunch of odd things. That Gray Cloud was surrounded by his family in the meeting chambers and Kitchi was there walking. That Alex and I were back in Espíritu Del Mar trying to surf, but it was super easy to paddle and stand. That Ava was performing, and when I asked her where her cast was she said, "I've never worn a cast."

The next morning, everyone woke up early because the light was peering in through the blast hole so brightly. Shay and I trudged out to the deck to decide where we could set up Ava, who was adamant that she could not sit in those quarter's all day long.

"Oy! Mrs. Mandeville's requested to see you two," said one of the roustabouts. He had a big pile of rope over one shoulder and with his free hand, he pointed towards the stern of the ship.

"Alright, thanks for telling us," I said to the man and then turned to Shay. "I forgot all about Caroline. Good grief, and she had it worse than the rest of us."

"Me too," said Shay.

"I wonder what she wants with us."

"I think she considers us more friendly than she used to."

"You've heard her think that?"

"Not exactly, but she's much warmer than before. Either way, she could probably use a friend right now."

As we walked across the deck, I hoped Reginald wasn't in the room with her. I didn't want to hear from him that morning. Up the stairs we went, and I knocked on the door that the roustabout had pointed to. When Caroline opened it, we could see the exhaustion in her face. She was all fixed up in her usual grandeur of fine clothes and meticulous grooming, but she looked weary and her posture was not the typically striking gracefulness.

"Come in," she said, and quietly moved to open the pathway to her room.

These quarters were by no means lavish, but a significant upgrade from what we had just slept in. A small bed in the middle of the back wall, a table with chairs, a couple windows on the back to view the wake, and a chandelier in the middle of the room. Caroline gestured to the chairs, and we sat at the table.

"Yesterday was horrifying. I can't imagine what you went through. How are you?" I started.

"Alright, I guess. Tired." She brushed her long blonde hair behind her ear. "Wish I had a smoke."

"You're out?"

Caroline tried to get more comfortable. "Actually, no. But that's a good segue to what I wanted to talk to you both about. It worked... I'm pregnant." She allowed a partial smile and her eyes brightened.

"That's wonderful!" said Shay.

"Wow! It worked. Wow..." I said, and then thought of the turmoil that ensued yesterday, "Oh my goodness! I bet you were even more terrified then."

"Yes, in more ways than you know," Caroline breathed.

"I'm so sorry."

"Hopefully everything is still alright. The debris hit my head, not my stomach, so…"

"You'll be fine," Shay said supportively.

"Anyway. The two of you have been quite good to me. I know I didn't say anything before, but I'm really grateful for what you both did for me." She paused and looked at each of us in the eyes.

"You're welcome," we answered.

I believed her; she did appreciate us. Maybe she just needed support or companionship right now. Caroline nodded politely and thought for a moment. "I need another favor of you both. It's very difficult for me to say this, but… I need help. I need people I can trust, and I feel like I can trust the two of you."

I'm sure we looked bewildered. Or at least I did. Maybe Shay knew what was coming. Caroline seemed to search for the right words to tactfully and cautiously communicate her next request. She was deciding how much information we needed in order to comply with whatever she was going to ask of us.

"This has been utterly quiet. Secret. Can I trust you?"

"Uh—Yes," we replied alternately.

"My being pregnant places me in a very vulnerable position for a number of reasons. As I get further along, I won't be able to perform and it will probably get harder and harder for me to keep an eye on everything that goes on. You know, to manage the troupe, but also other things."

"What other things?"

"Remember when you were attacked by Ceto in Merdwick?" Caroline asked me directly. She continued, "What did Ceto show you?"

"I think it was my fears."

"Do you think it also showed you what and why you should fear?"

I remembered how the vision made me realize how much losing Alex would hurt me. "Yes—I do think that," I answered.

"In a way, it was sort of like a warning then?"

"Yes, I guess so."

Caroline spoke carefully, "The vision I had was of a child being taken from me by someone I love. Not that the child was stolen. It was just that I had no relationship with it, no bond, no say in its life, because it was taught to follow someone else. Taught to stay close to someone else, to do as they do, follow in their footsteps, and to be far from me." She took a deep breath. "I want this baby to be mine. I want to teach it to be kind. I want to give it the life I wanted from my parents. You see, my parents didn't want me. They left me to an orphanage, put up for adoption."

We listened intently and watched as her guard dropped and she let us into her world.

"And no one ever picked me. No parents ever came. I was stuck there my whole childhood. And then, when I was about fourteen, one of the boys who had been there as long as I had actually escaped. He was older, and one night, he broke out and left. Rumors were that he hopped a train, a circus train. And he was miles away before the sun came up and the caregivers realized he was missing. I thought it was a wonderful story. I was rooting him on, hoping that the rumor was true. Couldn't stop thinking about it. So I spent the rest of my years in the orphanage stretching and practicing flexibility tricks, and when I was eighteen, I left to join a circus too. I never thought I'd cross paths with the boy again, and now we're having a baby together. Two orphans with a child of our own. To care for and love, the way we always wanted to be loved."

I took in all the wonder of her last statement. "That's pretty amazing."

Caroline quietly searched our expressions with great scrutiny.

"It's a beautiful story, but what do you need us to do?" Shay asked knowingly.

"Most of the troupe thinks I'm watching in the wings and sneaking around to keep tabs on them. To a certain extent I am, but there's more reason to why I do it. Let me start by saying I love my husband. Truly and deeply, to a fault. But it's no secret he can be volatile. He can be extreme, and at times he can be violent. It's my job to keep the peace. I feel like I have to protect the spirit of this circus, and sometimes protect the troupe members themselves. Which is why I stood up for you," Caroline said, looking at me. "And also—there have been times throughout the years where Reg struggled to remain loyal to me. He has moments of elation and moments of deep sorrow, and these changes in mood lead him to entertain the idea that maybe he's not good enough for me, or that maybe I'm not good enough for him. And he wavers. If someone else's arms are open nearby, me may go to them. But it's because he struggles, because he has a thorn from all those years ago in the orphanage. A thorn he can't remove, that will never be removed. And when he realizes what he's done, he goes to the edge. Tries to hurt himself, or worse. Anyway. Because of it, I fear for our child. And I need help."

"What exactly do you want us to do?" I asked.

"I need you to keep tabs on him and on the troupe, just as I did, when I need rest or when I'm tending to the baby."

I looked at Shay cautiously. "We want to help you. But how can we stop him? What can I do?"

"No one can stop him. You just have to redirect him, however you can at the time. I'll be around to do most of it. I'm just asking for a little help."

She looked so small and lost. I didn't know what else to say. "I'll try," I replied.

"We'll try," Shay added.

"Thank you," Caroline said quietly and solemnly. "Thanks for listening."

"You should rest now, recover. Have you heard how long we have left to Mezul?" I asked.

"The damage will slow us down. The captain is saying a week now."

"A week, huh," I sighed. "That'll be tough. Ava will flip."

Caroline smiled lightly. "Looks like I chose well. You guys take care of everyone, don't you?"

Continue The Series....

RINGMASTER'S RISE

Though it starts as a tumultuous journey, the voyage to Mezul yields many fruits. A tropical environment, welcoming locals, and a town bursting with color. It's the perfect climate for Janie and Alex's newfound romance to blossom.

The troupe is relieved to have more freedom and safety, but the Mandevilles are in between gigs and owe for the damaged ship they sailed in on. When a rich and beautiful heiress lends a hand, Reginald's cunning begins. The Marvels must use the old-fashioned ways of the circus, renting space for the big top. Though Caroline puts on a brave face, she struggles to keep up. Now she needs Janie and Shay to help her look after the troupe—and her husband.

While exploring Mezul, Janie finds a tourist map that
points to just how close she may be to reaching her
dreams of getting to Fimaldi Hunu. As she weighs the
pressure from the Mandevilles with a curious turn of fate,
she finds herself stuck in the daydream of a new life with
Alex. But will she sacrifice her friends turned family for it?

About The Author

J.E. Miller is the author of the captivating fantasy series The Marvelous Marvels. Her books have reached fantasy readers across the globe.

Miller has always had an affinity for the stories that imprint themselves on our hearts and change us forever. She is inspired by the ones that teach us how to grow and serve as a measuring stick for the genuine character we aspire to have.

To find out more, visit jemillerbooks.com or follow @jemillerbooks on TikTok, YouTube, & Instagram.